PLUCKING THE CROW

PETER CORBYN

PLUCKING THE CROW

MANOR HOUSE

First published in 1990 by
Manor House Publishing Limited,
57 Manor Way, Beckenham, Kent BR3 3LN, England

Copyright © Manor House Publishing 1990

Typeset by Saxon Printing, Ltd., Derby
Printed and Bound in Great Britain by
Billings and Sons Ltd., Worcester

British Library Cataloguing in Publication Data
Corbyn, Peter
Plucking the Crow
I. Title
823.914 (F)

ISBN 1 873056 00 1

To Liz

Acknowledgements

I would like to acknowledge all those ex-colleagues and friends in the City of London who gave me the encouragement and inspiration to write 'Plucking the Crow' and the other novels that are currently at various stages of completion.

In addition I would like to thank Mike Waudby for coming up with such an intriguing and apposite title.

One

Yamani Trucial States, 1971

At a little after five in the afternoon Trooper Jezail stopped screaming. To the seven exhausted men lying in the dried-up riverbed the silence seemed almost magical.

Keeping low, Lieutenant David Collins, Royal Marines, looked around him. The drawn, haunted faces of the shattered remnants of his platoon told its own story. Their dark Arab eyes were scrupulously avoiding his gaze, afraid of what further demands he might make of them, of what madness he might, even yet, prove capable. There was no fight left in them, he knew that, observing grimly that several had thrown away their rifles in the chaos of flight. All they yearned for was the onset of nightfall and the vague promise it held of a chance to get the hell out of there. The fact was, unless he came up with something pretty spectacular, and quickly, long before then all of them would be no more than a mess of bloody jackal bait. He ran a dusty hand across his eyes, feeling the weariness settle upon him. What a balls-up! What a monumental balls-up!

Up until that day, during the whole of his six month secondment to the Royal Yamani Defence Force, in military terms David Collins hadn't put a foot wrong. The exploits of his platoon, 'Allah's Fang' they were called by friend and foe alike, had become almost legendary among the government

1

counter-insurgency forces. On these regular 'shoot and scoot' incursions, penetrating deep into rebel-held territory, they had run up a body count that was the envy of every other unit.

Ambitious, and determined to make an impact in his new command it had been a tactic he had introduced into the, until then, rather defensively minded Yamani Forces. And success had rewarded his aggressive approach. Three times he had been summoned to the palace to be commended by Sheik Mohammed, the shifty old camel-thief taking his hand in a dead-fish grasp before kissing him, odorously and wetly, on either cheek. What was more important, he knew his efforts were viewed with equal approval back in the dusty corridors of Whitehall where faceless civil servants were hammering out final details of a deal to sell the Royal Yamani Air Force fifty English Electric Lightning fighter aircraft.

But now, three weeks before his contract expired and he was due to return home, this fiasco. To lead these men, tough, battle-hardened veterans but already combat-fatigued after five days in the field, straight into an ambush. Just like some bloody crap-hat fresh out of basic training. He expelled his breath in exasperation, trying desperately to get his brain working, as Sergeant Miller, head tucked down, came scrambling on hands and knees down the dusty wadi to crouch beside him.

'I gave him the last of the morphine, boss – all of it.' Neither the flowing robes, the cartridge belts that encircled his barrel chest, nor the long headdress, could ever hope to make the sergeant look in the least like an Arab. The massive shoulders shrugged philosophically: 'He was a gonner anyway, no point in prolonging the agony.'

Collins nodded approvingly. The man had taken half a pound of razor-sharp mortar fragments in the stomach during the first mad minutes of the ambush. Half-dragged and half-carried through their nightmare flight – 'guts hanging out like a fucking tripe shop' had been Miller's diagnosis – he had been an inconsiderately long while dying. A further seven of Jezail's fellow troopers had subsequently died, cut down in a series of brave but abortive counterattacks followed, as the day wore on, by increasingly desperate breakout attempts.

The rebels, holding the high ground, had harried and blasted them from one position to another. Each time his diminishing, despairing command gained cover and a moment's blessed respite, the mortars would cough distantly and take up their deadly, creeping pattern of fire, forcing them to pull back and out into the open. Once exposed, the accurate rifle fire of the rebel tribesmen picked them off like flies. Thus far, he reflected grimly, they had scarcely caught a glimpse of a solitary hostile; whoever was running things up there in the barren crags was a real professional. He suspected that there was a Lieutenant Collinski directing operations: his Russian doppelganger.

Their single glimmer of hope lay in the fact that they had succeeded in getting a Mayday off, seconds before a burst of HMG fire had blown both transmitter and operator to kingdom come. Whether it had been received back at base, however, he had no way of telling. Collins knew he had to work on the assumption that they were on their own and likely to remain that way.

'What d'you reckon Barney?' He nodded towards the Arab troopers, his voice no more than a whisper. 'If we try another break-out will they go along with it?'

The sergeant shook his head. 'I doubt it. They've had just about all they can take. I guess they're counting on us sitting tight here until dark and then slipping away. The only thing that will get them moving now is that fucking mortar up there and then it will be in any direction but forward.'

Collins considered the situation. There seemed precious little cover on the rocky plateau that lay beyond their position. Once they were driven out of this final sanctuary it would be all up with them. Somehow they had to hang on until nightfall and then, if possible, make their way back to base with their tails between their legs. Allah's Fang had been well and truly pulled. He looked at his watch, the story it told was far from encouraging: there was another hour and more of daylight yet. Pressing his back against the pebbly wall of the wadi, he felt the folds of his sweat-soaked robe sticking to his shoulders and ran a parched tongue over grit-filled teeth.

'What the hell,' he mused, 'is a member of the Special Boat Squadron, a qualified swimmer and canoeist, doing here in the first place? I've been trained to canoe white-water rapids, to plant limpet mines on warships and to swim out of the torpedo tubes of a submarine lying at twenty fathoms. What the hell am I doing in an Arabian wadi where the only water within thirty miles is in the water bottles of the bastards trying to kill me?'

He considered the book-keeping of the situation. Subtract, from Her Majesty's portfolio, one lieutenant and one sergeant of marines, add £50 million received for two squadrons of outdated aircraft. The fact that, ultimately, western pilots would have to be recruited to fly most of them was another bonus. That would be Whitehall's calculation, he guessed – the poor bloody Yamanis wouldn't even enter into it. Suddenly Collins knew precisely why he was there. He spat dryly into the dust. This was negative thinking and had to stop.

'Right, Barney, unless you've got a better scheme, this is the plan.'

Hardly had he finished speaking than there came the soft, almost tuneful, whine and dry deadly crump of the heavy mortar smashing into the earth away to their right. A pillar of dessicated yellow dust erupted high into the air, showering them with a small rain of crumbled rock. His eyes went to the remaining demoralised Arab troopers. As each man examined himself, unashamedly relieved to find that he had suffered no serious injury, it was clear that another mortar shell would be enough to break them. They were all well-versed enough in the lore of desert warfare to have long eschewed all thoughts of surrender; they valued their genitals too much for that. No, his guess was that the next incoming shell would send them running.

And so it proved. The second mortar round, crooning a low and murderous song in its brief arcing flight, burst with a deafening explosion fifty yards to their left, directly into the wadi. Sobbing and choking through the maelstrom of sand and smoke, the platoon that had been his pride broke and ran, scrabbling from cover and into the arms of certain death.

The two Englishmen lay still, moulding themselves into the dust as the sharp bark of rifle fire rang out above their heads and the pathetic remnants of Collins' command were picked off mercilessly. After a brief crackle of celebratory gunfire from the ridge above, all fell quiet. Opening his eyes, Collins found himself staring directly into the sergeant's grinning features. Despite their perilous predicament the man was smiling, apparently finding some perverse humour in the situation.

'Any chance of finishing early tonight, boss?'

'Fuck right off, Barney.'

Captain Ilya Krachov of the Speznatz, military adviser to the 147th Regiment of the Yamani Liberation Front, groaned inwardly as he watched his men run, tumbling and tripping down the escarpment like frolicking children on the beach. For more than eighteen months he had, with depressingly little success, tried valiantly to instil some sense of self-control. With the detached fatalism born of extended living in the desert he took his hip flask from his pocket and, throwing his head back, let a trickle of vodka trace a fiery course down his dusty throat. Yes, they were exactly like children these mountain Arabs, he thought, wild and dangerous children, capable of almost anything except disciplined action.

Following at an appropriate distance, intent on maintaining the dignity required of a Soviet officer, he was nevertheless keen to see what they would find on the bodies. He hummed softly to himself as he went; today would look good on his record.

The ambush had been a total success, achieving complete surprise, yet Krachov was professional soldier enough to realise that the enemy's withdrawal, inevitable in the face of such odds, had been skilfully handled. Too skilfully for local talent. A less well-led force would have been annihilated hours ago. The officer commanding had acted exactly as he himself, placed in the same position, would have done.

What would he find in the riverbed, he wondered? An American Green Beret? A British SAS man? They wouldn't be wearing uniform of course, anymore than he himself was, but you could usually tell from the arms they carried.

His rebel tribesmen, about twenty of them, filled with a sense of victory and eager to reap the spoils, were across the wadi now and stripping the bodies of the fallen. Assuming that the breakdown of discipline they had just witnessed had been total, they remained unaware of the two soldiers lying deathly still, half-buried in the dust. Within seconds they were ripping wristwatches from unresisting arms, sawing at fingers to gain gold rings. Their brand new Kalashnikovs, the finest assault rifle ever designed and weapons that Krachov had lobbied Moscow long and hard to provide, lay strewn about, forgotten in the scramble for loot.

Next, he knew they would probably mutilate the bodies, slitting noses and slicing off genitals that they would then, the ultimate insult, stuff between the dead men's gaping jaws. Krachov did not disapprove; it kept the government forces, who practised similar barbarities anyway, nervous and, more importantly, discouraged defections from his own ranks.

Leaving his, by now thoroughly preoccupied, Yamanis to squabble and haggle over the spoils, the Russian dropped lightly down into the bed of the wadi and approached the two inert forms that lay slumped, face down, in the dust. Both were well built, the shorter of the two, whom from his lanyarded revolver Krachov guessed would be the officer, lay with his cropped blond head pressed into the dirt.

He hooked the toe of his boot under the shoulder of the bulkier of the two bodies and turned it over onto its back. His features turned to stone. The corpse, far from being dead, was actually smiling. Not only was Sergeant Miller smiling, in his hand was a self-loading Luger that threatened to send a 9mm bullet through Krachov's Adam's apple and out of the top of his skull. The man's words were casual, almost amiable. Almost.

'On your knees, shagbag, or you'll be sprouting another arsehole.'

Krachov, the Geneva Convention suddenly much in mind, did exactly as he was told, relieved after his initial alarm to find he had, apparently, been captured by the British. He might well be a prisoner, and as such an embarrassment to his masters in the Kremlin, but, if his luck held, he might still come out of this with his balls intact.

The muzzle of his pistol inserted firmly in the Russian's right ear, the burly sergeant watched as Collins crawled snake-like to where the platoon's solitary Bren gun lay toppled in the dust alongside the stiffening form of Trooper Jezail.

Unscrewing the barrel he checked it out, blowing it clear of the dust of action, or rather inaction; all the long day they hadn't once been in a position to use the weapon and he didn't want it blowing up in his face. Satisfied, he deftly replaced the barrel and slipped home a curved magazine, first carefully ensuring that another two full clips lay close at hand. Then, with a quick thumbs-up to Miller, he took a deep breath and swung the gun up onto the lip of the gulley.

It was all over in less than five seconds. At such close range, without any chance to take cover and the majority of their weapons strewn uselessly about them, the tribesmen got no more than two or three shots off in reply before they were, to a man, cut down.

Although the first burst had killed or fatally wounded every one of them, Collins twice reloaded. Eyes blazing in a blood lust born of hours of terror and frustration, he continued to pour a hail of fire into the disintegrating mound of tattered rags and bloody flesh that jerked and heaved under the savage bite of 7.62mm bullets. Even then he wasn't satisfied. He nodded at Krachov.

'Send him up first, Barney.'

Encouraged by the Luger, the Russian raised his head cautiously above the parapet and then, very slowly, stumbled up the bank ahead of them towards the carnage.

It was an unnecessary precaution. Already the flies, attracted first by his own slaughtered men, were swarming about this new and unexpected harvest, tentatively exploring nostrils and ears, drinking at wide, dead eyes. High above, the ravens and kites were already wheeling in the purpling sky. Soon the vultures would arrive, scything in from miles away, and the feast could begin.

Binding Krachov's arms behind him and laying him face down in the sand, Collins went across to examine his handiwork. Barney was already busy, collecting up arms and carefully searching each corpse. A pyramid of rings, watches, amulets and bracelets lay glistening in the sun, a small fortune in gold that represented a handsome supplementary income to a sergeant-of-marines' pay. Collins gritted his teeth and averted his gaze as Miller, picking up a still warm cartridge case, inserted it into a dead mouth and with a quick wrist movement prised free a golden incisor. This done, and with the hoard safely stowed in his field pack, he drew the slim fighting knife that hung at his side and, flies settling thickly on his hands and forearms, proceeded to slice the left ear off each enemy corpse.

The government security forces were paid a bounty on each rebel ear – left ears only drawing the bounty to avoid paying twice for one rebel. It was a practice Collins did not entirely approve of, but was conscious that it ill became him to disapprove of a man who had played such a crucial part in the long day's fighting. Oblivious, or indifferent, to his officer's moral qualms Barney cheerfully waved his bloody windfall under Collins' nose.

'Should get a few sovs for this little lot, boss. Be able to give you a proper send-off in the mess now.' He looked wistfully down at the prone figure of Krachov, who stared at them over his shoulder in some alarm. 'I don't suppose ...' There was no profit in prisoners, even Russian prisoners. Collins smiled but shook his head.

'No, Barney. Better not.'

With the sun standing like a brazen disc on the western horizon and the shadows of the distant peaks stretching out towards them across the plain like dark fingers, there came the distant, dry threshing of the Chinook. Five days previously it had dropped a disciplined fighting force of twenty Yamani troopers and NCOs, under the command of Collins and Miller. Tonight it would return with three weary mercenaries, each indescribably happy to find himself alive. That, and enough dead meat, all locally bred, to fill a small abattoir.

Once inside the drumming whale's belly of the chopper, Collins strapped himself into the canvas seat and stretched out. Opposite, Krachov, manacled now, stared pensively out at the night, while Barney was already asleep, snoring gently. Following his example, Collins closed his eyes. It was his last operation; in three weeks he would return to Britain and civvy street.

*

'Despite being ambushed by a significantly superior enemy force...' after eight pints of Tiger and a couple of whisky chasers Barney maintained a firm and steadying grip on the bar as he continued in somewhat mocking vein, '...armed with heavy machine-guns and 4.2inch mortars, Lieutenant Collins conducted a skilful withdrawal, inflicting casualties as he went. During a five-hour action, in which he suffered the loss of almost his entire force, he continued to resist vigorously. Thanks to a display of the resourcefulness for which the Royal Marines are renowned, he ultimately succeeded in killing no less than twenty-three enemy tribesmen and capturing a foreign military adviser, as well as recovering a considerable quantity of arms. For his valour Lieutenant Collins is awarded the Yamani Star.'

With a snort of disgust Miller handed the vellum citation back, incensed at what he saw as a slight on Collins. 'Fucking Yamani Star?' It might have been a boy scout badge they were discussing. 'You'd have got an MC back home for that last little romp.'

'Ah, but we're not back home, Barney. The fact is we're not supposed to be here at all. Anyway, I don't want the bloody thing, you have it – you deserve it just as much as me.' He laid the slim, silk-covered box on the bar. 'Something to show the kids.'

In an appreciative silence that was the biggest concession either man would make to emotion, Barney nodded and slipped the case into his pocket. He drained his glass and waved it in the air absently to gain attention.

It was late, well after midnight, and the Yamani steward in the sergeant's mess sighed. He had long abandoned all hope of shifting this pair of increasingly maudlin drunks, or for that matter of seeing his wife and family that night. Signing the mess chit Barney sipped his Scotch, lapsing into an awkward silence. Collins knew what was coming.

'You really going outside, boss?'

10

'That's right, Barney. This time next month I shall be wearing a bowler hat and driving a desk in the City of London.'

'After all this? You'll hate it.'

'Hate it? Hate it? Next time you're out there in the field, up to your arse in muck and bullets and combing crabs out of your bush, Barney, think of me running amok among all those luscious office girls.'

Collins' sharp blue eyes grew thoughtful as, shaking his head, Miller eased his rump from the stool and made his uncertain way across the deserted mess in search of the heads. As if to reassure himself Collins slid a hand inside his jacket, taking out the letter that had arrived that morning. It had a boldly embossed letterhead that read: Martin & Nicholson, International Financial Services Advisers. Flattening it out on the bar he scanned it for the twentieth time that day.

'Dear Mr Collins,' it read. 'This is to confirm your appointment as an account executive on the staff of Martin & Nicholson as of Monday June 3rd. As we discussed at your last interview, you will initially be working with John Latimer who is one of our most promising young executives and from whom I feel certain you will learn much.

Your decision to join the company gives me great satisfaction since I have always been of the opinion that some form of military training ideally fits a man out for a career in the City. Here in the Square Mile, unlike many other other walks of life in contemporary Britain, the virtues of self-discipline and loyalty are still valued. I look forward to welcoming you to the company in June.'

Beneath the scrawled signature was a brief postscript. 'PS. Congratulations on the gong.'

The letter bore a cryptic reference – SM/PCW. PCW was Sir Peter Campbell-West, chairman of Martin & Nicholson and his future boss. Who, he wondered, was SM? Could she possibly have been the sloe-eyed houri who, with aloof politeness, had offered him coffee before his final interview and, the ordeal over, had arranged for a car to return him home?

Observing Barney returning, he slid the letter away. While perhaps easier in the bladder the sergeant had not, it appeared, yet come to terms with the inevitable.

'I still think you're making a mistake, boss. How old are you, twenty-two, twenty-three? With your track record you're guaranteed to pick up your captain's rank within a year and after that, who knows, you could be the youngest major in the Corps.' His tone suggested a man could aspire to nothing higher.

Collins threw back the last of his drink and, smiling cruelly, indicated to the despairing steward that yet more refills were required.

'Forget it, Barney,' he said flatly. 'I've had enough soldiering to last me a lifetime. From now on my plan is to become a walking shagging machine. I want to be up to my nuts in guts – permanently.'

Two

London, June 1974

'My God, but I love this place,' said Campbell-West softly. He stood, glass in hand, a powerful figure silhouetted in the window of his twentieth-floor office, gazing out at the City skyline that stretched away, from Tower Bridge to St Paul's, along the shimmering, half-hidden ribbon of the Thames.

Despite the hour – it was nearly seven – the mid-June sun still stood high over the fast emptying canyons of the streets below, falling warm into the office and onto the faces of the two young men who sat in respectful silence as their chairman continued.

'I have always considered myself privileged beyond measure, you know, to have been permitted to play a part, albeit a minor one, in the City's progress. Don't misunderstand me, I recognise that my role has been no more than a supporting one. But just to think of all the diverse traditions, the rich talents that have combined over nearly a thousand years to produce this unique City, makes one very aware of how much of a privilege it is simply to work here.' He sipped carefully at the smokey malt, his eyes fixed upon the vista before him, as though unable to break its spell.

'Oh Jesus,' thought Latimer as Campbell-West gathered himself, 'here we go again. We're going to get the Dick Whittington bit.' He was right.

'It must be difficult for young men like yourselves to imagine but when I came here first, in 1946, the City of London had been devastated by the Luftwaffe and the whole country was virtually bankrupt. Yet here we are, nearly thirty years later, and just look at all the old institutions. The Old Lady, the Stock Exchange, the Baltic, Lloyd's – all of them going stronger than ever. Each doing their damnedest to maintain the faith and keep the country afloat, while the bloody unions strike at the drop of a hat and let the Japs and Germans grow ever richer at our expense.

Believe me, this is a very special place, a place that has for centuries been a haven for the imaginative and the innovative – the best business minds of their time. Generation upon generation, each building on the traditions of honour and good faith laid down by the last.' He swung round to face them, jaw set hard, the fist of his right hand smacking solidly into the cupped palm of his left. He was almost shouting now.

'And it's up to those of us who care about these things to make sure that the creeping curse of socialism doesn't destroy everything they have built.'

His tantrum, despite the sincerity of the underlying emotion, was received with a silence that bordered on the embarrassing. He blinked, the handsome leonine features easing a fraction, and smiled apologetically. Perhaps such eulogising would be lost on these power-hungry youngsters, keen only to get ahead and make their mark in the world of finance. He shrugged.

'Forgive me if I seem to romanticise about what is, of course, a very hard-nosed world, but after all these years I have become something of an addict, I'm afraid. Still, I imagine that the pair of you are not totally immune to the spell that the Square Mile weaves over a certain type of man. Men of integrity and ambition, keen to carve their own path and tough enough to take destiny by the throat.' His expression grew serious. 'Indeed, I pride myself on being no mean judge of character and it is largely because I have always felt you both to be kindred spirits in a sense, that I have taken rather more than a passing interest in your careers over the last year or so.'

He went to the darkly gleaming walnut cocktail cabinet, producing an already depleted bottle of Glenfiddich and, having replenished their glasses, returned to his desk, smiling paternally at his audience.

They remained silent, outwardly relaxed but coiled and watchful, like hunting dogs on the leash, eager to learn what sort of hand fortune was about to deal them. In selecting these two he had, thought Campbell-West, chosen well.

John Latimer was twenty-four and only recently married, a fact, in view of the lateness of the hour, of which he was more than usually conscious. He knew that Charlotte would be on tenterhooks at their new home in stockbroker-belt Surrey. The champagne would be ready, chilled to celebrate whatever further opportunities his recent appointment to the main board of Martin & Nicholson was about to yield up. If only CW would spare them this, by now familiar, socio-historical tirade and come to the point.

Despite his desire to get on with the business in hand, however, Latimer was far too smooth an operator to interrupt when this man, revered and feared as a minor and sometimes vengeful god among the lower echelons of the company, was in full flow. Anyway, he understood, felt was perhaps a better word, well enough what the older man was saying. On this glorious summer evening the City of London, slumbering under the heavy sunlight, exuded a tangible sense of history, like a precious, skilfully crafted artefact set in amber.

He took a healthy pull at the Scotch in his hand and, without for one second relaxing his attention to what was being said, allowed his eyes to wander about the elegant room.

When in 1968 Campbell-West, after a year of bitter internecine strife, finally achieved the chairmanship of Martin & Nicholson, he had commissioned Sergei Lestrange, then the gilded darling of the international design scene, to construct this office. It had been his equivalent of a triumphal arch.

The desk and cabinets had been purchased in a wild profligate hunt through the auction rooms of Europe that had seen more money spent than the average clerk in the company could expect to earn in twenty years. The Sarandin prints that hung upon the walls had likewise cost a king's ransom. It was an office that had been crafted, in line with CW's specifications, to make a definitive statement about its occupant. What it said to Latimer was that this was the lair of a wealthy, powerful and potentially dangerous animal. Had the skulls and bleached carcasses of the man's business rivals been strewn upon the Kazak carpet, it would not have been totally inappropriate.

Although all this had taken place before Latimer joined the company, the successful power struggle that it celebrated was still spoken of in hushed tones among the longer serving staff. Campbell-West, it appeared, had been regarded as the outsider for the chairmanship. Only when allegations of involvement with male prostitutes by his main rival, Simon Green, appeared in the yellow press, had the struggle begun to go CW's way. How the press had got wind of this in the first place was never fully understood. Certainly even the man's closest colleagues had never suspected his indulgence in such activities. Whatever the truth of the matter, Campbell-West had been elected and Green, by all accounts a popular and capable man, had committed suicide eighteen months later.

On the wall behind the desk were maybe a dozen small, expensively-framed photographs, encapsulating in visual shorthand the career of Sir Peter Campbell-West MC. There was a beaming CW, ten years younger and immaculate in morning dress, parading with his wife and daughters outside the railings of Buckingham Palace on the day of his investiture. There was CW, resplendent in the slightly ridiculous robes of a sheriff of the City of London, officiating at a state visit to the Guildhall and CW in the livery of the Worshipful Company of Limeburners, most senior of the three liveried companies that had, to date, welcomed him, his wealth and his influence into their ranks.

In less formal vein there was a kilted, jocular CW, his arm round an attractive blonde and letting his hair down with a vengeance at some charity Burns Night or other. Elsewhere, an oilskinned CW looked grimly to windward from the helm of his beloved yacht *Ashanti* during the 1969 Fastnet race and a pink-jacketed CW brandished a stirrup cup in the saddle prior to the chase.

Above all these was mounted the Samurai sword that, as a twenty-year-old captain of the Parachute Regiment, he had accepted from a surrendering Japanese officer at the end of the Burma campaign. It was a trophy that, these days, had increasingly often to be discreetly removed whenever any of Martin & Nicholson's burgeoning number of Japanese clients demanded a personal interview with the chairman. Peter Campbell-West had certainly fitted a lot into his fifty or so years, thought Latimer.

'We both know precisely what you mean, Peter.' It was Collins who spoke, always the more dynamic, more direct of the two younger men. Even so, he was still tinglingly aware of the privilege of the omitted 'Sir'. It was a privilege that had only come with his and Latimer's apotheosis as full directors of the company two weeks earlier.

He was now twenty-six and had prospered in his time with M & N. Despite his comparative lack of experience he had, thanks to a forceful approach and a tireless application to whatever task he was charged with, climbed rapidly. Despite often making enemies on the way up, he now held equal status with the better qualified and longer serving Latimer.

Somewhat surprisingly, considering the latent rivalry in the relationship, Latimer was the only man in the company Collins actually regarded as a friend, a bond based on a mutual liking for rugby union, beer and fast cars. Six months previously Collins had been best man at Latimer's wedding.

'We're both Citymen, through and through,' he said. 'It's just that we're intrigued by the special assignment you mentioned when we first came onto the board. We're just keen as mustard to get on with it, that's all.'

Campbell-West nodded approvingly at this reaffirmation of their zeal, contrasting the stocky, fair-haired Collins with the tall, slim and darker Latimer. When he was gone, he wondered, who would come out on top in the ensuing dogfight? His money would be on Latimer. The quiet ones were always harder to read, more devious and every bit as ruthless when the moment came to plant the knife. He held up a placatory hand.

'Bear with me just a moment longer, David, and I will explain everything.' He pressed the small telephone switchboard on his desk, leaning forward as he spoke. 'Would you come in for a moment please, Sarah, there's a couple of letters I'd like to go off tonight.' Instinctively, the younger men's eyes pre-empted her appearance in the door, eager to make the most of even this brief opportunity.

Even discounting her striking good looks, their interest was understandable. Academically, Sarah Mendelsohn was better qualified than any member of the board, or for that matter anyone else in the entire company. She had come down from Oxford with a cum laude in economics and, as a favour to her father, a fellow City alderman, Campbell-West had taken her on as his personal assistant.

The appointment had been on the understanding that the position would carry a career progression to executive level, providing she proved herself. This she had done in no uncertain manner yet remained, some three years later, in her original position as Sir Peter's PA. Olive-skinned and beautifully Jewish, she stood patiently over him as he carefully reread the letters before scrawling his signature upon them. He smiled up at her.

'Thank you, Sarah, that's about it for today I think. I'm likely to be here for another hour or so, so perhaps you'd like to switch the phones through to my extension before you leave.'

Without comment save for a brief good night to them all, she went, gliding tall and full-breasted, across the room. Latimer marvelled at the way they managed to maintain such a businesslike relationship in the office when it was common, though strictly unspoken, knowledge throughout the firm that CW had, for two years now, maintained her in a plush apartment in the Barbican. It was an apartment he shared during the week before returning dutifully to Fairview, the family home in Oxfordshire, and Lady Campbell-West at the weekend.

More than twice his own age, Campbell-West had retained a zest for the pleasures of life that sometimes made Latimer envious. More importantly, he had accumulated the all-important means of affording them. As she closed the door behind her CW laid down his pen and came to the point. He was in his bluff, no-nonsense mode now; the history lesson was over.

'Right, let's get down to business. In a nutshell, what we, or rather you, David, and you, John, are going to do is to set up an offshore subsidiary of this company.' He frowned, clasping his hands on the desk before him. Politics was a messy business, thank heavens he was just a simple businessman.

'I'm sure I don't have to spell it out. Thanks to the balls-up the Heath government has made in its handling of the miners' strike, it's clear we are going to be stuck with a socialist regime for the next four years at least. As a result, from the point of view of the people we act for, especially the big foreign punters, the tax position in the United Kingdom looks guaranteed to get worse rather than better.

If we hope to continue attracting blue chip clients at the rate we have achieved over the last decade or so, we are going to have to find somewhere new to operate from. Somewhere that won't confiscate hard-earned profits to subsidise inefficient nationalised industries, or to pay Danegeld to the unions. If Scargill and his bully boys can bring down Heath they can, sure as hell, bring down any socialist government that won't play their game. Wilson knows he's only in power thanks to the miners – he's not going to rock the boat.

Until the Tories have sorted themselves out and Westminster returns to sound fiscal policies we must be able to operate from somewhere that offers tax levels which won't frighten clients away. I refuse to let the company stagnate just because – please God only temporarily – the lunatics have taken over the asylum.

We are in the financial services business which means, putting it in its crudest terms, making as much money as possible, within the right and proper constraints of the law, for those people who entrust us with their personal fortunes. If we can't do it as efficiently as our competitors then those clients – and who's to blame them – will take their business elsewhere. I, for one am not prepared to see that happen. Not without a fight anyway.'

His eyes came up to bear on them. They weren't even listening to his lecture and he smiled inwardly. It was understandable enough for he could imagine what they were thinking, presented with an opportunity like this, a chance to establish themselves as big-league operators and earn serious money. He understood, thoroughly approved, and wished he were thirty years younger.

So that was it, Latimer thought, they were going offshore. Well, it made a lot of sense. But offshore where exactly, and

20

would it mean a permanent posting overseas? That might not go down too well with Charlotte, just settled into married life, possibly pregnant and blissfully contented among the up-wardly-mobile trappings of middle-class suburbia. While he digested and evaluated the possibilities, again it was Collins who spoke first.

'It's a natural move of course, Peter. Several of our main rivals have already set up offshore operations. But where are we going – the Channel Islands, Lichtenstein?'

Campbell-West shook his head. Getting up he went to the ornate Georgian bookcase, drawing forth a heavy, leather-bound atlas. Setting it down on the desk between them he flicked through the crisp, whispering leaves until he came to a double-page projection of the Caribbean. After a moment's closer examination, he placed a forefinger just north of the coast of Venezuela.

'Ever heard of Algoa?' he enquired, continuing without a pause for their admissions of ignorance. 'I have to admit that I hadn't until about six months ago. Well, it's a small island in the southern Caribbean. Along with Aruba, Curaçao and Bonaire it used to form part of the Dutch West Indies. It remained a Dutch colony up until 1961 when, after a great deal of agitation by Venezuelan-backed activists, it became independent. By supplying arms and moral support at the UN, the Venezuelans had hoped that, once the Dutch pulled out, the island would quickly be absorbed into their sphere of influence. They had reckoned, however, without the in-tervention of a local politician, a remarkable man by the name of Caruso Sandarte.

After a few weeks of chaos and near civil war, the good people of Algoa, accustomed as they were to the philosophies of siesta and mañana, quickly wearied of the demands that democratic rule placed upon them. Sandarte was able, thanks to the promise of healthy pay rises to the police and the discreet removal of several of his main political opponents, to establish himself as President. It's a tribute to the man's political skills that he has remained securely in that position ever since. While some of his practices might not appeal overmuch to those of us used to life under the Mother of Parliaments, he has maintained law and order for over thirteen years now. Today Algoa is a stable and, by Caribbean standards, prosperous state.

Up to now the island has relied for its wealth almost entirely on the sugar cane trade and, to a lesser extent, on tourism, mainly from the United States. But Sandarte is keen to put the economy on a broader base than that. To achieve this he has, over the past couple of years or so, been actively canvassing firms on both sides of the Atlantic, trying to encourage banks, insurance companies and organisations like ours, in the financial services sector, to establish subsidiaries on the island.

His message is plain and clear. Come to Algoa, build offices, employ and train local people, and we will offer you a rate of taxation that pales into insignificance when compared to those prevailing in the recognised financial centres of the world. In effect, there is no direct taxation of investment income on the island: an almost unique situation. What Sandarte is looking for in return is a commitment to setting up a strong trading infrastructure and to putting Algoa on the map in the world of international finance.

I have, on behalf of the board of Martin & Nicholson, been in contact with the Algoan Minister of Finance for some months now. From the very beginning of negotiations he has made it crystal clear that his government will offer us every assistance possible in the event of our opening an office there. Well, that decision was taken several weeks ago and so, what you two will be required to do is to go out there and get things moving.

You'll have to obtain suitable premises. You will also need to recruit a small team of appropriately qualified staff; a balanced team sufficient in size and skills to enable us to service a significant proportion of our existing accounts from Algoa.'

Standing, he returned to the window, his back to them, chin drawn into his chest, hands clasped behind. There was something Napoleonic in the pose. 'You should be aware that there is one aspect of this project which will need very careful handling. Because of the tax implications, which are far from clear at the moment, it is essential that we, the parent company that is, maintain as low a profile as possible.

The Revenue's attitude towards the taxation of funds held offshore is ambivalent at the moment. However, since it's an option that more and more investment companies are likely to take up now that the comrades are in power, they will certainly be looking for means of getting their bite of the cherry one way or another. One thing we can't afford is to find, at some future date, that our operations are saddled with a monumental tax bill. So, as far as possible, we will treat the new company as being independent. It won't stop the Revenue sniffing around of course, but it will make their job that much more difficult.' He smiled conspiratorially. 'As we all know, tax evasion is illegal and very reprehensible. Tax avoidance on the other hand is the City's national game.

One special feature of the deal requires us to support the local banking community. Sandarte's ambition is to establish a system based on the Swiss model. There's a lot of hot money circulating in Latin America these days, much of it generated by some very suspect deals indeed. A secure bolt hole close to home is sure to attract billions.

The Banco del Carib is a joint venture between the Algoan Government and the private sector. All M & N funds will be held and serviced by them. They've recruited some top-class banking talent from the States and what little I've seen of them suggests they are a pretty slick outfit. I don't foresee any special problems with the arrangement.

You'll find, when you get out there, that some of the groundwork has already been carried out so you won't be starting from scratch. We recruited a representative early on, an American woman by the name of Chantelle Kolowitz. She's an ex-commodity broker from the New York Exchange and she's been acting on our behalf for the last four months or so.

As of this moment you two are appointed joint managing directors and, of course, will have the final say in all matters. Mrs Kolowitz – she's divorced incidentally – will report directly to you. On matters of public relations and in your dealings with the Algoan Government I recommend that you listen to whatever the lady has to say.

Having seen what she has achieved in the short time she's been with M & N it will be to everyone's advantage, I feel, if she is given the widest possible scope for individual action. I've met her on a number of occasions now and she's a most resourceful young woman and one, moreover, who has excellent contacts both on the island and back in the States. I am confident that she will bring a number of lucrative accounts with her, once the new company is operational.

As I say, you two are joint bosses, let there be no mistake about that, but treat the lady with respect, she's a pretty tough cookie who could attract a lot of nice business. With your agreement, once the thing's up and running and you've had a chance to see her in action, we will appoint her operations director.' His eyes came up, a wicked twinkle in evidence. 'As if that wasn't enough, she has the looks of a film star and, so far as I can ascertain, is currently unattached. I really envy the pair of you.'

Collins raised his glass, clearly delighted at the prospects in hand. 'Here's to the new company.'

Latimer sipped carefully. 'How soon do you want us out there, Peter?'

Campbell-West made a show of considering the matter as

24

though it had not, until then, occurred to him.

'Let's see. Today is Friday. You are, as of now, relieved of all your previous responsibilities. Indeed, I imagine most of the past two weeks have been spent handing over to your appointed replacements. I suggest you take a few days leave and then fly out at the back end of next week sometime. It's a rather long-winded journey at present, I'm afraid. There are regular flights from Schiphol. The nearest major airport is Willemstad on Curaçao, about thirty miles east of Algoa and from there you'll have to charter a private flight.

Whether or not you eventually decide you need to be permanently based on the island I leave entirely up to you. In the event of your upping sticks the company will, naturally, pay all your relocation expenses. I suspect, though, you may well find that, once things are running smoothly out there, you could operate from London and visit on a monthly basis, just to keep an eye on things. As I say, you'll find Chantelle Kolowitz is a very competent administrator.

Anyway, I want the whole shooting match up and running by the end of August. We have already drawn up a list of suitable accounts that could, at short notice, be transferred to Algoa without any problems with the Revenue. After that we start work recruiting abroad and convincing as many as possible of our current British clients, with overseas assets, to transfer them to the new company.'

Returning to the cocktail cabinet Campbell-West produced a bottle of Dom Perignon, holding it aloft with a flourish for their approval. 'I think the occasion calls for a special celebration, gentlemen.' The cork exploded spectacularly and he carefully poured out three foaming tulip glasses, pausing before handing them round. 'Since too blatantly Anglo-Saxon names tend to attract the attention of the British tax man, Martin & Nicholson will on this occasion be sailing under false colours.' He raised his glass. 'Here's to AFS – Algoan Financial Services.'

Suddenly thoughtful, Latimer watched as, beyond the double glazing, a helicopter, a black dragonfly, drove swiftly and silently across the golden evening. They had, he knew, been presented with a fantastic opportunity. Even so, it was likely to bring problems. For a start, what would Charlotte say? Apart from holidays her horizons had always been limited. For her, Guildford was the centre of the civilized world. She liked it there, living close to her mother. Rigidly middle class, he knew she was not cut out for life on a tropical island. Nor was she in the least adaptable to change.

'Charlotte will make a perfect mother,' her own mother had told him. Soon to be put to the test, this was probably true, for she freely admitted that it was her ultimate ambition. Equally true was the fact that she would never learn to live with the demands of his work.

Collins smiled across at him. 'To fame and fortune.'

Campbell-West, however, had the last word with the ancient masonic toast: 'That profit and pleasure may be the outcome.'

Three

Algoa, April 1980

When Collins woke, to sunlight and the plangent call of the oriole, he thought for one moment that Chantelle had risen early. Then he smiled, becoming aware of the gentle yet insistent tugging of her mouth, working, hot and moist, beneath the sheets. Closing his eyes, he arched his back languorously, curling strong fingers in her thick mane, pulling her hard onto him. When she had finished, hungrily drawing the final surge of quicksilver seed between wicked scarlet lips, she reappeared, surfacing beside him like a lovely mermaid. Slightly breathless, her blonde hair was tousled, her breasts gleaming damply under a sheen of sweat.

'Good morning, darling,' she drawled, 'how about a swim before breakfast?'

It was a regular opening gambit. Without ever becoming mundane, their lovemaking had fallen into a well-rehearsed pattern; they traded orgasms as others traded stamps. Like most American women Chantelle regarded sexual fulfilment as a God-given right; something that should have been written into the Declaration of Independence. What she was saying was: 'That's one you owe me.' Collins considered the situation. Today, despite her skilful ministrations, his erection lingered. If he seized the moment he might yet pay his debt on the nail.

With one swift move he mounted her, bringing a low moan of delight as he entered, a practised, almost casual, thrust of his hips sliding him easily into her welcoming wetness. She stared up, eyes wide with surprise and pleasure yet at the same time almost resentful at the dismissive ease with which he had taken her. Slowly at first, he pumped away with a relentless persistence that, devoid of all tenderness, nevertheless quickly took her, writhing voluptuously, into a carnal dance.

'Come on,' he hissed. 'Take it. Take every inch of it.'

Chantelle's hands clawed at the pillow and her legs locked about him; she grunted sow-like as the first galvanising bolts hit home. Then she screamed, head thrown back, the dancing static that darted and played about her very core swelling irresistibly into an electric tide, pounding through her like a shaft of flame.

'Oh, yes,' she gasped, eyes pressed tight, 'oh, yes.'

As the moment passed and the flood subsided he felt her loosen beneath him, limbs softening into a dreamy torpor. He kissed her eyelids gently, yet there was a mocking edge of triumph in his words.

'Right then. What about that swim?'

Collins was, by any standards, a very fit man, working out regularly in the gymnasium to maintain the hard edge that had served him so well in his service career. Nevertheless, for the best part of a thousand yards she matched him stroke for stroke until, with Collins applying the pressure and drawing away, she rolled onto her back with a low laugh.

'OK, Tarzan, I give in. I'll see you at breakfast.'

He ploughed steadily on for a further fifteen minutes then, having showered, he joined her at the poolside table where Anita, the Filipino housemaid, was setting out the breakfast things beneath a wide yellow parasol. Leaning over he kissed Chantelle on the cheek, his hand straying inside her bright orange robe to squeeze a ripe breast; a hand she lightly slapped away in mock disapproval. Well aware that he had bedded both the maids she took the occasion to let Anita, who was now concentrating hard on achieving a geometric perfection to the table settings, know just who ruled the roost. She had long since realised he was promiscuous by nature and was, within reason, content to let him have his head so long as her hegemony at home and in the office was not threatened.

'David, will you please behave. What would Sir Peter say?'

Clasping his hands behind his head, Collins stretched back in his seat, looking up at the scarlet frigate bird that had cruised in from the bay, hanging motionless above them in the azure sky before side-slipping away on the wind.

'Peter Campbell-West would say, I'm sure, that you and I can do whatever we please so long as we continue to attract the kind of clients and produce the same calibre of business that we have over the past five years. He knows full well that, if it wasn't for our operation here, Martin & Nicholson would still be a middle-sized, middle-of-the-road, middle-of-the-pack outfit, instead of the market leader it has become. Anyway, hopefully you'll be able to ask him yourself today. That's assuming he turns up. If he's spent the last twenty-four hours kicking his heels at Schiphol, he's sure to be in a foul mood. I hope he's happy with the arrangements we've made for him.'

'He should be. I've booked him and Miss Israel into the Parmelia for a change. Separate but adjoining suites, I hope that wasn't too extravagant.'

He smiled. Although they had met on no more than half-a-dozen occasions there was little love lost between tough, streetwise Chantelle and the precious, cossetted Sarah.

'Of course not. With the sort of profits the company's shown this year I think we can afford to spend a little on the luxuries. I'm going down to meet them at the airstrip this morning. Will you be coming along?'

'No. I'll just make sure everything is up to scratch at the

office before Sir Peter does his tour of inspection. I wouldn't want José trying to sell him lottery tickets or offering him a discount on Consuela's body.'

Collins poured a tall glass of iced orange before attacking the scrambled eggs the housemaid had laid before them.

'By the way, we're all invited to dine with Sandarte up at the Residence tomorrow evening, I had hoped we might dodge it but Peter's keen that we maintain a high corporate profile. He's going to use the occasion to announce the company's intention of setting up a scholarship for Algoan students in London. It's all good public relations from our point of view, so I suppose we shouldn't complain.'

She didn't comment and he watched as she spread her marmalade, even this mundane task receiving her complete concentration; she frowned as she attempted to achieve a perfectly even layer that covered the triangle of toast precisely. She was not tall and the full breasts and buttocks would certainly have begun to sag on a less active woman. On her, however, thanks to regular tennis and riding at the local country club, everything was as firm as on a fifteen-year-old, an age which, in fact, was exactly half her own.

They had become lovers during the first hectic months when he and Latimer had arrived on the island to take charge of AFS. Initially he had suspected that it had been a cynical ploy on her part, designed to safeguard her position in the company and, with equal cynicism, he had accepted the affair on that basis. However, after five years of working together, he was now well aware that she had had no need to feel insecure about her ability to meet the demands made of her. The truth was, the effort she had put in prior to their arrival, fixing local authorities, greasing palms and all the while establishing useful contacts, had made their task painfully simple. It was thanks largely to her single-minded approach that AFS had been in commission a full month ahead of Campbell-West's deadline.

Collins recognised now that, as a young, healthy woman whose marriage to a Boston lawyer had collapsed, publicly and messily, six months before, he had arrived on the scene at precisely the right moment to satisfy her unfulfilled physical needs.

She was tough and highly efficient and, in the early days, had hired and fired without fear or favour. As a result, these days the company boasted probably the best qualified and most loyal staff of any firm on the island, with dozens of hopefuls, young blacks from the shanty towns mainly, keen to escape the cane fields or hotel kitchens, applying for jobs every week.

It had been their flowering relationship, and the subsequent decision to set up house together, that had resulted in the current arrangement. He and Chantelle had elected to provide the permanent M & N presence in Algoa, while Latimer, under the lash from his increasingly waspish and regularly pregnant wife, had opted to operate from London. He visited the Algoan office every three months or so for consultations and at the time of the annual audit. All in all, Collins reflected, it was a management structure that had worked out very nicely for everyone concerned.

Certainly, they had done exceedingly well on a financial level, both for the company and for themselves. The house, Villa Franche, one of the largest properties in the fashionable Calicas Bay district and which he owned outright, stood in several acres of carefully tended plantations and gardens. It would be guaranteed, he knew, should they ever choose to sell, to realise well over two million US dollars. They maintained a household staff of two maids, a cook and a gardener, as well as a chauffeur who, since Collins hated to be driven anywhere, had little to do. As a member of the island's Chamber of Commerce and patron of a number of local charities, he had become a respected figure in Algoan society. His relationship with Chantelle, he reflected, had been the icing on a very substantial cake.

She looked up, her eyes catching his, and smiled, bare toes caressing his leg beneath the table. Despite his indiscretions and the inevitable emotional attrition of the years, there was still a strong bond between them. They were, as he usually pointed out when he had been caught with his hand on the wrong knee, a good team.

'When is John due out next? It seems like ages since he was here last,' she asked.

Her question was not entirely ingenuous. On his previous visits to Algoa she had become his confidante to some extent, and he had spoken freely about his own unhappy marriage. From this had developed a relationship that was now ambivalent and which she found rather unsettling. She had begun to anticipate his arrivals with a furtive sensuousness.

'Next month sometime, I think. We'll have to find somewhere new to take him this time. I thought we might charter one of the yachts down in Lambura Bay. I heard that Salazar's just had a brand new ketch delivered from the States. If we could get hold of something like that we could spend a week cruising, sail down to Maracaibo maybe. You know John, put him in a boat and he's happy. More to the point, he won't have Charlotte and those cretinous kids with him this time, so we can hopefully manage to enjoy ourselves without a continual discourse on pisspots and post natal piles.'

Four and a half thousand miles away, there was a definite feeling of spring in the air that April morning as, having parked his company Jaguar, newly delivered that week, Latimer walked briskly up Fenchurch Street, the coffee and bacon smells of the breakfast bars assailing his nostrils. Broad shafts of saffron sunlight slanted down the narrow streets. The heavy winter coats of a few weeks before were today out of fashion as City girls, as always, proved quick to display their physical charms at the earliest opportunity. Breasts and legs, that had been in deep hibernation since the autumn equinox, were today very much in evidence and he could do nothing but approve.

Latimer, in fact, was feeling pretty good all round that morning. And not without reason. With Campbell-West out of the country for three weeks at least, it promised to be a very pleasant interlude. Not that he harboured any personal dislike of the chairman, far from it, for the man had been largely instrumental in launching them all on a seemingly endless upward spiral. It was just that during his absences abroad, these having become increasingly frequent of late, Latimer was quietly easing himself into the role of acting head of the whole group. It wasn't official of course, but its tacit acceptance by the other senior directors augured well for the future. And he was having fun too. Already his diary was filling up nicely, mainly with expensive lunches and dinners, the all-important, and pleasurable, chore of entertaining current and potential clients.

He reminded himself to double-check that his secretary had booked him into the Great Eastern on Thursday. If Ali Mubarek was coming over to discuss the portfolios of those members of the Bahraini royal family who, to the dismay of the competition, were currently contemplating using Martin & Nicholson as their financial advisers, it was sure to mean a night of gambling and hard drinking. Also, if past experience was anything to go by, it was likely to culminate in a tour of the more arcane and nastier parts of Soho. With Charlotte and the children away at her mother's, breaking the news of official confirmation of a third happy event in the Latimer household and their impending move to a larger house to accommodate this mini population explosion, there would be no point in driving back to Surrey. Indeed, in view of Mubarek's capacity for champagne, it might well prove positively dangerous. No, he would stay up in town.

Saluting smartly, the bemedalled commissionaire held open the plate-glass doors at the entrance of the M & N Building and then marched stiffly ahead of him to the lift, pressing the button while, politely but firmly, directing other would-be ascenders of lesser corporate eminence to await the next lift.

While he waited, snakeskin briefcase in hand and rather enjoying the impotent resentment around him, it occured to Latimer, not for the first time, that until the family returned at the end of the following week, he was a free agent. As he rose, in silent and splendid isolation, he examined his image approvingly in the half-mirrored walls of the lift, returning a knowing smile. Perhaps it was time to give Victoria a call.

By 12.30, with all the important business of the day satisfactorily dealt with, he looked towards the phone, the exquisite blend of guilt and anticipation bringing the usual delicious frisson at his groin. No, not yet. Better just check that all was well in Algoa first. He did a quick mental calculation of the time differential between London and the island; it would be early morning there now. No matter, it would look good if he phoned to ensure that CW had arrived safely. It would show that he was concerned for his colleagues' welfare and, more importantly, that he still kept an eye on the business, albeit from the other side of the Atlantic. He didn't want to give Collins and the gorgeous Chantelle an opportunity of upstaging him.

It took a good ten minutes to get through to the island, Chantelle's voice coming, crystal clear, down the line.

'Jesus, John. Do you know what time it is? We're just having breakfast.'

'Sorry to disturb your bacon and eggs, darling, but I'm not going to be around for the rest of the day. Just checking that CW arrived safely.'

Her initially aggrieved tone ameliorated somewhat as Collins' arm entwined vinelike round her inner thigh beneath the table and, smiling wickedly, she shifted her position.

'As a matter of fact he hasn't turned up yet. They were due yesterday afternoon. Dave went down to the airstrip to meet them but they weren't on the regular inter-island plane. We checked out Curaçao, but they had no record of them being on the flight from Amsterdam. I guess they must have stayed over an extra night – probably turn up today sometime. Anyway, if he contacts you in the meantime, let us know what his plans are, will you?'

'Sure. Is David there?' There was a brief delay, as Collins disengaged himself from the highly personal massage he was applying to Chantelle's nether regions, and took the handset from her.

'Hi, John.'

'What's all this with CW then? I suppose the old bastard's taken the opportunity to give Sarah a right royal seeing-to in the Amsterdam Hilton. Anyway, never mind all that, what delights are you laying on for my forthcoming visit to your tropical paradise? Only three weeks away you know. Nothing too lavish, you understand, just spoil me something rotten – that will be quite sufficient.'

'We thought you might like to get some sailing in. I'm going to see if I can charter a boat. We can try and get down to the mainland – Venezuela or Colombia maybe. It's only a couple of days away. I might bring Anita along to do the cooking – that's right, the one with the big jugs – so all we'll have to do is sail the boat and get a suntan. Does that meet with your approval?'

'Sounds terrific. Love to Chantelle. Talk to you later.'

Putting down the phone, Latimer stared thoughtfully out of the window. Despite his studiedly casual reaction to the news of CW's delayed arrival on Algoa, it had set alarms ringing in his head. He buzzed his secretary, or rather the latest in a line of incompetent temps that had filled in since the departure of Joanne. His regular and, it would appear, grossly overpaid secretary had, with minimal notice, embarked on a three-week safari in Kenya with a 'super guy' who had picked her up in some wine bar. The new girl, black and helpful, but no more capable than her hastily discharged predecessors, looked round the door warily.

'Will you get onto the Amsterdam Hilton please, Maxine. Find out if Sir Peter has checked out yet and, if so, when. If by any chance he's still there I'll have a word with him.'

After half an hour she returned. Yes, Sir Peter Campbell-West had definitely checked out earlier that morning. According to the hotel register, his next port of call was to be Curaçao en route for Algoa.

'Thanks, Maxine. I shall probably be out of the office for the rest of the day. If anyone wants me I'm with the people from Drysdales all afternoon. I shall have my phone with me, so you can always get in touch if anything really important comes up.'

Reassured, he waited for her to leave the room before picking up his personal direct line.

'Good morning, good afternoon rather, it's John Latimer here, can I speak to Lady Campbell-West please?' He doodled idly on his blotter while he waited, diminishing spirals that led nowhere, luxuriating in anticipation of her voice. 'Hallo, Victoria? It's me. I was just sitting here, staring out of the window and wondering what Oxfordshire is like at this time of year ... Yes, I imagine it must be. As a matter of fact I was experiencing an overpowering urge to come and see it for myself. Can you make dinner at The Plough tonight? ... Terrific, I should be with you sometime round about four. I'll phone first and book a room – who shall we be this time? Something simple but dignified, I think. Carruthers has a certain ring about it, don't you think? ... Yes, we'll be Mr and Mrs Carruthers. See you in the bar.'

The Plough was a converted coach house, not far from Banbury, that charged, and readily obtained, outrageous rates for the privilege of eating superbly in largely genuine Jacobean surroundings. Latimer had discovered it in the course of visiting clients in the area and now used it regularly for its impeccable standards of service and discretion. Equally attractive was the more prosaic consideration that he could, thanks to its location close to the estates of several gentlemen farmers who used the company on occasion, safely charge it to expenses without fear of awkward questions being asked by accounts department. As he drew across the broad tarmac forecourt, he was pleased to see Victoria's gleaming emerald-green BMW already parked outside.

She was sitting in the otherwise empty bar, an example of that endangered species, a correctly assembled Pimms, in her hand, a double Scotch on the table, awaiting his arrival. As he kissed the offered up cheek, the fragrance of her perfume came to him and he laid his hand on the elegant nape of her neck, feeling her tremble under his touch.

Victoria Campbell-West remained, despite her forty-seven years, a strikingly beautiful woman. Tall and elegant, the lines at her wide brown eyes only served to emphasise the Nefertiti-like beauty of the high cheek bones, while the regular cosseting of health farms had kept her figure trim yet sufficiently well fleshed to appeal to men half her age.

Although not naturally given to casual carnality, her husband's constant infidelities, of which Sarah Mendelsohn was only the latest in a long and distinguished line and in which he made little attempt to exercise discretion, had, from an early stage of their marriage, led her to develop a life of her own outside the family circle. Latimer had first met her socially at a company dinner when, as a promising young associate director, he had fallen under the spell of her austere beauty and natural grace. From the initial, unmistakeable establishment of eye contact, he had pursued her remorselessly until, almost a year ago now, at a time when CW was being especially unpleasant, she had succumbed to his persistence, his flattery and to her own increasing loneliness.

'I do hope you haven't been waiting long, darling,' he said, drawing up a chair beside her, 'the traffic on the M40 was absolutely awful.'

'Five minutes, no more. I went into Oxford this morning to get a few things.' She reached down into the carrier bags grouped about her feet. 'I guessed you wouldn't think of it, so I bought you a change of shirt and underwear. Can't have you going into the office looking less than smart tomorrow, can we?'

She ran a moist tongue across her lips, casting a cautious glance over her shoulder to ensure they were not being watched. 'I bought myself a little present too. I hope you approve.' She smiled naughtily and, unbuttoning the short, silver fox jacket she wore, allowed it to open slightly, revealing a solitary diamond pendant nestling snugly in the deep cleavage between her naked breasts. 'What do you think?'

Throwing his Scotch back in one he took her hand, kissing the soft flesh of the palm.

'Shall we go up?'

Four

Côte d'Azur, South of France

Conchita Pacino looked about her in wonder, hugging herself close in delight. Yesterday she had been in Algoa, today she was on the Côte d'Azur. When you mixed with men like Ramone Enriques things certainly happened fast. Her eyes went about her again. The only thing that she could recall as being even vaguely comparable to the lounge of the Caravel Hotel was the directors' suite back at the bank. The offices she had swept and dusted, grateful for the work, until her dark Indian beauty had caught Ramone's ever-hungry eye.

The lounge, with its gleaming steel fittings, marble tables and deep pastel carpet, exuded an air of tasteful excess. In every corner a waiter stood poised and eager, almost desperate to fulfil the most outlandish caprice; to satisfy the merest whim. Screwing up her courage, Conchita raised a tentative hand, bringing the nearest hurrying to her table.

'A tequila please.'

She knew Ramone, had he been there, would not have approved, it was not ladylike, he always told her, to drink tequila. It was a peasant's drink. Ramone only drank champagne.

She looked down at the glass in her hand, the slightest of frowns creasing the bridge of her classic nose. On the back of her right hand was a small tattoo, a faded blue and red flower. She had had it put there to celebrate her first serious emotional attachment, at the age of thirteen, to Paco Santana, the huge negro cane cutter who had initiated her into the mysteries of carnality. Now, three years later and the mistress, no, future wife, of a government minister, she regretted it.

Ramone disapproved of tattoos, as he did of so many things, and had hinted that a plastic surgeon he knew could remove it quite simply. For Conchita a hint from his direction was as a tablet of stone. It was of no great importance; in return for all this, she could accept some minor discomfort. She sipped at the burning drink naughtily. Paco had been a wonderful lover, young yet experienced, with the body of a panther. Ramone was fifty-five, very fat, and with an unfortunate tendency to sweat under pressure, physical or mental. She did not mind, Paco had lived in a dirt-poor shanty town and talked of going to America. Most likely he would continue doing both until the day he died. Ramone, on the other hand, had taken her on business trips to Miami and Havana. And now, the pinnacle of sophistication, France.

Outside, across the black oily waters of the bay, she could see the lights of the *Amaryllis*, a string of yellow pearls tracing the lines of the ship's masts and superstructure on the velvet backdrop of the night. Soon she would be dining on board with Ramone at her side, making polite conversation with an English knight and his lady.

Once he had completed his business he would send a boat to collect her, Ramone had said, and from her window seat she would be able to see any vessel coming alongside at the hotel's private jetty. Smoothing her dress down over her knees she raised her hand to indicate that another tequila was required. This time, greatly daring, she clicked her fingers. If she was going to be an asset to Ramone, she told herself, she would have to assert herself.

*

MY *Amaryllis* had originally been Her Majesty's Canadian Ship *Chippewa*, an anti-submarine destroyer of 1600 tons that, redundant after the end of the Second World War, had been a snip at $20,000. Now, nearly forty years old, thanks to regular refits she remained a sleek, fast ship, still capable of twenty-five knots at a pinch.

Between decks, however, she bore little resemblance to the warship that had played cat-and-mouse with Hitler's wolf packs for the best part of four years. Her new owner had paid maybe five times the purchase price to refit her to a standard that escaped the charge of ostentation by the merest whisker. On the foredeck, where 'A' and 'B' turrets had once stood guard over fat convoys bound for beleaguered Britain, a heated swimming pool now waited to receive the lissom bodies of society's darlings. At the stern, where A/S mortars had once hurled screaming death into the depths, parasols and loungers were set out in preparation for tomorrow's sun worshippers to make their offering of flesh.

In the panelled state room, despite the air-conditioning, Ramone Enriques was sweating profusely. He was getting too old for this sort of thing. How did Campbell-West manage to maintain his infuriating English sang-froid? He took a delaying sip of the special cuvée Champagne, trying to compose himself. The ship was very quiet, the only sound the distant hum of a generator singing softly to itself two decks below.

'You have the passports?'

Campbell-West laid two leather-bound booklets on the table between them.

'As agreed, Ramone, one US passport for you and one Venezuelan passport for your companion. In the unlikely event of trouble, dual nationality can be such a godsend. You have the money?'

Enriques lay his hand-tooled briefcase on the table.

'The final transfers, ten million in US Dollars, five million in Swiss Francs and another five in Deutschmarks, have all been successfully deposited in Geneva. In six months they will be converted into whatever currencies are at that time attractive and moved to our previously established accounts in Basle. Trying to get information about one numbered account is hard enough; by the time the funds have been through two or three banks and currency conversions they will be virtually untraceable. As agreed we will not touch any of these monies until the end of 1982 at the earliest.' With a click he opened the case and began drawing out banded wads of crumpled $10 dollar bills, laying them in neat rows on the table. When he had finished he looked to Campbell-West, the merest hint of a challenge in his eyes.

'Precisely $250,000. Do you want to count it?' Campbell-West looked pained.

'My dear chap, of course not. We're friends – and men of honour.' Enriques, shamed by the other man's open-handedness, relented. He dabbed at his forehead with an already damp handkerchief.

'Forgive me, Peter. I'm very tense tonight. It's taken a lot of planning, and these last few days – the pressures have been enormous.' He pinched his brow between thumb and forefinger as Campbell-West topped up his glass. Clearly the man was troubled. Having locked the money away in his desk he came and laid a consoling hand on the Algoan's shoulder.

'You really must learn to relax, Ramone. It's over now. We've done it. By tomorrow we will be away from here, the richer by tens of millions and free to live the rest of our lives howsoever we choose.' His eyes brightened. 'I tell you what, old man, before we send the cutter ashore to pick up ... er, Conchita, why don't you let me take you down to the sick bay and ask our resident nurse to give you something for your nerves. She's a marvellous girl. I'm sure she'll be able to prescribe something.'

In the brightly lit sickbay, amid equipment guaranteed to make the most devout hypochondriac feel immortal, Miss

Lee listened sympathetically. In her time on the yacht she had seen many businessmen brought to the verge of a breakdown by the pressures of work. 'Poor dear,' the almond eyes seemed to say. She laid a cool hand on the sticky brow and took a podgy wrist to check his pulse. Then she smiled brightly.

'Nothing serious, I think. Just a touch of hypertension – you've been overdoing things, Señor Enriques. I can give you drugs if you wish but, for the best results, I would recommend a short course of acupuncture.' Enriques looked doubtful; for him the art of acupuncture smacked of quackery if not downright black magic. Moreover, the mere thought of needles under the skin made him shudder; he had a very low pain threshold. She was quick to reassure him. 'It is entirely painless – Sir Peter will tell you. He swears it's the only thing that will lift his migraine. In ten minutes your tension will have vanished entirely.'

'She's absolutely right, old man. I'd been a martyr to it for years until I met Miss Lee here.' He paused tellingly. 'Doesn't hurt either.' Not wishing to be thought a coward as well as a worrier, Enriques took the plunge.

'Very well, if you really think it will do the trick.'

'Splendid,' Campbell-West was standing in the doorway now, keen to leave them alone. 'I'll send the cutter off to collect Conchita in five minutes. By the time they get back, you'll be as fit as a fiddle. We should all be ready to eat by 9 o'clock.'

As the door clicked shut Miss Lee came close.

'Take off your clothes please, Señor Enriques, you may keep your underpants, and sit in the chair.'

Settling himself into the padded dentist's chair he watched as she carefully collected his scattered clothes and, neatly folding each garment, placed them in a clear plastic wallet. From one of the stainless steel lockers that lined the bulkhead she took a slim leather-bound case. Laying it flat she slid back the brass clasps and stared down thoughtfully at its contents, before lighting a flickering alcohol burner he assumed would be to sterilise her instruments of torture. Her preoccupation allowed him the chance to run a tutored eye over her slim figure. She was pretty in a small-breasted way, he thought, with nice knees that peeped out between her overall. Already he was relaxing.

'Where did you learn acupuncture, Miss Lee?'

'Shanghai. In China I am a doctor. In the west I am only a nurse.'

'What can you treat besides nervous complaints?'

'Many things. Muscular problems, cancer sometimes, impotence. Many things.' Ramone's interest grew.

'Where do you put the needles for impotence?'

She laughed. It was a question they all asked.

'Not where you might think.' She came to his side. At the press of a button a motor hummed and he was raised and extended like an Aztec sacrifice as the chair converted into a horizontal couch. She looked down at him, sufficient concern on her face to convey professionalism, and laid a hand on the taut, sweat-oiled parchment of his gross stomach. 'No need to worry. First I put two needles here,' tingling fingers he could not see indicated a point midway between genitals and navel. 'These are just to relax you.' Ramone gritted his teeth.

To his surprise and relief, however, it did indeed prove to be totally painless. What was more, within a minute or so he was feeling more relaxed than he had for many a long day. Another five minutes or so passed and Miss Lee returned.

'How you feel now?'

'Good. Very good.' Her hand played on the golden needles, vibrating them between slim fingers, radiating a warm glow that spread until it eventually extended to his groin. At first it was just a pleasant sensation then, to his surprise and embarrassment, he felt his organ begin to stir. She laughed aloud at his confusion and released her hold on the needles.

It was with mixed feelings that Ramone felt his customary flaccidity returning.

'You see. Acupuncture good for many things.' The tone was teasing.

Relieved to find that she was deliberately flirting with him he grew bold enough to stroke the tight roundness of a buttock. At something of a disadvantage in the world of fringe medicine, when it came to sex Ramone was on firmer ground. A pretty young nurse on a rich man's yacht must get lots of chances to make extra cash with tricks like that. What might take a nymphet like Conchita an hour's work, and even then with no guarantee of success, Miss Lee could produce in seconds.

'Do that again.'

'Not now, maybe later, first two more needles – here.' She touched the junction of shoulder and bloated neck. 'Then all tension be gone. Five more minutes and we finish.'

She went to the long case and selected two more short needles, briefly waving them over the dancing flame before inserting them beneath the loose flesh. Ramone was feeling better than ever now and when, standing over him, she began to unbutton her short white overall, he could hardly believe his luck. Ten minutes ago he had felt like death. Now it seemed he was about to get laid.

She was naked beneath, the soap smell of her tea-coloured skin coming to him, as she played coquettishly with the needles in his stomach again, conjuring the same tumescent surge. This time she slid a hand down into his jockey pants, gently grasping his shaft and pulling back the skin in one smooth, tantalising movement. He closed his eyes as her words, whispered lovingly, came to him.

'One more needle and then we finish treatment.'

'One more? I feel terrific right now.'

'This one make you feel terrific for ever.'

His eyes remained closed as she withdrew her hand and

returned to her case of instruments. She stared down, careful in her selection. The final needle was longer than the others, maybe four inches or so, not gold but stainless steel and not round but flattened, like the blade of a tiny sword. She twisted it in the flame until its point glowed crimson.

'Where does the next one go?' he asked, drowsily indifferent. She leant across him, gently biting his right lobe, her breasts brushing his lips.

'In your ear!'

With one sharp thrust the skewer seared through the membrane of his left ear drum, penetrating the cortex to find the precise centre of his brain. With no more than the briefest yelp of pain, the black core of Enriques' skull exploded into a supernova. For a second, as though triggered by some powerful electric charge, the fat man, already quite dead, sat bolt upright, eyes staring into eternity. Then he slumped back with a dry rattle.

Withdrawing the needle, Nurse Lee tutted. Normally this would have been a clean job but, somehow, she had hit a vein without cauterising it and a thin trickle of blood ran down between her breasts. It was a good thing she had removed her uniform. It did not matter. The man was dead and she would collect another $5,000. Soon she would have enough saved to continue her training; she would be able to go to America and qualify as a real doctor.

Removing the remaining needles from the sagging flesh she briefly purged them in the flame and laid them back in their case. Closing the case she grew thoughtful and, returning to the corpse, she again ran a questing hand over the man's genitals. Nurse Lee smiled, gratified to find her medical assessment confirmed. At the moment of death Enriques had come.

Sarah Mendelsohn loved *Amaryllis*. This was her third visit to the boat and, coming out of the blue like this, was all the more exciting. Peter really was a naughty boy: arranging a Mediterranean cruise as a surprise for her thirtieth birthday. If nothing else, coming after eight years, it showed he remained an incurable romantic. Until that morning she had genuinely thought herself bound for Algoa and a fortnight of typing letters, checking cash flows, and attending an endless round of boring social events. Then, in the departure lounge at Schiphol, he had calmly advised her that they were free agents for two whole weeks. How the dear man had kept it such a complete secret was a miracle to her. Everyone in the office, including tight-arse John Latimer, the only one with sufficient clout to warrant consideration, had carried on as though nothing in the least unusual was planned. It had been the most wonderful, most fantastic surprise.

She wandered round the suite, as luxurious as any five-star hotel. Of the several yachts she had stayed on, she by far preferred this one.

Even the fabulous Onassis boat, *Christina*, had smacked of slightly tasteless luxury. Moreover, she had never forgiven the man himself for calmly asking her, within five minutes of welcoming her aboard, how it felt to sit on the biggest penis in the world. Still young enough to be embarrassed, she had been thrown into total confusion by the elf-like tycoon's question. Peter, gallant as ever, had come to her rescue, explaining gently that the stools on which they all sat had been upholstered with the foreskins of whales. Ari asked every woman who came on board the same question; it was what passed for wit on the *Christina*. Sarah shrugged off the memory. She was certain that the owner of such a vessel as *Amaryllis*, whoever he was, would never sink to such boorish levels.

Two decks below, alone in the spotless galley, Billy Bates wandered to and fro in a similarly pleasurable frame of mind. He took in the banks of equipment with a professional eye.

Ovens, grills, toasters, microwaves and spit-roasts – everything the most demanding chef could ask for had been provided. There were dish-washers and dish-dryers. There were fridges and deep freezers. Best of all, there was the big commercial mincer. If Billy had been a chef he would, in truth, have been in Nirvana.

But Billy wasn't a chef, although he had for a time worked in the food trade as a butcher for one of the big burger chains. It was during these formative years, compelled by an increasingly disapproving judiciary to find gainful employ, that Bates had found his niche in society. If, he had reasoned, the shit mashers that processed a thousand burgers a day could grind a pig's skull to an edible consistency, it could certainly achieve an acceptable result on a human carcase. It had been a turning point in his life and, thanks to already established links with the fringe of Glasgow's underworld, his fame had spread. These days he travelled a great deal. London, Berlin, Stockholm – business was brisk. Billy's trade was specialist, esoteric almost. Billy saw himself as part surgeon, part anatomist and part undertaker.

He jabbed a forefinger at a red button on the bulkhead, the strip lights overhead dimming momentarily as the steel mincer growled ravenously. Case-hardened steel cogs and teeth meshed and turned, grumbling like a dyspeptic troll. He recalled from his far-off Sunday school days the phrase that always came to him at times like this. 'It is easier for a camel to pass through the eye of a needle than for a rich man to enter into the Kingdom of God.' While getting a rich bastard through the Pearly Gates might be beyond his abilities, given the right equipment the camel should pose no problem at all.

Staring down into the open hungry mouth of the feeder he nodded with approval and his gaze went to the two forms stretched out on what, tomorrow, would be the confectionary chef's bench. By that time Billy hoped to be back in Glasgow

– he had tickets to watch Celtic in the afternoon.

One was slim, a young olive-skinned girl in an expensive red dress. Bates feasted his eyes on the long, silk-clad legs, sheer shantung drawn way above the knee, and the swell of her exposed left breast. A traveller now beyond modesty's narrow confines, Conchita stared indifferently at the deck-head.

The other corpse was big, gross almost, a fat man in soiled jockey shorts that Bates knew meant extra work for him. 'If you was paid by the pound, Billy,' he grunted to no one in particular, 'you'd be a bloody rich man by now.' He un-stoppered the bottle of Bacardi he carried and then surveyed the task in hand. His head jerked to and fro in a little dance. 'Eeny, meeny, miny ...'

With a shrug he grasped the tattered neckline of the dead girl's dress, with one sharp tug ripping it away and tossing it aside. His eyes ran over the once lovely body. This had been a nice-looking kid, once.

Selecting a short, wooden-handled knife he took an unre-sisting hand, his fingers feeling expertly for the wrist joint. Satisfied, he inserted the point and with one deft movement sliced through skin, flesh, muscle and sinew until the girl's right hand was severed. For a second he hesitated, staring at his trophy. There, just below the thumb joint, was a small tattoo, a faded flower. He snorted in disapproval: 'A kid that age with tattoos.'

Bates shrugged and tossed the hand into the mincer. The gears did not falter in their task and a bloody slurry of viscous bone and tissue oozed into the bucket below. He took a solid belt of the Bacardi and then turned his attention to the girl's elbow; it was going to be a long night.

'I'm afraid Enriques has had to leave rather earlier than expected,' said Campbell-West as he fixed his bow tie before the mirrow. 'It looks as though we'll be dining alone after all.'

49

Sarah didn't mind in the least; Enriques had pinched her bottom once. She curled a loving arm through his, laying an adoring head on his shoulder.

'Let's eat on board, Peter. That would be nice.'

He smiled apologetically at her in the mirror.

'I'm afraid the galley is out of commission at the moment. The captain assures me it'll be fixed by tomorrow but we'll have to eat ashore tonight.' He looped a scarlet cummerbund about his girth and slid his tuxedo on, checking himself in the mirror. 'Just one quick phone call, darling, and we can be off.'

In the cramped radio room he ran an eye over the banks of electronic equipment as, in Macau, Mr Chang's personal telephone jangled to life.

'Good morning, Mr Chang.'

'Good evening, Sir Peter. Is everything proceeding to plan?'

'Yes, we are due to leave here tomorrow.'

'And Enriques?'

'Ramone has moved on to higher things.'

'He was born for it. Until next month then.'

'Goodbye, Mr Chang.'

'Goodbye, Sir Peter.'

Sarah was waiting for him on the quarterdeck. She seemed excited, standing at the safety rail pointing down.

'Come and see the fish, Peter. I've never seen so many.'

He stood at her side and stared at the brightly flood-lit waters about the ship's stern where the cutter crew waited patiently to take them ashore.

Below, the whole sea was alive with fish, from tiny silver sardines to barracudas a yard long, all cruising in graceful synchronised shoals through the illuminated stretch of sea. Occasionally, the dark undulating form of a small shark would thread its sinuous path through the vast submarine fleet, death at the banquet. On the face of the sea a thin reddish scum drifted, attracting surface feeders, tiny min-now-like creatures who sucked hungrily. Campbell-West looked at his watch.

'Best be off. I don't know about you, my dear, but I'm famished.'

Five

London

Thanks to an overturned tanker at Uxbridge, the journey back to London from Oxford took nearly three hours and, by the time he reached the office, Latimer was in a foul mood. His frame of mind was not improved on finding several urgent messages on his desk from the previous day, all requesting him to ring Algoa at the first opportunity.

'Why the hell didn't you get me on my own phone?' he snapped at the unhappy Maxine, well aware that the moment he and Victoria had quit the bar of The Plough he had switched the thing off. 'Get me Collins straight away. I don't give a monkey's what time it is in Algoa. Get him out of bed if you have to.' Fifteen minutes later he was speaking to Collins.

'What do you mean, he still hasn't turned up? He left Amsterdam yesterday. I checked.'

'That may well be so, but he certainly didn't come here – there's no plane to Curaçao on Mondays. We checked.'

Latimer felt a thin film of sweat lubricating his palms. He didn't like the sound of this one bit. Surely CW hadn't come back to the UK? If he had returned unexpectedly, and if he had found the office unmanned and Victoria away from home for the night, he was surely astute enough to put two and two together. But no. It simply didn't add up; there must be another explanation.

'Perhaps he's coming by another route. You can fly down to Curaçao from Miami I think.'

'The next flight from there is not until Thursday, we checked that too.'

'I could try ringing Sarah's flat I suppose, there's just a chance they may have gone there – though for what reason I can't imagine. I'll try phoning and then I'll get onto Fairview as well.' Latimer instinctively crossed his fingers. 'He may have gone home. In the meantime, perhaps you can check out all the other airlines flying into Curaçao, just in case he's taken some roundabout route. I'll ring you back when I've covered everything at this end.'

At Sarah's flat all he got was her cut-crystal drawl, announcing like an automaton that Sarah Mendelsohn was not at home just now but, if he cared to leave his name and number, she would get back to him as soon as possible.

Victoria was not at home either but, as far as the housekeeper was aware, Sir Peter was abroad on business, somewhere in the Caribbean she thought, and was not expected to return to Fairview for two weeks at least. So far as she knew, he had not been in contact since his departure on the previous Friday. That, at least, was some comfort, he thought. Providing this puzzling turn of events posed no threat to either the corporate, or his personal, status quo, he wasn't too concerned. CW and Sarah were quite capable of looking after themselves. However, just to cover his tail, it wouldn't do any harm to advise the police of their mysterious disappearance.

The desk sergeant who took his call was polite without being over excited about his tidings and Latimer fell in with his mood. No, he wasn't really worried; they would probably turn up today sometime. No, no need for a manhunt yet, it was a misunderstanding on someone's part most likely. He would keep them advised of any developments but, for the moment, he was just putting them in the picture, that was all. Considering his civic duties fulfilled, his thoughts turned to more attractive matters.

Lunch, at Wheeler's, was a pleasant interlude. His guest, Sandy McColl, was a veteran journalist whose capacity for alcohol had resulted in a peripatetic career that had included working on the financial columns of most of the quality papers as well as, during those periods when his legendary bouts of boozing increased in ferocity, several of lesser standing.

It had always been a policy at Martin & Nicholson to maintain good relations, in the shape of regular distributions of largesse, with influential pressmen, and McColl, when he was on a tight rein, was certainly a respected figure in Fleet Street. Today, however, the horse showed all the signs of having bolted with a vengeance and Châteauneuf-du-Pape was vanishing by the case. No matter, thought Latimer, better this shambling wreck, who at least had an inexhaustible supply of jokes and anecdotes, than the earnest, pinstriped youngsters who drank Perrier and asked awkward questions. Moreover, as the detritus of the meal was cleared away and the pressing matter of the moment became which port to accompany the Brie, McColl was to become the bearer of good tidings. With a cautious glance about him he tapped a heavily veined nostril.

'I shouldn't really tell you this, John, because, in theory, I shouldn't be in a position to know, but what the hell, that was a bloody good meal so the least I can do is sing for my supper. I happen to know, don't ask me how, that Martin & Nicholson are down for a Queen's Award to Industry.'

'You're joking.' Latimer stared into the craggy features. 'I mean, how do you know?' McColl licked his forefinger and dabbed at a spot of tartar sauce on his frayed cuff.

'I'm not joking. It's absolutely kosher. I've had a sneak preview of this year's list. I reckon you should hear officially next week sometime, until then keep it to yourself. Of course, it's mainly thanks to the business AFS is bringing in that the award's come your way but, naturally enough, the recognition will go to the parent company.'

The coffee and two large ports arrived and McColl fell silent, stretching a shaky hand towards the newly set-down glass.

My God, thought Latimer, they had done it. A Queen's Award, and all down to AFS. Wait till Campbell-West hears about this, he'll be over the moon. If things carried on the way they were going the sky was the limit. Who knew what would happen next? He lifted his glass.

'Cheers, Sandy old friend, and thank you very much for that information. I will, of course, respect your confidence absolutely. Everyone in the company is aware just how much the piece your paper ran on the offshore business helped to publicise our activities – brought us several interesting enquiries as well.'

He sipped thoughtfully at the rich, dark port. 'Oh, I almost forgot – the gîte in Combourg – it's free that week. Just turn up when you feel like it. I'll phone ahead and tell them you're coming. It's always kept fully provisioned, so you shouldn't need to take anything. If you find you do, we have an account in the village – just charge it to Martin & Nicholson.'

He looked at his watch. It was nearly three. Out of the office all yesterday afternoon and now a three-hour lunch; he didn't want to give his enemies in the company too much ammunition. 'One more port and then I think I'll really have to be gone,' he said. His words went unheeded as McColl responded with a gentle snore and dozed happily on, the dregs of his toppled glass expanding in a crimson blossom across the tablecloth.

As, in slightly euphoric mood, Latimer walked back to the M & N building, he considered the longer-term implications of the award. Who knows, he thought, a few more years and

Campbell-West might not be the only knight on the board. Sir John Latimer had a certain ring about it.

On his return to the office he purged his breath with a burst of Gold Spot and drew a sobering lungful of air before entering. He was surprised, but not initially concerned, to find two policemen waiting in his office: Inspector Ellis, a middle-aged man with an air of world weariness about him, and a nameless constable, so young he must have been fresh out of Hendon. Both sighed audibly at his arrival, three hour-lunches were a luxury not often enjoyed in the force. Clearly, Latimer thought, when someone with a title and a double-barrelled name went missing the City police went on full alert.

He briefly sketched in the situation, at pains to convey his appreciation of their diligence in this matter while stressing that he was not at this stage over-concerned by Campbell-West's disappearance. Having told them everything he could imagine might be of use, he sat back in his seat, waiting for the wheels of justice to go into action. They, however, seemed in no great rush to dash off in search of the missing pair; indeed, for reasons that at first escaped him, they seemed more interested in the operations of AFS and its relationship with M & N, than in locating the missing chairman, title and double-barrelled name notwithstanding.

'Tell me, who exactly is in charge of ...' the inspector frowned down at the note pad on his knee, 'Algoan Financial Services, sir? Who sits on the board?'

'David Collins, who is a resident of Algoa, and I are the joint managing directors. Sir Peter is a non-executive director and Mrs Kolowitz is also a director.'

'How long has the company been operating, sir?'

'Five years, six this July. We opened the office out there in 1974.'

'And when was the last audit carried out?'

'April last year, we're due to complete this year's audit at the end of the month. In fact, I'm scheduled to fly out there the week after next to tie the whole thing up.'

'Have you ever come into contact with the Banco del Carib in the course of the company's business affairs, sir?'

'Of course, BdC have been our bankers ever since we set up the company – it was part of the deal with the Algoan Government. But really, Inspector, I don't see what all this has got to do with finding Sir Peter Campbell-West.'

The policeman eyed him ingenuously for a moment.

'I take it then, sir, that you were not aware that Sir Peter was a major shareholder in the bank?'

Latimer blinked. This was news to him: news that carried all sorts of nasty implications, implications that had not, thus far, entered into his calculations. Better tread very carefully here, he thought, regretting the final port.

'I don't understand, Inspector. What's all this about?'

'We have reason to believe that substantial funds have, over the past five years or so, been transferred from Martin & Nicholson, the parent company, to its subsidiary, Algoan Financial Services. Is that correct, sir?'

'Certainly,' confirmed Latimer, a modest suggestion of indignation creeping into his tone. 'It's all perfectly above board. We have submitted regular reports and audits to the Algoan Board of Trade and to the British Inland Revenue. The funds were transferred because at that time we could get a better tax settlement for our clients out there than we could here. In fact, since Mrs Thatcher came to power the situation has changed somewhat and a fair proportion of those accounts will shortly be transferred back to the UK. There's no mystery about it – we can provide chapter and verse on every penny that has been invested in Algoa.'

'Then again, it's hardly pennies we're dealing with, is it, sir?' said the inspector, brushing back the sparse hairs that sprouted from his freckled pate. 'Just how much, in approximate terms, would we be talking about here?'

It briefly crossed Latimer's mind at this point that he would be well within his rights to refuse to disclose what was, after all, privileged information. Perhaps it was time to get legal advice. However, sensing something was going on that might, if he played his cards right, be turned to his own advantage, he decided that it made tactical sense to be as cooperative as possible. If Campbell-West was going to get his knuckles rapped for an undeclared vested interest in BdC and if, a not impossible consequence of such conduct, that knuckle rapping subsequently led to his disgrace and resignation, there might well be advancement in the offing. All the possibilities, all the potential pitfalls and advantages of this unexpected revelation, threaded through Latimer's mind in the elapse of a second. He clasped his hands on the desk before him, frowning slightly to convey just how hard he was trying to be helpful.

'In broad terms, taking the dollar at its current rate, I suppose we'd be talking about something in the region of £60 million in all since we first set up in business. Our current reserves, held by BdC, which, of course, include other funds apart from those transferred from the UK – such as investments from the US and elsewhere – stand at something like £84 million.'

The young constable, who until this point had done little other than pick delicately at the large red spot on his chin, reached down into the briefcase at his feet, retrieving a sheaf of papers which, after a moment's consideration, he handed to his superior. Ellis, after a brief reference to the documents, continued to eye Latimer thoughtfully as though debating whether or not to take him into his confidence.

'When did you last see Sir Peter Campbell-West, sir?'

'Five days ago. The day before he left the country.'

'So far as you know, what time did he actually leave the United Kingdom?'

'He was certainly on the 10.40 morning flight from

Heathrow to Schiphol, his chauffeur will be able to confirm that, and, so far as we can tell, he was in Amsterdam that afternoon and all the following day. Look, Inspector, if there's something going on that I should know about, I'd be grateful if you would tell me. What is all this? I phone Wood Street Police Station because the chairman of the group, a City alderman and former sheriff, and his personal assistant, have gone missing, then you come along and start giving me the third degree about the company. What exactly is the problem?'

Both policemen stared at him bleakly as though giving his demands some consideration. Then the inspector nodded his head, apparently satisfied with Latimer's progress thus far, and prepared to open up a little.

'The fact is, Mr Latimer, the activities of Banco del Carib have been the subject of an intensive but discreet investigation by a number of police forces for nearly a year now. You tell me you were unaware that Sir Peter Campbell-West was a sleeping partner in the bank. You will therefore be equally surprised, no doubt, to learn that Señor Enriques, the Algoan Minister of Finance, also had a large interest. We have reason to believe that assets amounting to something in the region of £220 million have, over the course of several years, been misappropriated by Sir Peter Campbell-West, in league with Señor Enriques and several others. Some of that, perhaps as much as 10 per cent, came from AFS, the rest was defrauded from a whole range of other companies who, at the insistence of the Algoan government, banked with Banco del Carib as part of the deal under which they were allowed to set up in business on the island.'

Latimer's mind was racing. Things were beginning to get out of hand.

'But at the annual audits,' he protested, 'everything was fine. Why didn't any of this show up then? I went through them, line by line, each year, everything was in perfect order.

I signed them,' his voice faltered as the full implications of this statement sunk in. 'We all signed them.'

'It would appear that the auditors who, under Algoan law, had to be approved by the Algoan Board of Trade, were carefully selected by Señor Enriques. They were kept advised, presumably by sources within BdC, of precisely what the financial position of each of the bank's accounts was expected to be, and adjusted their final figures accordingly. So long as none of the defrauded customers needed to make a large call on their reserves, there was sufficient in the vaults of BdC to service them all. It'll come as no surprise I'm sure if I tell you the senior partners in the auditing company have also disappeared.

While I realise it's no great consolation to you, the relationship between AFS, the bank and the auditors, convoluted though it may appear, is comparatively straightforward in comparison to some of the other companies that have been swindled. I imagine the lawyers will be feathering their nests until the end of the decade on the strength of this particular bit of skulduggery. Apparently the shysters are flocking into Algoa like a swarm of locusts.' Ellis, it appeared, was not enamoured of the legal profession.

'What happens next?' asked Latimer, already mentally drafting the report to his fellow M & N directors. 'What can we do to recover the situation?'

'Warrants have been issued for the arrest of Campbell-West and his fellow conspirators, both here and in Algoa, as well as in the United States where, incidentally, the majority of the victims of this little scam are resident. I suspect, however, that by now the whole thieving rat-pack will be safely installed in some banana republic that doesn't know the meaning of the word extradition.

Enriques has vanished too and President Sandarte, who is by all accounts very angry indeed at all the bad publicity this will mean for his island, is calling for blood. I understand that both Mr Collins and Mrs Kolowitz are under close arrest and that the assets of AFS have been frozen, pending a full inquiry into the affair.'

'But David and Chantelle would have had nothing to do with all this, I'm sure. They would have been as unaware as I was about what was going on.'

Inspector Ellis shrugged his shoulders indifferently. In ten years with the Serious Fraud Squad he'd seen it all before. To him the fate of a couple of overprivileged whizz kids who had got their fingers burnt was clearly a matter of supreme indifference. He gathered up his papers, tapping them into a neat square sheaf on the corner of Latimer's desk.

'I don't know about them, Mr Latimer, but if I were in your position, I think I'd be more worried about what your bosses are going to say to you. You did say you'd signed the annual audits for the last five years, didn't you? It's been my experience in these matters that, regardless of whether you knew what was going on or not, someone always has to carry the can as they say. What with Campbell-West doing a moonlight, and your friends banged up in an Algoan jail, I'd say their choice of sacrificial lamb was pretty limited, wouldn't you?'

Six

Vancouver, British Columbia, February 1984

Every morning at eight Mr Ling hung the birds outside the Happy Valley Diner. These days it was one of the few of his chores he enjoyed, smiling as he spoke to each, watching their nervous flittings as he suspended them beneath the canvas awning. For each saffron finch, cockatiel and cardinal, he had an affectionate word as they swung in their bamboo cages, their chirping ringing down the narrow side street. Macquarrie Street was the Fifth Avenue of that mile-square microcosm of Shanghai: Chinatown, Vancouver, British Columbia. The ghetto was an oriental transplant, alien and inscrutable, grafted onto an increasingly resentful white Canadian body politic that threatened rejection. These days Mr Ling seldom ventured beyond its strictly defined limits.

When he had fed, watered and placed each bird in position he would wipe the tables clear of the crusted remnants left by the previous night's customers and place the chairs in position. This done he would sit in the sun, smoke a cigarette and read his copy of that morning's *Vancouver Oriental*. He hated the paper; it was progressive. It called for assimilation and integration: acceptance of North American values. He saw its malign influence in the baseball-capped children that came into the place demanding cola and pretzels. They filled their minds with the same trash as they did their bellies: the fast, the flashy and the superficial. Worse still, they laughed at their elders.

Mr Ling was old. Not in years especially, for he was still several years short of his seventieth birthday and regular exercise had kept the flesh firm upon his face, but old in the evil ways of the world. Born of illiterate Xiangtan peasant stock, at the age of ten his parents, caring and wanting the best for their eldest son, had apprenticed him – sold was nearer the truth – to a Cantonese drug trafficker. For the next three years he had accompanied his master on his business trips. These had taken him on illegal and dangerous forays into Burma, Thailand and what was then French Indo-China. It had been a formative period in which Ling's native astuteness, toughness and loyalty had marked him out. On his fourteenth birthday his master, appreciative of services rendered, had presented him with an ancient Mauser rifle, a trophy from the Boxer rising, a purse containing thirty English guineas, and a twenty-year-old Han woman who, he was quick to assure Ling, was a virgin.

While the birds sang in the sunlight overhead Mr Ling smiled as he recalled the woman; she must have been the most experienced virgin in history. On his next trip to Burma he had exchanged her for an almost new British Lee Enfield and a case of ammunition. With the guineas he had bought a shipment of raw opium. It was a modest enough beginning yet, by the time he was twenty, Ling had raised enough money to buy his release from his master and to go into business on his own.

It was not until he was twenty-five, when the Japanese occupation of Manchuria had developed into a full-scale invasion of China proper, that his remarkable career reached a watershed. The spirited, if incompetent, resistance put up by the uneasy coalition of Chiang Kai-shek's nationalists and Mao's communists had, for the first time in his life, presented Mr Ling with something of a moral dilemma.

He had by now achieved the status of a minor warlord with a limited but undisputed sphere of influence along the Burmese border, 150 square miles of jungle and rice paddies, within which his word was law and where no one travelled or did business without paying tribute.

Although, as the Sino-Japanese war continued to ravage the country it seemed that the Nipponese devils must eventually raze the whole of the country to the ground, in his own little world Ling – now General Ling – continued to prosper. Within his domain he carefully and ruthlessly controlled the age-old cross-border trade in arms, drugs, women and, lately, the increasing amounts of other saleable war materiel coming onto the black market in a world seemingly gone mad.

Occasionally, a trader might be tempted to try to cross Ling's territory without making the customary financial arrangement. Inevitably, the man would be detected and punished, perhaps a simple beating for a first offence, possibly castration or hanging for a persistent offender. He was no worse than most of his kind and a great deal better than many. The local peasants, glad of strong government, supported Ling and for several years they all flourished and the war remained far away. Then, in the spring of 1942, the Japanese arrived.

His scouts had warned of their approach, a big fighting patrol with heavy machine-guns and mortars, coming up the track from Tengchong. Ling had his desk set out in the dusty sunshine of the courtyard among the strutting fowl, put on his best uniform and awaited their appearance.

Lieutenant Haro, imbued to his fingertips with the philosophy of Bushido, bowed just sufficiently deeply. He was conciliatory, even flattering, in his approach; the Emperor had heard of the powerful General Ling and had sent gifts of guns and money in the hope of establishing good relations. There was no reason that they should not come to an under-

64

standing: the General could continue to operate as before providing he was prepared to supply information of any British military movements across the border in Burma and agreed to hand over any Allied airmen who might be forced to land in the General's area.

Ling smiled broadly. No reason for him to concern himself in politics. In normal circumstances it would have been an offer worth considering. Standing, he beckoned the Japanese to come forward.

'Please, Lieutenant, you have had a long march, let us go inside and discuss these matters.' A wave of his hand brought forth a gaggle of local girls bearing trays of drinks. 'I have given orders for your men to be attended to.'

Inside the hut it was cool and shadowy. Observing protocol, Haro waited for Ling to settle himself before sitting, taking the offered bowl of rice wine gratefully. 'We are rather cut off here, I'm afraid. Tell me, Lieutenant, how is the war going? They say the Americans are growing stronger every day; building ships and aircraft faster than the Emperor's soldiers can destroy them.' Haro frowned. 'How could this bandit come by such information?' He thumped the table – so much for the niceties.

'It is all lies! Lies! Everywhere the Emperor's forces drive all before them. Soon we shall have liberated India and the whole of the western Pacific. Everywhere the people of the east are welcoming the establishment of the Japanese Co-Prosperity Sphere. It is only a matter of time before the colonialists sue for peace.'

Ling held up a calming hand, pleased to know the man's circulatory system would be working the harder, but not eager to arouse this touchy samurai too soon.

'I'm sure you're right. We all know what liars these westerners are. But what of the war in China? I hear your soldiers are making big gains.' Haro relaxed.

'Indeed, General. Three weeks ago we took Xiangtan.'

'Ah yes, Xiangtan. There was much damage I hear, indiscriminate bombing. Many civilian casualties. Atrocities some say.'

'Allied propaganda.' Haro felt his own words boom in his skull and he shook his head. 'The Imperial forces do not make war on civilians.' The room seemed suddenly hot and he stared stupidly at Ling who by some strange trick of the light had become suddenly remote, as though separated from him by a wall of thick, slightly flawed glass. Setting down the wine he mopped his brow, growing suspicious as Ling's smile grew insolently confident. 'Why do you smile bandit? What I tell you is ...'

There was a gun in Ling's hand now and instinctively the Lieutenant's fingers, grown strangely clumsy, pawed ineffectively at the leather of his holster. Half rising, he staggered forward as the room began to swim sickeningly in and out of focus, only to slump helplessly back into his seat.

'Have no fear, Lieutenant,' Ling stifled a yawn. 'I shall not shoot you. There is no need to waste a bullet. The paralysis you are experiencing is just the first symptom. Taken by mouth the venom of the swamp krait enters the system only slowly. If you lie still you may live for, who knows, maybe another twenty minutes. But, if you become agitated ...' he gave an eloquent shrug.

Ignoring the jerking figure in the chair, Ling rose with regal self-assurance and strode to the doorway of the hut. Across the compound the first flames were licking at the sides of the long house that held the lieutenant's unsuspecting, and now half-comatosed, patrol. White smoke wreathed through the latticed leaves of the roof as his men circled the fire in a ragged, almost contemptuous, ring, loosing off random shots into the quickly crackling pyre. It was time, the General thought, to slip quietly across the border. The souls of his parents could rest quiet.

*

'Any chance of a coffee, buddy?' Officer Rourke's gruff tones broke into Mr Ling's reverie. The big policeman had entered the diner unseen and clearly felt that he had been kept waiting long enough to be served. 'I thought that was what you people were supposed to be in business for.' Without comment Mr Ling laid his paper aside and shuffled inside, wishing he knew where he could lay hands on a convenient swamp krait.

The end of the war had found him in Macau where, in the tightly sewn-up world of the long-established tongs he could not hope to achieve his previous status. Nevertheless, his special skills quickly found him useful and lucrative employ in the colony's underworld.

Just one more displaced person in the flood of refugees that swarmed into Macau in the forties, he had originally had to settle for work as a foot soldier in Mr Chang's private army. Mr Chang came of an ancient and powerful family and when Mao assumed power on the mainland the implacable hatred Chang had displayed towards the occupying Japanese was swiftly revived and switched to the communists. The US consul was a regular visitor to the house and there were rumours that the Changs worked for the CIA.

Twice Mr Ling was despatched by boat across the Pearl River estuary into Kwangtung province with orders to erad- icate straying agents who had tried to play both ends against the middle. The first man had been a known CIA agent who had been turned, but the second, he learned later, was not political but a commissar with a penchant for the horses but, sadly, lacking the funds to meet his gambling debts. To Ling it was a matter of supreme indifference. He was a natural: he never fouled up, never asked questions and was accordingly well rewarded for his troubles. Until the early seventies he was supremely happy serving Mr Chang in whatever capacity was required: assassin, courier or bodyguard – Mr Ling could do it all.

Then things began to change: people began to mention 1999. The talk in the bars and godowns was of what was likely to happen when the Portuguese departed and Macau was handed back to China. To Mr Ling 1999 seemed a long way off, but to Mr Chang it might have been tomorrow. Slowly the assets of the Chang empire began to be moved abroad – to Lisbon, to London, to California, and to the west coast of Canada.

Mr Chang, an honourable man by his own standards, had treated all his soldiers fairly. Passports and money had been provided as the empire established new and healthy roots in the world beyond. Mr Ling's services had been especially valued and Chang had personally invited him to the big house overlooking Calbaros Bay to discuss his future.

'You and I are no longer young, Ling,' Chang had said, 'it would be unfair to expect you to continue in your former position. I have bought up several establishments in Canada through which I intend to merchandise our goods for the North American market. You will manage one of them – it is a position of responsibility and honour.'

Thus, in the fall of 1980 Mr Ling, rather reluctantly it must be said, found himself manager of the Happy Valley Diner and a Canadian citizen.

He placed the coffee in front of Officer Rourke and returned to his paper and his reminiscences.

Before he quit Macau for the last time, Ling had gone to the temple at Kun Lam to have his fortune told. The priest, renowned for the accuracy of his predictions, had demanded $100 for a full reading. It would, he said, be a bargain, carried out in accordance with ancient practice, and would assuredly reveal the whole of Ling's future. He considered it money well spent.

Within the priest's cramped cell, where tallow lamps burned fitfully, the two old men faced each other across a bare wooden table. A sacred tortoise, oiled and polished to a fine finish, was prepared and placed between Mr Ling's hands, his grasp restraining the creature's dry scraping as it attempted to free itself. Then the priest produced a small charcoal brazier into the glowing heart of which he thrust a thick steel spike, watching in silence as it glowed red, yellow and, finally, white. In Ling's hands the tortoise struggled with stiff stabbing thrusts of its scaly legs, almost as if it sensed what was coming.

'Let your thoughts be of your ancestors,' said the priest as, first ensuring it stood above the exact centre of the shell, he plunged the spike into the centre of the carapace, leaning his whole weight on it to ensure it penetrated through to the table below. The shell cracked sickeningly, blood boiled and hissed, and the stench of seared flesh filled Ling's nostrils as the creature writhed and then stiffened in death. When he looked he saw that, in its death throes, the tortoise had shit on his right hand.

The priest beamed. Not only was this in itself a favourable omen, the fissures in the shell radiated in a most auspicious pattern. 'Most propitious. I see that you must go on a journey but that you will return. Your bones will lie among those of your ancestors.' He ran a wizened hand over the shell. 'Also you will earn much honour ...'

For another fifteen minutes he interpreted, in infinite detail, things revealed by the shattered shell. Fame, fortune and honour, it was all there. But Mr Ling was no longer listening: he had heard enough.

Despite his antipathy to his new country, Ling was appreciative of Chang's generosity. The money he had received, together with the takings of the diner, meant he could employ a good team of chefs and waiters who took most of the work off his hands. But for a man of action, even an ageing one, it was degrading. All he had to do these days was occasionally hold certain packages on the premises until the heat died down and keep his ear to the ground for any information that might be relevant to the Chang empire.

It was in the latter capacity that the Englishman had first come to his notice. Three evenings in a single week the man, just a tourist at a loose end he claimed, had come into the Happy Valley. At first Ling had hardly noticed him, just another loudmouthed dogface who couldn't hold his drink, joshing with the waiters and flirting with the girls. But the man had asked too many questions. Who owned the place? He was looking to buy a place like this – was it for sale? Did anyone know where he could get some 'special stuff'? If it wasn't for the fact that he had acted rather too drunk when, to Ling's knowledge, he had taken no more than a glass or two, the deception might have worked. Ling, sensing an opportunity to be of service to his master, had telexed Mr Chang in Macau and awaited orders. To his disgust, Mr Chang had sent the despised Danny Yap up from San Francisco. The birds chirping above Mr Ling's head brought Danny to consciousness.

Swinging his feet to the threadbare carpet Yap slipped a scurf-clogged comb from his hip pocket and stood before the mirror, scraping back his oiled hair. Danny Yap was American-Chinese, a hitman whose name was whispered fearfully in every chinatown on the west coast. Just twenty-three years old, he had killed fifteen men, some for business purposes, others for the pure hell of it, and never spent more than an overnight stay in police custody. Danny Yap never left anything to chance. Regarding himself approvingly in the full-length mirror he sucked his flat belly in and flexed his ridged pectorals. Man, was he in good shape! Returning to the bed he roughly shook the sleeping boy.

'Hi, come on sleaze-ball. It's time to go.' The young man, opening his mascara-lined eyes, recalled the tawdry events of the previous night and dutifully tried to look seductive. He was wasting his time. 'Get your things on and get out,' Yap snapped. 'I gotta busy day ahead.' The boy pouted sulkily but did as he was told. When he stood in the door Yap handed him a twist of dollar bills. 'Remember, shit-for-brains, I want a first-class hooker for this job so don't try cutting yourself a slice of the action. Get the best-looking whore on the block. I want the Englishman to enjoy himself – it's gonna be the last fuck he ever gets.'

When he was alone Yap went through his daily exercise programme. For half-an-hour he stretched and postured as he performed the graceful ballet-like movements of his karate routine. Following this with a further half-hour pumping iron, he stole one final admiring review of his sweat-sheened body and pulled on a stained jogging suit. Running lightly down the stairs and through the deserted restaurant he went out into the street, blinking in the sunlight. With a quick glance either way he trotted easily towards the harbour, past Mr Ling who, lowering his paper, watched him thoughtfully as he went.

Seven

When Collins arrived the Happy Valley was crowded, noisy with the sing-song shouts of the waiters and the excited, slap-punctuated chatter of the mahjong players. On the heavy atmosphere the aroma of 100 exotic dishes mingled with the stink of stale cigarette smoke and cheap perfume. Swaying uncertainly in the doorway his eyes flicked around the packed room. Seeing no table free, he made his way to the bar and settled himself on one of the high stools. The barman smiled easily and set a bowl of pretzels before him.

'Evening Mr Forester, sir. Had a good day?'

'Fine thanks, Sam.' He ran a weary hand across his face. 'Drank a little too much bourbon at lunch though; my head's going like a jackhammer. I could sure use a pick-me-up. What do you recommend?'

'How about if I fix you a snakebite? Most of my regulars swear by it.'

'Sounds fine to me. Guess you better make it a double.'

Collins wondered why he was still persisting with this charade. He had all the information he needed now and that afternoon had told Chantelle he'd be home at the first opportunity. If he had any sense he wouldn't be here at all; he'd have been on the first Air Canada flight to Heathrow. Still, the food at the Happy Valley was good and, what was more, he was feeling distinctly horny. What the hell, there was sure to be another flight tomorrow. Why not indulge himself for once? As though she had read his thoughts the girl with the legs slid onto the stool next to him. She eyed the bustling scene about her.

'Do you think it's worth waiting, Sam?' she asked the barman.

'Can't really say, Miss Sue. We're pretty busy tonight; you may have to share.'

As she considered the prospect her gaze, it seemed by the purest chance, met Collins' and they both smiled.

'Always the sign of a good restaurant,' he said, his wicked eyes revelling in the expanse of silken thigh revealed as she crossed her legs. She glanced impatiently at her watch, keen to convey just how tenuous was her stay there. She was gorgeous, blonde, tall and slim, yet with breasts full enough to reveal a tantalising valley of golden cleavage above the scarlet silk of her dress. Suddenly he didn't want her to leave. 'Look, I'm next for a table I think. I'm on my own so you're welcome to share with me if you want.' He lowered his voice. 'The backsliding monk is fantastic.'

She frowned. 'Backsliding monk?'

'It's a traditional Macau dish: abalone, chicken and ham served with mushrooms and herbs. It's called that because it's supposed to be delicious enough to tempt vegetarian monks.' His eyes twinkled. 'I'm a bit of a backsliding monk myself.' Huge violet eyes came to bear on his face. Her smile said she was not too deterred by what they saw and she held out her hand. As she did so the resident photographer came up and they put their heads together, the better to fit in the frame. As they blinked away the lingering image of the flash the photographer ripped off a ticket and, handing it to him, was lost in the crowd.

'Thanks. I'm Sue Anne Ramirez.' Collins took the offered hand gently in his own, his fingers, almost imperceptibly, stroking the warm soft flesh.

'Charles Forester.'

'Do I detect from your accent that you're not from these parts, Mr Forester?'

The stairs up to Sue Anne's flat were steep and provided an agreeable opportunity for Collins to make a first-hand assessment of the curve of her finely turned calves. At the head of the narrow staircase, beneath the dull light of an art deco lamp, she fumbled in her bag for the doorkeys. It was funny, he thought, she hadn't once mentioned money throughout the whole evening.

Inside it was dark, the only light a regular but intermittent blue glow from a distant neon. Collins sniffed the air, the window was half open and a fresh breeze caused the fragile nets to lift and dance lightly on its stream. The air should have been pure, cool Pacific Ocean yet it carried something extra: a slightly sweet amalgam of perspiration and hair oil. Collins doubled up, clutching his stomach and the girl looked round in alarm.

'Are you OK, Charlie?' Her tone was edgy, concerned, though not necessarily for him.

'Not really,' he gritted through his teeth, 'must have been that bloody crab.'

'You get into bed, honey, and I'll get you a seltzer.' There was a brittle urgency in her voice that he knew meant she was keen to be gone from that suddenly claustrophobic room. Still doubled over he stumbled against her, clumsily pulling the silk from her shoulder. She gave a little gasp as his arm, suddenly strong and purposeful, went around her, swinging her bodily between him and the darkness. In a pulse of blue light he watched as the etched features of Danny Yap stepped from the shadows and felt, rather than saw, the blade of the stiletto slide into the unresisting softness of the girl's stomach. With the merest of groans she sagged in his grasp and

74

he knew instantly she was gone. As a warm stickiness seeped over his hand, Yap clicked the light on and Collins, almost gently, laid the dead weight of the once lovely Sue Anne on the bed. Yap was shaken, for once things hadn't gone to plan, yet he managed to compose a confident smile.

'Was that really necessary?' Collins asked easily, nodding at the relaxed form of the girl lying on the bloodied counterpane. 'I thought you were supposed to be a professional.'

Yap smiled without humour. His carefully rehearsed routine had been shattered by the girl's death and now he had to reprogramme himself to complete the job. He was off balance and Collins wasn't about to let him recover.

'Pretty sloppy work. Still, I guess you only get what you pay for – Chang must be a real cheapskate.'

Furious, Yap moved in, but too quickly and without measuring the space between them.

'You dirty English bastard. Don't talk about Mr Chang like that ...'

As the stiletto came up toward Collins' heart the Englishman stepped to one side, his left arm describing a broad, windmilling arc that diverted the blow harmlessly away to the side. As Yap steadied himself and tried to draw back, off balance and wide open, Collins drove his fist, in a classic Aikido move, hard up into the man's ribcage. It was a murderous blow, shattering bone like matchwood, compressing the tissue of the right ventricle up into the atria and ripping the aorta open. With the valediction of a bloody belch, Danny Yap's eyes rolled skyward and he was as dead as the girl whose bed he now shared.

When Mr Ling was called to the scene he smiled. He gave the worried janitor, a Korean illegal fearful of police involvement, a $100 bill together with a stern warning to silence. Alone in the room, he wandered absently around, his eyes on the two bodies.

Picking up Sue Anne's bag he took out all the folding money and checked the serial numbers – $300. His smile broadened – Yap had drawn $500 from funds to pay for her services – what a world. After a search of Yap's wallet he was able to tuck close on $1,000 into his own back pocket. Then he picked up the phone, dialled and waited.

'This is Mr Ling in Vancouver. There is trouble.'

There was a brief but disconcerting delay before Chang responded. Ling knew this was because it was coming via satellite; the kids who came into the diner had said so.

'What sort of trouble?'

'Mr Yap is dead. A woman has died too.'

'And the Englishman?'

'He killed Yap.'

'What do you know of him?'

'Nothing, apart from the fact he was asking too many questions. But we have a photograph.'

There was another, longer delay.

'I think you should come to Macau, Mr Ling. There are matters we need to discuss. Do whatever you consider necessary to retrieve the situation over there. Spend freely – it is the best policy. Be here within five days.'

As the phone went dead Ling considered his position. Stepping over the body of Yap he felt a sudden urge to be back at the Happy Valley; no one would think to bring the birds inside and it was a cool night.

Eight

Southampton Water, England

The grey waters of the Solent were, that late winter's morning in 1984, devoid of all sailing craft save one. In the dismal bleakness, a solitary yacht was tacking into the keen south-easterly breeze towards the barely visible finger of Ryde pier. Its progress was unsteady and from time to time the helmsman seemed to misjudge his manoeuvres, the little boat hanging with the wind on the nose and then falling back onto her original tack.

'Come round, you bitch,' yelled Latimer, as though this aberration was the boat's fault and not his own. 'Fuck you. Come round!' He luffed up again, this time successfully as, with a resentful crack of her jib, the bow came through the eye of the wind and she headed off down the intended track. Like a jockey reining in an ill-tempered mare, he sheeted the jib in hard, panting slightly as he slumped back in the cockpit. He glanced at his watch, running his tongue over salty lips; it was nearly eleven. The pubs would soon be open ashore and he briefly toyed with the idea of going about and putting into Cowes for a couple of pints. He shook his head. No, better not; someone might remember him and the ugly fracas of his last visit. There was no point in risking another run-in with the local yobs. He'd come well prepared anyway. Briefly quitting the helm he darted below, returning to the tiller before his truculent steed had time to head up to windward, a bottle of Scotch and a plastic mug clutched to his chest.

The wind was bitter, whipping the crests of the short steep waves into small, icy shrapnel that slashed at his face, yet he wore only a pair of jeans and a sweater, apparently oblivious to its bite. Pouring out half a mugful of the Scotch, he took a good solid belt straight from the bottle before stoppering and laying it aside and settling himself down in the cockpit. Astern, a solitary gull hung in his wake, mewing forlornly. Another mile or so and he would come about and head back to the Hamble. In the cockpit sole, the whisky bottle rolled to and fro with a slow, desultory motion that seemed to match his mood. He smiled knowingly to himself: plenty left in the bottle and he was in no great rush.

Never fat, he was these days down to under 165 pounds and his thick black hair, once so carefully and expensively groomed, now hung in greasy rat-tails about his collar.

During the three years and more that had passed since the AFS affair had broken, since the subsequent furore in the press and Parliament, and his own enforced resignation from Martin & Nicholson, he had spent many days like this. He would sail aimlessly, sometimes for several days on end and in the foulest weather, ranging up and down the south coast, anywhere from Dover to Land's End. Indifferent to the elements he would hammer through the roughest seas until his food or, more likely, his booze, ran out, at which time he would return to his mooring at a rundown boatyard on the Hamble River and the little cottage which represented his portion of the separation deal he had negotiated with Charlotte.

Despite circumstances which had made his resignation inevitable, the terms of his parting from M & N had not been ungenerous and this, together with his half of the divorce settlement, meant that financially he remained, had he so chosen, in a position to live moderately comfortably.

Instead, since the collapse of his marriage, an event that had been on the cards for some time and only hastened by his rapid descent to near alcoholism, he had chosen to exist like a virtual recluse. A strange, uncomfortable figure in the local community, he was often drunk these days, potentially violent and shunned by his fellow villagers. Twice to date he had been arrested for unruly behaviour: drunken scuffles with local louts he considered had insulted him in some obscure way. The second occasion had resulted in a £50 fine and being bound over to keep the peace.

On those evenings he did not choose to ride out at sea, he would make his way to the Jolly Sailor, the regulars falling silent at his unwelcome entrance as they attempted to gauge his uncertain moods. Here he would sit drinking alone, staring out into the night, indifferent to the surrounding ambience of nervous contempt and rejection. At closing time he would depart, staggering into the darkness.

'There goes the nodding donkey,' some local wag would say, careful first to ensure that he was well out of earshot. 'Twenty million quid gone out of the till and he doesn't even know about it. Bloody nodding donkey's just about right.' Sometimes the uneasy laughter that ensued would reach him and he would turn in the darkness, glaring at the lit windows of the pub, debating whether to return and face his tormentors. Then with a curse he would continue on his way.

The term, if not original, had been used to devastating effect by the lawyers acting on behalf of disgruntled AFS clients. Nearly all of them had lost money to a greater or lesser extent as a result of the monumental fraud that Campbell-West and his colleagues had perpetrated. To a man, they wanted their pound of flesh and didn't give a damn where it came from. In the form of Mr Stamford Millbrook QC, they had selected a very competent butcher.

'Do you really expect this court to believe, Mr Latimer,'

he had asked, 'that over five successive years you and your colleagues, professional financial advisers of considerable experience, accepted at face value audits that we now know to have concealed a monstrous conspiracy? A swindle that resulted in the loss to your clients of nearly £30 million?' Heavy Semitic jowls turned towards the bench, a broad smile of theatrical disbelief upon his face. 'If that really is the case, My Lord, I can only say that the accused brings a new dimension to the term, "nodding donkey".'

The following day, several of the national newspapers quoted the lawyer verbatim and the *Sun* carried the spitefully gleeful headline: "£30 million goes missing – on the nod." It was a damning indictment and, despite the fact that Latimer had been cleared of all complicity in the fraud itself, his professional standing had been compromised beyond recall. His career in the City was at an end.

Eventually, as these things always do, the affair blew over. Thanks to strategically placed insurances, M & N somehow found the means to replace the missing funds although, despite their efforts, no further mention was ever heard of any Queen's Award to Industry. Today, the press seldom even mentioned the Algoan affair, apart from sporadic reports of the peregrinations of the villain of the piece, the absconding Sir Peter Campbell-West. He had been in Spain for a while; an Australian journalist had been set upon and badly mauled by Rottweilers while trying to interview him. However, with that country's entry into the EEC drawing ever closer, its days as a haven for British crooks were clearly numbered and later that year he was seen in Brazil. The last sighting, three months ago, had been at a casino in Uruguay where he and Sarah were reported as playing, and winning massively, at the high table.

In its usual perverse way, as day by day during the court hearing the full details of his enormous swindle came to light, the British public had rather taken to Campbell-West. He seemed a glamorous figure, larger than life and now, thanks to his piratical initiative, richer than Croesus. He had gambled for high stakes and had won. More importantly, as many were quick to point out, no one, apart from wealthy investors, had got hurt – and they would be well insured wouldn't they? Now he lived in style and tropical ease with the lovely Sarah to grace his bed.

As he stumbled homeward through the freezing rain Latimer heard the wind picking at the leafless trees above him: 'Nodding donkey, nodding donkey, nodding donkey.'

Once within the shabby, uncared-for surroundings of the cottage, he went directly to the drinks cabinet. Shit! He had left the Scotch on the boat. Never mind, there was still some gin in the bottle. He poured himself a stiff one and then slumped down in front of the unlit fire, his eyes straying to the table. The three airmail letters still lay there among the congealing dishes of yesterday's, or was it the day before's, breakfast. All bore American stamps and were addressed in the same neat, familiar handwriting. The earliest was postmarked over three months previously, while the most recent had arrived only two days before. They were all unopened. He looked away, wanting no part of anything relating to his past. All that mattered to him now was to escape. Whether it was to the cold, clean anonymity of the sea, or the warm, mind-melting oblivion of the bottle, he didn't care. All he wanted was to be rid of the taint of the City and his disgrace. He certainly didn't want any part of Collins or Chantelle.

Of course, despite his bitterness, he recognised that he had fared better with British justice than they had under the Algoan version but that, so far as he was concerned, was just the luck of the draw. Collins had spent six months in jail and Chantelle would almost certainly have served a similar term but for the intercession of the American consul. The consul, sensitive to Sandarte's priorities, had tellingly pointed out to El Presidente that it could well stem the flow of high-spending Yanqui tourists if she were to be imprisoned.

In the event she was kicked off the island in summary fashion and, the last he had heard, had returned to the States to await Collins' release. So far as Latimer knew, no such intervention had been made on Collins' behalf and he supposed that the British Department of Public Prosecutions, aware that the real culprit had flown the coop, had been equally cognisant of the fact that its own monolithic strivings were unlikely to have any success in bringing him to book. They had, he assumed, considered that so long as someone went to jail, regardless of guilt or innocence, it made the statistics look that much better.

The final twist of the knife, at the express orders of Sandarte himself, had come in the form of the sequestration of all of Collins' and Chantelle's assets on the island. Everything they had built up over five years of hard work, the house, cars, furniture, absolutely everything, was seized and sold off to placate the fine moral outrage, and salve the bruised wallets, of the cheated investors. Overnight, moral rectitude had become flavour of the month in Algoa and, in a mood of 'pour encourager les autres', Collins had been made the scapegoat.

It had been the same in London. Everyone held up their hands in horror, amazed and dismayed to discover that such things could happen. A few discreet resignations followed, usually on grounds of supposed ill-health, and there were a few unexpected board shuffles. But the line held and there were no more scandals; everyone was squeaky clean.

Latimer ran a hand round his unshaven chin; all that was another world, another time. For him the past had ceased to matter and he pushed these troubling thoughts from his mind. What would he do tomorrow? He frowned. More to the point, what was tomorrow? Tuesday? Wednesday? He shook his head, grinning savagely. What the hell did it matter anyway? Tomorrow morning he would head westward on the ebb tide. If the wind stayed where it was, and he made an early start, he could be in Poole by lunch time. A couple of pints in the Lord Nelson, something to eat, and then maybe he'd go round to see Mary. She, at least, would be glad to see him: whores always were.

He took another long pull at the neat, perfumed gin, his eyes straying to the letters once more, their very presence frustrating his quest for oblivion. Damn it, he'd settle this once and for all. Taking them up, he screwed the flimsy blue papers into a loose twist, tossing it among the long-cold ashes of the hearth before putting a match to it.

'Bollocks to the lot of them,' he grunted as the flame caught and consumed the browning shards of paper, curling and crumbling to powder beneath his gaze.

At three in the morning he woke with a start, shivering in the chair and went to bed.

'What do you mean, she doesn't live here?' Latimer demanded, his words ringing along the street of little terraced houses.

From his vantage point in the doorway at the head of the flagstone steps, the dreadlocked young black looked up and down the street nervously. A cocaine pusher on probation and presently holding enough stuff on the premises to put him away for several years, the last thing he needed was this dosser causing a scene. He kept his voice low.

'I told you man, Mary moved out weeks ago. She went back to Glasgow. The pigs busted the joint – all the girls have gone. Look, if you're desperate for it, I can give you a phone number.'

Swaying slightly, Latimer stared suspiciously up at him. The couple of pints in the Lord Nelson had stretched to five and had been reinforced by a couple of large whiskies besides. He grew very dignified.

'What exactly do you mean, you can give me a telephone

number?'

'You know – a number where you can get a woman.'

A small, fierce flame, like a gas burner, ignited in the fuddled labyrinth of his head. 'How dare he,' thought Latimer. 'How dare this jumped-up nigger talk to me like this, as if I was some down-and-out, desperate for a quick screw? Who the hell does he think he is?'

'I don't want any of your bloody clapped-up black whores, thank you very much. I want Mary – she happens to be a personal friend of mine. Now, will you go and fetch her, or do I have to come in and do it myself?' He was shouting now, the noise of his annoyance causing considerable agitation behind the net curtains along the street. Coming to terms with the fact that logic would not suffice in this argument, the young man shrugged his shoulders indifferently, although his eyes grew hard as he replied.

'Look, I told you, she's not here, man, now just let it go, OK? Just let it go. Do yourself a favour and fuck off, OK!'

As he turned on his heel and made to close the door on his unwelcome caller, Latimer, by now in drunken high dudgeon at being deprived of Mary's dubious ministrations and outraged at such dismissive treatment, charged unsteadily up the steps, attempting to wedge a shoulder into the narrowing gap. Under his weight, the door swung inwards sharply and, overbalancing, he sprawled full-length up the narrow passageway. While, momentarily winded, he lay there gathering his wits, the heavy thump of feet on the stairs thundered in his ears as the other inhabitants of the house came running to investigate the ruckus. Burly black arms snaked about him, binding and smothering his frenzied but fruitless struggles, as he heard the voice of the young man, still soft and reasonable above his own colourful abuse.

'Don't hurt him, he's pissed. Fucking nutter keeps saying he wants Mary. I told him she'd gone.'

Determined to be rid of him but, nevertheless, employing

84

only the minimum force required to achieve that end, three of them hoisted him aloft and dumped him unceremoniously on the pavement outside. Then, as a group, they hurried back inside, eager to get the bolts on the front door before the wild man had recovered sufficiently to make a nuisance of himself again.

'Come out, you black bastards,' he yelled, staggering to his feet and tottering backwards into the road. 'Come on out.' He was still making his displeasure manifest as he stepped directly into the path of an oncoming Volkswagen, executing a graceful somersault over the bonnet and sliding earthwards into a loose, untidy heap.

Shaken but not badly hurt he muttered a subdued oath and set about examining himself for signs of damage. This, he was relieved to find, was minimal and, the shock having sobered him up, he began to experience an overpowering urge to be away from the circle of curious eyes that had gathered. However, the driver of the car, a middle-aged woman with a mouth that set like a badger trap, and who moreover had apparently cultivated the ability to detect alcohol at a hundred yards, had other ideas. In full self-righteous flow she insisted the police be called.

'I've been driving twenty-five years and never once been in an accident,' she kept repeating, while he sat on the kerb, shaking his head. 'Twenty-five years and never an accident.' She leant tentatively towards him, intent on testing the alcohol content of his breath. Seeing the gleam of red-eyed madness in his stare, however, she retreated a step or two, taking up a more defensive position before passing judgement. 'And you've been drinking, young man. Haven't you?'

Steadying himself against the car Latimer, now very keen indeed to be elsewhere, stood up and began to walk away on legs that threatened to buckle under him, ignoring the woman's shrill protests. He had taken no more than half-a-dozen paces when a police car, whistled up, no doubt, by some responsible citizen among the small band of onlookers who had assembled, came round the corner. The driver, taking the scene in at a glance, drew to a halt a little way down the street; both coppers got out and advanced grimly on Latimer while he, becoming aware that events were getting rather out of hand, tried desperately to convey an impression of puzzled innocence. They were not, however, men to be readily taken in.

Released the following morning with a stern admonishment about his behaviour, and sent on his way with the ominous hint of possible further proceedings from the desk sergeant, Latimer stepped jauntily out into the bright morning and, whistling softly to himself, began to walk briskly back towards the town quay and the boat. On the quay, it was almost low water, he looked down and frowned. The boat was still there, securely moored to the wall, but now the forehatch was open, something he knew he would never have overlooked when he came off. Someone was, or had been, on board.

He climbed swiftly down the rusting ladder careful, as he stepped on board, to place his feet as near amidships as he could so as not to make the boat heel over, and alert whoever might be below to his presence. Looking down into the forepeak he could see nothing apart from a couple of badly bagged foresails, whilst from the saloon came the sound of the radio and the smell of coffee.

At the base of the mast a heavy winch handle, several pounds of solid chromed steel, was secured in its bracket and it was to this that his hand went. Casual theft and vandalism were a continual problem along the marinas of the south coast and Latimer was in no mood to see his boat treated in such a manner. The weightiness of the winch handle in his hand a comfort, he drew a deep breath as he prepared to face the intruders. However, before he could make another move, a pale face crowned with ash-blonde tresses appeared in the hatchway below him, wide blue eyes looking up with a smile that might have been of pleasure or triumph.

'Hi, John, you're just in time for breakfast!'

Chantelle had found him.

Nine

Poole Harbour, Dorset

'What the hell are you doing here?' Latimer demanded belligerently although, for all the impact his aggression appeared to make, he might as well have saved his breath. Chantelle smiled sweetly and turned her attention to the bacon that sizzled in the pan. She looked good, even if no longer the perfectly manicured, silicon-breasted clone he remembered from Algoan days and, guiltily, recalled desiring on certain drunken tropical evenings when the port had been passed round. No longer the soap-opera beauty of times when they had all lived high on the hog but, in the burgundy jogging suit and with her hair pinned up, she still exuded an exciting sensuality. Even so, he wanted none of her. His attitude precluding the need for niceties, she got straight to the point.

'David sent me,' she said simply. 'He's got a proposition for you. He wants you to come up to London and discuss it.'

'I'm not in business anymore,' he said sullenly, 'and I don't go up to town these days.' Brushing past her, he went to the chart table, switching on the VHF radio and the Decca navigator. Pointedly turning his back on her, he began to scrutinise the tidal tables in the nautical almanac. 'It's nice to see you again, Chantelle,' he said over his shoulder, 'but I'm in a hurry right now. Eat your breakfast and go, will you?

I need to get underway as soon as possible if I'm to make best use of the tide.'

Ignoring his rudeness, she examined him closely, shaking her head slowly. Uncomfortable under this unsolicited scrutiny, and aware just how much his appearance had deteriorated, he kept his eyes fixed on the book before him, unable though to prevent a tidying hand straying to his hair.

'Christ, John, you look a goddamn mess. What've you been doing for the last couple of years?'

Unhappy at finding himself on the defensive he pulled open a locker, producing the half-empty bottle of Scotch. Shaking the contents into a yellow lather he waved the bottle at her with an unpleasant grin.

'This mainly, and some sailing and whoring. What about you?'

She stared in silence as he poured half a mugful of the Scotch, taking a healthy swig at it before twisting sideways in his seat to face her, exuding an air of resentful mistrust. He held the bottle towards her, his head to one side questioningly, a gesture she waved away.

'No thanks. It's a little early for me.' Aware she wasn't getting through to him, she tried to change the subject or, at least, her approach. 'I've had the devil's own job tracing you. When you weren't at the cottage I almost gave up. The people at the pub made it quite clear they didn't know or care where you were, just so long as you weren't on their premises. It was the people at the boatyard who thought you might have come here – they said something about a woman.'

She paused, inviting some comment. Seeing none was forthcoming, she went on. 'You don't exactly seem to be flavour of the month in that quarter either. I saw Charlotte and the children a few days ago, they all send their love by the way. She told me then that you were drinking pretty hard when she saw you last. Does it help? You used to be a pretty sharp operator at one time, John, I didn't think you would go down hill like this. What happened?'

His eyes grew wide with disbelief at her question and his tone, when he replied, was low and mocking.

'What happened? The fucking sky fell in, that's what happened, or perhaps you didn't notice.'

'It was our sky too, remember? OK, so you lost your job. We all lost our jobs. Dave spent six months in a stinking Algoan jail too. Have you any idea what the Algoan penal system is like? They base it on the US system, they claim, but of course that's without the expense or aggravation of prisoners' rights and suchlike liberal concepts. Dave worked fourteen hours a day, on chain gangs and on the rock pile, when he was just as innocent of any crime as you or I were. On top of that Sandarte confiscated our entire personal fortunes – everything. Dave lost the lot, yet he's not whining or drinking himself into an early grave.'

She lay a cool, conciliatory hand on his. 'Come and talk to him John, just listen to what he's got in mind. He flies in from Vancouver on Monday, come up to London and see him.' She smiled. 'We've got a really big deal going down and we need your help. We both want you in on it with us.'

Despite her placatory approach, his manner continued to reflect his obstinate resentment of her presence. He looked down into the mug that he nursed close between locked fingers, a spiteful, nasty smile upon his face.

'Well, that's very flattering, I'm sure, Chantelle, but never mind David's past problems, what about you? You're still looking pretty good, despite everything. Oh yes, I forgot, Uncle Sam and the US cavalry came to the rescue didn't they? With the exchange rate the way it was at the time, the severance settlement with M & N must have worked out pretty well in financial terms I guess. All in all, you didn't come out of it too badly did you? No rock piles for you, eh?'

She stared at him, not showing any signs of being angered by his baiting but wearying, it seemed, of his infinite capacity for self-pity.

'I lost my baby, John,' she said simply. 'That's all. I was pregnant when the shit hit the fan. David and I were going to be married. It's ironic, isn't it, you were in line to be best man and godfather, and then, as you say, the sky fell in. Along with everything else I'd worked for and built up over six years, I lost the baby. I'm thirty-four now and the doctors tell me, thanks to the way the miscarriage was handled – Algoan gynaecology leaves a lot to be desired I'm afraid – that I'm unlikely to conceive again.'

He was angry now, angry with himself for being so heart-less, angry with her for being totally and absolutely right, angry with the whole bloody set-up. He ran a weary hand over his eyes.

'Look, I'm ... I'm sorry. I had no idea. It was all so long ago. Please, just go will you, Chantelle. The tide's on the turn and I have to be moving on. Tell David, thanks for the offer, but no thanks. It's not for me.'

She stood up sharply. On the bunk beside her lay a large book, a scrapbook so far as Latimer could tell. Picking it up she tossed it onto the saloon table with a solid thud that made him blink, and there was a vein of icy contempt in her voice as she spoke.

'Suit yourself, John. I guess that if your – what do you Brits call it – bottle? If your bottle's gone, then better forget it anyway. It's not going to be the kind of thing a broken-down lush should get involved in.' She pointed to the book. 'In the meantime, take a look in the family album. If you change your mind you can get me,' she handed him a card, 'on that number.'

With that she was gone, climbing lithely out through the forehatch like some wrathful feline predator, frustrated in her hunting. The boat bobbed in a nervous little dance as she pulled herself off and upwards.

So abrupt was her departure that for a second or two

Latimer sat blinking stupidly after her, turning off the gas she had left burning under the frying pan. He carefully picked a crisp rasher from the pan and, dropping it into his mouth, chewed ruminatively. Then, in a rush, as though to ensure she was truly gone, he followed. By the time his head was outside, she was already on the quay side.

'Chantelle,' he roared, heads on neighbouring boats turning towards the kerfuffle, 'this business you and David had in mind. What sort of thing is it?'

She turned, hands on hips and, looking down on him, laughed aloud, the harsh sound of her mirth taken up by the uneasy marauding gulls scavenging along the waterfront.

'Revenge, you drunken arsehole, revenge. What else do people like us have to live for?'

Latimer did not sail on that tide, nor the next. Neither for that matter did he drink heavily in the next twenty-four hours but sat, through the rest of that day and far into the early hours, sipping a thin whisky, poring over the pages of the book she had left him.

As the night drew on and the unheated cabin grew damp and chill, he pulled another sweater on and took to his bunk. Propping the thick volume against his raised knees his eyes flickered over the pages under the soft yellow light. Outside a slack halyard rapped out a ringing tattoo against the mast in the fitful wind. Normally he would have gone topsides to secure it but tonight he was oblivious to its irritant ringing.

What Chantelle had left him was indeed a scrapbook, neatly laid out and presented, and compiled largely, he guessed, by her own fair hand. It was an overstuffed, broken-spined volume, jam-packed with press cuttings, each carefully pasted down on the coarse grey pages. All related to the AFS affair, the earliest dating back more than three years, and to the careers of the main protagonists. His own name appeared frequently in the earlier clippings, sometimes with the hated epithet, 'nodding donkey', and here he turned the page quickly, without dwelling overlong on the detail.

Further on, he read more carefully for almost all of the second half was filled with extracts chronicling the progress of Sir Peter Campbell-West and the lovely Sarah Mendelsohn. Slowly and thoughtfully he turned the pages and, as the evening grew late, even the sounds of the Friday-night revellers on the quay did not distract him. There were cuttings from many sources, mainly glossy magazines, often in Spanish or Portuguese, and there were many pictures.

There was a full page photograph of Campbell-West after water skiing on the Copacabana. At nearly sixty he was still physically powerful, distinguished features tanned to a deep teak beneath the sleek silver hair. Sarah was at his side, a little older – she would be thirty-five or six now he calculated – but still undeniably gorgeous, the magnificent breasts testing, almost to destruction, the scrap of yellow bikini assigned to restrain them, her arms clasped tightly round her paramour as they stared at the camera, smiling broadly.

While most of the cuttings were taken from magazines of the superficial 'high society' paparazzi type, there were also extracts from serious newspapers and financial journals. Latimer's languages weren't good enough for proper translations but from what he was able to glean there could be little doubt that Campbell-West, a thieving pariah, hounded out of his own country, was still wheeling and dealing out there in the wider world.

Insurance exchanges, 'to rival Lloyd's of London' the papers said, were being set up in Paraguay and Argentina. Large sums were being invested in Brazilian hardwoods and arms deals were being broked and financed in South Africa, Israel and Chile. Every so often clippings from Hansard appeared, chronicling predictable set-piece parliamentary exchanges in which some of the more vitriolic socialist back-benchers demanded, in high moral indignation, that action be taken to bring CW to book. Extradition was often mentioned in the government's replies but it was clear that the Department of Public Prosecutions, despite lengthy discourse on the subject and considerable expenditure of public resources, had long abandoned all hope of ever getting a result.

In general, though, moral indignation was a theme that had quickly lost its attraction and the later cuttings were content to reflect a regime of high living and the fat of the land. The rogue English knight, Sir Peter Campbell-West, he still insisted on the 'Sir' apparently, dined with dictators in comic-opera uniforms that groaned under the weight of medals, and relaxed with bare-breasted film stars at the poolside. The most recent picture, taken less than a month before, showed him, in a Rio nightclub, shaking hands with the train robber, Ronald Biggs. With the same affinity that Livingstone and Stanley must have felt in the darkest Congo, a pair of thieves greeted each other like kindred spirits in an alien world.

After a good night's sleep Latimer woke to the heavy throb of fishing vessels leaving harbour, their wash causing his boat to chop and snub impatiently at her moorings. Pulling on a pair of faded cotton trousers he went on deck, blinking in the bright, but wintry, sunlight, his breath hanging on the frosty air. It had been a sharp night and a thin crust of ice covered the deck, welding the carelessly strewn gear to the deck beneath a fragile crystal glazing that crunched dryly underfoot.

He cast an unenthusiastic eye over the untidy state of affairs he found there. Having taken little care of his vessel he now, for the first time in maybe a year, set about making reparations for his previous neglect. Sheets and warps that hitherto had made the cockpit a treacherous snakepit, were carefully coiled, cheesed and flaked. Crumpled and creased sails were dragged from their bags to be carefully folded and packed away. Finally, the deck was bucket sluiced and scrubbed down. After two hours he stood in the stern and surveyed his work approvingly. She was beginning to look like a boat he could take pride in.

Once the vessel was tidied to his satisfaction, below decks as well as above, he went ashore to the showers on the jetty, intending, with no great hopes of success, to perform a similar transformation on himself.

As he examined his image in the tarnished mirror, he understood how Chantelle could have been so unimpressed with him. His eyes were sunken and darkly underlined and, as the razor, painfully blunt it seemed to him, sheared away the tangled excuse of a beard he had permitted to sprout, he saw the lines around his mouth, thin incisions in the pallid sun-starved skin. 'Christ,' he thought, 'I'm thirty-four and I look fifty.'

This assessment was, in fact, something of an exaggeration and, by the time he had blasted away the accumulated grime from his lean body under the steaming lash of the shower, he was able to regard himself in a less jaundiced light. Rolling up his toilet gear in his towel he quit the shower and made his way back to the boat, the air cool on his newly bared features, only the merest suggestion of hesitation coming when he realised the pubs were open. It was a temptation, however, that was manfully resisted and, once back on board, he brought the engine thumping to life, allowing it to warm up while he set about singling-up the lines. Ten minutes later he was out in the middle-ship channel and heading towards the harbour entrance.

He looked about him and smiled foolishly at the childlike pleasure he was experiencing at having put the boat to rights. There was, however, one thing still missing. Rummaging in the lazarette, he pulled forth the ensign, still tightly furled in its plastic cover, the red duster that had never flown at the stern since he had first purchased the boat out of his severance pay. As he released the bright new scarlet flag and watched it crackle and sport in the stiffening breeze, he began to sing softly to himself: 'Row, row, row the boat, gently down the stream. Merrily, merrily, merrily, merrily, life is but a dream.'

Once clear of the sheltered waters of the harbour, the brisk westerly breeze heeled the boat over and she bowled with a will down the fairway. He eased out the mainsail and then hoisted the biggest foresail he carried. As she drove willingly onward under this extra press of canvas, Latimer cut the engine. Now he moved about the boat with a new-found sense of purpose, trimming the sails with a care that bordered on fussiness, easing sheets and tightening the outhaul with a delicacy he had not practiced for many a long month. When all was to his liking he put his head to one side, listening to the music of the elements: the hiss of the bow as it sliced through the water and the solid percussive slap of the waves on the hull. Above everything, the backstay moaned dolefully, like the lower register of a huge organ, under the insistent strumming of the rising wind, and he felt the old thrill tingling down his spine.

The sun was shining brightly now, splintering and glancing off the low, bottle-green waves as he busied himself about the boat, stowing mooring warps and fenders before returning to the helm. At hand was the scrapbook and, almost compulsively, he reached out and turned the leaves. It fell open at a picture of Campbell-West and Noriega, the Panamanian President. Beneath was pasted a clipping from an American shipping magazine; apparently they were opening a new container facility somewhere on the canal.

'General Noriega and the British financier, Sir Peter Campbell-West, are pictured', the caption read, 'opening the new Coronadona facility near Christobal. In his speech the General paid tribute to the consortium of British backers who had put up the money for the new scheme, saying it represented the realisation of a long-standing dream.'

'Dream on CW.' Latimer murmured softly to himself. 'Dream on, while you can. We're coming to get you.'

Ten

Savoy Hotel, London

The Riverside restaurant at the Savoy had always been a favourite of Latimer's, for its varied menu, its swift yet unobtrusive service and its ever changing views of the embankment and river. He had, however, chosen it as a venue for his meeting with Chantelle and Collins for the more practical reason that it seemed to present less chance of bumping into any embarrassing faces from the past than might be the case had they lunched in the City. As he sat sipping his second, very thin, whisky, gradually becoming more at ease in these civilised and once familiar surroundings, he considered his situation.

As Chantelle had no doubt intended, the contents of the scrapbook had served to focus his thoughts and emotions to a level of clarity and intensity that now excluded all else. Whatever plan they had in mind for bringing Campbell-West in, no matter how extreme or dangerous it might be, he knew he would go along with it.

On the pristine linen tablecloth lay the scrapbook that had formed his sole source of reading material in the three weeks since Chantelle had visited him on the boat. Almost compulsively he flipped it open again, each picture and press cutting now as well known to him as the pages of his Latin grammar at Winchester. He had, slowly and painstakingly, translated each cutting and interpreted each picture until now he could decline and conjugate every move, regular or irregular, business or social, that Campbell-West had made in the past two years.

He stared out at the river where a fleeting shaft of weak sunlight played briefly on slack water and flat, low-tide mud, before being engulfed by the ragged basalt of the cloud. Whatever else happened, he now recognised that, until he came face to face with the man who had wrecked his life, there could be no rest.

In the past couple of weeks he had, apart from boning up on all the available information, also made some effort towards getting back into reasonable physical shape. Indeed, he had deliberately delayed the meeting to ensure that when they finally got together he would not find himself at too much of a disadvantage. To his surprise the task had not proved as daunting as he had expected. Before the Algoan affair he had been a good club class squash player and despite his drink problem his basic metabolism remained sound. Daily swimming and jogging, excruciatingly painful and lung wracking to start with, had, now he had a firm objective in mind, imperceptibly transmuted into a labour of love. Or was it hate? A spartan regime had begun to ameliorate the excesses of his previous lifestyle and, although he still drank it was, in the main, in moderation. Indeed, today, dressed in a smart broad pinstripe and with his hair once more subject to reasonable discipline, he looked as at home in that starchy atmosphere as any other West End businessman. As, his glass near empty, he considered at some length the wisdom of ordering a third, it came as a relief to see Chantelle and Collins, shepherded by the head waiter, approaching the table. His crisis had been temporarily resolved.

They both looked fit and well. Collins, tanned and grinning delightedly as he came forward, had retained the squared shoulders and flat stomach of a trained Marine and still walked with the slightly bow legged strut that comes with regular weight training. As he pumped Latimer's hand in the old powerful grip Chantelle, simply dressed in a navy two-piece and blouse, stretched up and kissed his cheek. As they sat down Latimer attempted to stammer out a well rehearsed apology.

'I'm sorry I gave you such a hard time on the boat, Chantelle. It came as rather a shock, your turning up out of the blue like that. I thought that part of my life was dead and buried. Anyway, I'm sorry. I behaved like a perfect shit.'

She laid an understanding hand on his arm, smiling at this uncharacteristic admission of fault and, perhaps, approving of the marked change in his appearance since their last encounter.

'Forget it, John. We're all back together again, that's what matters. What we've got to do now is to get on with the job in hand.'

'That's right.' Collins rubbed his hands together in glee, as though they were contemplating some minor dormitory prank. 'I think the occasion calls for a little celebration. Why don't we crack a bottle of the Bolly, order lunch and then get down to business?' It took the merest raising of his eyes to bring the wine waiter hastening to the table.

As the meal progressed and Collins unfolded their plans Latimer, maintaining a firm grip on his alcohol intake, listened carefully and critically to what was being proposed. With the cold analytical skill for which he had been renowned during his time at M & N, he assessed in detail every aspect of what they were putting forward, much as a few years previously he might have weighed up an investment prospect. In the main, he had to admit that what Collins was suggesting held a substantially better than fifty-fifty chance of success. There were, undoubtedly, areas where luck might play a larger part than he would have liked, but all-in-all it was a plan that he could go along with. As the second round of coffee and brandies were cleared away, and a third laid before them, Collins summed up.

'The crucial factor is that for the first time since he did a runner, Campbell-West will be setting foot somewhere that has an extradition treaty with the UK. If we were to grab him anywhere else, even if we got him back to Britain, we would, most likely, be the ones to end up in the slammer on a kidnapping charge, while he would be sent back to Brazil or wherever at the expense of Her Majesty's Government. So, given that he will be paying a visit to the Azores – Portuguese territory – at the end of next month, we must strike while the iron's hot. We've got to be in position, ready to make our move, then. We may not get another chance for years.'

'Why don't we simply tell the authorities? Surely Interpol could pick him up the moment he landed?' Even as he made the suggestion Latimer knew, precisely, the reason why.

'With Campbell-West's contacts, any moves we made through official channels would be common knowledge long before he left Brazil. Even supposing we found an honest copper, it would only take the least delay in arranging the extradition formalities to give our man plenty of time to fly the coop.'

'You seem very sure about this visit to the Azores, Dave. How come?'

'For nearly three years now, starting from the time when I was banged up in Huertos Jail, Chantelle has been working on this project, building up a comprehensive dossier on Campbell-West and his movements. The scrapbook there is only a very small part of what she has managed to glean and we have, in the process, established a very effective intelligence network that reports back to us whenever CW so much as passes wind. Naturally, we were doubtful when we first heard he was going there – especially as the information originated from a source we hadn't previously used. I know it's totally out of character for him to take any chances with his personal security but, knowing the man and, more importantly, the kind of deal he's hoping to put together on São Miguel, it all adds up.

He'll be acting, although they would deny it absolutely, I'm sure, on behalf of the South African government. His meeting, to be held at the Almirante Hotel in Ponta Delgado, will be with a man by the name of Chang Tau, although knowing CW's penchant for security we must be prepared for the venue to be changed at the last moment. Chang is an ex-tong war chief from Macau, Portuguese territory again. Holding Portuguese nationality and passport he feels safe on their territory, hence the Azores. Anyway, aware of the impending communist takeover of Macau and not wishing to leave things to the last moment, he set up retail and restaurant businesses in Vancouver a few years back. Part of his business is legit, bamboo furniture, jade artifacts, that sort of thing, but that's just a cover. As a sideline he also deals in the two commodities most in demand today – drugs and arms. Just to confirm our information was correct I've spent the last couple of weeks in Macau and Vancouver, checking on Mr Chang. Sure enough, he's scheduled to be in Madeira, a couple of hours' flight from the Azores, at the same time Campbell-West is in the Azores – there's no doubt about it John, the deal is on.'

Latimer frowned.

'What sort of deal are we talking about? Just what does it take to tempt Campbell-West to take a chance with his freedom?' Collins drained the last drops from his brandy balloon.

'Basically, what it comes down to is that Pretoria needs high tech weapons to keep on top of the Cubans and Nationalists in Angola and Namibia. In this case it's a shipment of infra-red nightsights which, because it's convenient and also less easy to trace than hard cash, they intend to pay for in high grade heroin. It's a drug they've acquired in large

102

quantities during their raids into Angola. Havana keeps its revolutionary heroes well supplied with the stuff. Incredible though it seems, the trade's run by a consortium of top brass in the Cuban forces and narcopoliticos – politicians who learned their business in Colombia. Normally it's Colombian cocaine they traffick but, since the US drugs agencies have tightened-up, there's a lot of heroin on the market looking for a home. You can see the logic of the set-up; while it lines the pockets of Fidel's cronies it also serves to keep the fighting soldiers' minds off the fact that AIDS is decimating their ranks more effectively than the South African security forces. Of course, the whole thing has become a vicious circle with the AIDS virus, contracted from the locals in the first place, now being spread by the use of dirty needles.

Chang has access to the nightsights, the best Uncle Sam can supply, thanks to his contacts with certain South Korean Generals. He also has a ready-made distribution network for the heroin through the chain of stores he has established in the Chinese quarter of most of the major cities on the west coast of the States and Canada.'

Latimer frowned, his enthusiasm for the venture un-dampened, yet soberly aware that they were going to be playing for very high stakes.

'What sort of money are we talking about?'

'From what I hear the South Africans are looking for enough sights to equip at least ten infantry battalions and, because of the nature of the deal, they will expect to pay well over the odds – maybe double the market price. I'm no expert on these things but I would be surprised if we were talking about less than £20 million. The Israelis would have supplied them more cheaply but wanted hard cash – they won't dirty their hands with drugs.'

'What sort of commission would Campbell-West expect to get from the deal?'

'Ten per cent. Ten per cent on both commodities, that is.

Four million. It's only when you realise the sort of money involved that you can understand why he is prepared to take the risks involved. This would be the biggest coup he's pulled off since he mega-crapped on us in Algoa.'

Latimer looked down at the table, his hands folding his serviette into ever smaller squares.

'We're going to be up against some pretty unpleasant characters in this. Don't get me wrong, I'm 100 per cent with you, but people like Chang could get very miffed indeed if they thought we had queered their pitch.'

Collins thought of an unconsummated tryst in a Vancouver hotel room: of Danny Yap and Sue Anne Ramirez. Best to say nothing, he thought. 'Absolutely, that's why our planning must be spot on. Chang intends to be on São Miguel for one day only. He flies in by private plane from Madeira, does the business, and then flies out. We must grab Campbell-West immediately the deal is completed. Once he has the drugs Chang won't give a stuff about what becomes of CW or the nightsights. I'm with you, John, I don't want to spend the rest of my life looking over my shoulder.'

Latimer looked up sharply, meeting the other man's eyes which, like his own, were smiling.

'Great. When do we fly out?'

'We don't. Campbell-West will have an advance party on the island long before he arrives. They'll be watching the airports and the harbours. He's almost certainly got a few police officers and customs men on his payroll as well. We'd be spotted immediately. No, what you and I are going to do is sail down there and lie low on the north coast of the island while Chantelle flies in and does the reconnaissance work for us in advance. I take it that boat of yours will get us there?'

So that was why they were so keen to have him along, thought Latimer, they needed him to get onto the island undetected and then to bring CW off. He instantly approved of the plan, it gave them an edge. Even a wily old bird like

CW would hardly be prepared for an operation like that.

'Of course it will – there and back again – but surely Chantelle will be spotted just as easily as we would. I don't get it.'

Chantelle shook her head.

'No. I have, in the course of my investigations, made a virtue of being extremely clumsy and unprofessional. I have deliberately made my presence known whenever I have been in Campbell-West's vicinity. So far as he is concerned I am currently writing the definitive account of the AFS affair, in the hope of clearing my own name, that's all. I have written to him on a number of occasions, inviting him to give his side of the story. He didn't reply, of course, but have no fear, he considers me a minor nuisance and no more. More importantly, he doesn't associate me with either of you two any more, so I will be perfectly safe.'

Collins looked about him, clearly considering that the subject had been thoroughly discussed, and looking now to settle the bill.

'Right, John, how long do you think it will take us to sail down there? The meeting between him and Chang is scheduled for five weeks time. We will need to be within striking distance of São Miguel at least a week before that.'

'I shall have to have a look at the charts, but I reckon three weeks would give us a good margin for bad weather and any other hiccups. I'll need a few days to get the boat stored and tuned up, so if you were to come down, say, next Saturday, we could get away the next day – or even that night if it would be better.'

'Fine, I'll be in touch before then, but you can expect us next Saturday. I'm looking forward to seeing the boat. What's she called, by the way?'

Latimer shrugged.

'She hasn't got a name at the moment. I bought her new from the yard and never bothered to give her one. I suppose that I should: we don't want to arouse the suspicions of the Customs Service. I'll give it some thought; we can have a little naming ceremony when you come down.'

With the bill paid, they had barely stirred from their seats before the over-attentive wine waiter was fussing about them, clearing away.

Once he had left the Savoy, Latimer went straight to the nearest pub, a gloomy place just off the Strand and, at that hour of the afternoon, happily almost deserted. Settling himself into a corner seat he sipped his beer and considered the venture to which he was now committed. Certainly it seemed a plan that just might succeed. Chantelle and David had thoroughly researched it and he had no doubts as to his own ability to get to the island or, for that matter, to bring CW off. Nevertheless, there could be no harm in carrying out a little investigatory work himself; you could never be too careful. Slipping the battered address book from his inside pocket, he went to the telephone.

'That is the first time I have made love with anyone since you and I spent that glorious afternoon at The Plough, the day Peter disappeared.' Victoria Campbell-West lay back across the bed, her eyes closed, the back of one hand resting lightly on her forehead. 'It must be best part of four years ago now.'

Latimer drew back the brocade edging of her silk gown and, leaning forward, took the soft puckered flesh of her nipple in his mouth as she sighed and shifted under his touch. He could well believe she had been chaste for so long, for he had just witnessed her experience such an urgent and powerful orgasm that she had half-fainted beneath him, climaxing so swiftly he had barely realised she was coming.

He had not finished but, for the moment, was not concerned, there was plenty of time. He was pleased that he had been able to ease her so rapidly and effectively. It would make her all the more amenable to his questions. Sliding his tongue wetly across the plane of her belly, questing for her navel, he began his careful inquisition.

'Do you ever hear from CW these days?' he enquired casually. There was a pause, as she gathered her scattered thoughts, and when she spoke her voice was deep and dream-like.

'Strangely enough, I received a letter from him only yes-terday. The first word I've had since he went off. From Paraguay I think. The bloody cheek of the man.'

His hands lightly teased along the inside of her readily parting thighs and she raised herself onto one elbow, smiling down at him as he probed ever deeper.

'What did he want?'

'Oh, he only wants a divorce, would you believe! Appar-ently he's managed to get that slut Sarah Mendelsohn in the club and wants to make sure his son and heir – he always wanted a boy – isn't saddled with the stigma of being a bastard. It would be most appropriate if you ask me – like father like son.'

Not in the least interested in the conversation she reached down, gently grasping his half erect organ as she manoeuvred herself into position. As she bowed forward, her mouth hovering lasciviously, her eyes fixed on his, he fired off his last question.

'What did you say?'

'I told him to go and fuck himself.'

Later, as she lay half asleep in his arms, she murmured softly.

'It's funny, you know. They say things run in threes. First Peter writes; then you turn up out of the blue and tomorrow I'm due to meet a Mr Ho from Hong Kong to discuss God knows what about Peter's affairs in the Far East. To tell the truth I never knew he had any.'

She looked down and smiled; Latimer was dead to the world.

Eleven

Latimer whistled cheerfully to himself as he scrubbed away at the teak decking for the second time that morning. Overhead the sun peeped fitfully between the creamy cumulus that rolled in from the west on a stiffening breeze. The weather forecast had not been particularly encouraging, promising gale-strength winds later but, just now, nothing could spoil his mood. The boat was fuelled-up and provisioned for a month at least. They were ready to go.

In the weeks since his meeting with Chantelle and Collins he had buffed and polished her to perfection. Nor had his efforts been for purely cosmetic effect. Every item of both standing and running rig had been removed and examined. Sails had been patched where needed and the big Volvo diesel had been stripped down and given a thorough servicing. His vessel, once the disgrace of the river and the subject of much self-righteous tut-tutting in clubhouse bars, was again a living entity of strength and beauty. Staring up to the gently swaying cross-trees, Latimer felt the emotion rise in his throat, his eyes misted, and he coughed away his embarrassment.

His mood was not born entirely of the day. He was high on expectation. Today John and Chantelle were due to arrive and, for reasons he couldn't exactly quantify, the prospect of seeing her outweighed the more substantial consideration of their imminent departure. His elation was not to last long, however.

As Collins' Range Rover, riding low on its suspension, slewed into the little boat yard, his heart sank. He had spent the last two days carefully victualling the boat in preparation for the journey south. Now it appeared he was expected to find room for another load. What was worse, Chantelle was nowhere to be seen. Perhaps his consternation showed for Collins was quick to explain.

'Essential equipment, my boy. I managed to get hold of a couple of Klepper collapsible canoes. Two-man jobs – one for you and one for me. We won't be able to sail right into Ponta Delgado you know. Don't worry, we won't set them up until we arrive, then we can lash them to the foredeck. You wait, you won't even know they are there after a day or two.'

'What about that little lot?' Latimer pointed into the rear of the Range Rover which, apart from the canvas canoe packs, was stacked to the roof with heavy wooden crates. 'She's a Bermudan-rigged sloop and not quite forty foot overall, Dave. What exactly were you expecting? The fucking *Nimitz*?'

Collins, however, was in no mood for such defeatist talk, slapping him heartily on the back. 'As the Bishop said to the actress: have faith my child – it'll all go in.'

And so it proved, although it took the best part of an hour to stow the extra equipment to Latimer's satisfaction and entailed utilising all the after-cabin space and part of the forepeak too. The after-cabin was no great loss so far as he was concerned. With only two of them on board for the outward leg their was plenty of room in the main saloon. However, he was less happy with the clutter up-forward, obstructing access to the sail locker as it did. If the weather was to catch them out and they needed to carry out a rapid sail change it might well make things awkward.

'What's in the crates, anyway?' he demanded hotly. 'I've stowed enough food and booze to see us to New Zealand and back. I thought that you'd come aboard with a small toilet bag and change of underpants. What the hell is all that stuff?' Aware of the real cause of his irritability, he came to the point, his tone suddenly casual. 'Where's Chantelle? I thought she was supposed to be coming with you.' Collins looked at his watch.

'She's in the village. I dropped her off to pick up a few final bits of shopping. She going to see us off then drive the wagon back to London. Her flight doesn't leave for a week or so yet.' he raised a questioning eyebrow. 'I take it we can get away tonight as planned?' Latimer, preoccupied now with the prospect of seeing Chantelle nodded and Collins smiled. 'Right, then I suggest we take this opportunity to throw a few pints down us. It might be the last chance we get for quite a while.' He looked directly at Latimer, a challenging glint in his eye. 'Race you to the pub – loser buys the first round.'

Collins won his bet, but only by half-a-yard or so for, to the surprise of both men, Latimer pressed him hard all the way down the narrow High Street, startled heads turning as they stampeded past. When they stood outside the Kings Arms, gasping for breath but laughing like scrumping schoolboys who had evaded the farmer, Collins murmured his approval of this unexpected evidence of fitness in the other man. 'Not bad, Johnny boy. Not bad at all.'

Chantelle was waiting for them in the bar. She seemed rather withdrawn that morning, Latimer thought, putting it reluctantly down to her imminent separation from Collins. Her welcome for him was warm enough however, throwing her arms about him, her eyes on his. For a second there was an awkward silence and, sensing the hiatus, she moved firmly to break the spell.

'Everything aboard?' she asked easily, releasing her hold

110

on him and proceeding to elbow her way through the noisy throng of midday drinkers with trans-Atlantic single-mindedness.

'Yes. We can leave anytime we choose now.' Latimer looked at Collins pointedly but kept his voice low. 'I'm just intrigued to know what all that junk Dave has brought along is for. I do recognise ammunition cases when I see them, you know. I thought the motto of the Special Boat Squadron was "By guile not strength"; I didn't expect to be going in like John Wayne.'

Not until they had collected their drinks and were seated in a comparatively quiet corner of the bar did Collins deign to enlighten him.

'Think of it as insurance, John. A few Armalite rifles, a brace of Skorpion machine-pistols, enough ammunition to hold the Khyber Pass, and a family pack of fragmentation grenades.' Pre-empting Latimer's not unexpected reaction, he raised a hand. 'Please – let me finish. Hopefully none of that stuff will ever come out of the crates, but we have to accept that we could find ourselves in all sorts of trouble if things go wrong. We must be prepared for any eventuality.'

Latimer, eyes fixed on Collins' face and still not prepared to take anything for granted, lifted his glass without comment. It was for Collins to justify his position. He proceeded to do just that.

'Don't expect the Campbell-West we are going after to bear much resemblance to the smooth-talking bastard you remember from the old days. Forget about all the charities he used to support so enthusiastically. Forget the whales, the seals and the underprivileged children – all that was just window-dressing. It's always been obligatory for City elders to present the acceptable face of monumental greed. I have to tell you, I'm afraid, that altruism doesn't feature largely in his philosophy these days. He carries a side arm, a Smith and Wesson .38, everywhere he goes. What's more, he knows how to use

111

it. And, as if that isn't enough …', he produced a handful of photographs, black and white prints that Latimer had not seen before although the faces seemed vaguely familiar, presumably from the scrapbook, '… he has a couple of minders who would put the fear of God up anyone. Take a look at these little beauties.'

Collins laid the top picture on the table. It showed a gaunt giant of a man, dressed in a camouflaged combat jacket, a pump action shotgun slung on his shoulder. He stood over what, at first glance, appeared to be a bundle of rags. On closer inspection Latimer saw, however, that it was in fact a human body. The giant, grinning, was giving a triumphant thumbs-up to the camera.

'That one is Luis Behan. Not an Irishman, despite the name and general appearance, but a third-generation Argentinian. He is thirty-eight years old, stands six feet five inches tall, and weighs two hundred and twenty pounds. About the only good thing that can be said for the bastard is that he played front row forward for the Pumas back in the sixties.

He served as a regular soldier for eighteen years, was commissioned from the ranks and ended up as a major in Grupa 606 – the dago equivalent of the SAS. In 1982, when the Argies threw their hand in in the Falklands, Behan refused to surrender. He and his men who, incidentally, were the first to go ashore in the invasion, dug themselves in on Beagle Ridge overlooking Port Stanley and refused to budge. They held a whole company of Ghurkas at bay for nearly twenty-four hours after the ceasefire.

Eventually, rather than risk British lives, it was decided to whistle-up the artillery and blast them out. For four hours the area was well and truly stonked. Milan anti-tank missiles, 105 millimeter HE shells, mortars – the lot. However, when the barrage was lifted and the Gurkhas finally took the slit trenches, it was found that Behan and his men had slipped away under cover of darkness. As if that wasn't enough he then contrived to steal a small fishing boat, sail right through the exclusion zone and get back to Mar del Plata – right under the nose of the Royal Navy.

Anyway, once back in Argentina he was, for a while at least, treated like a hero. It was a commodity which, you may remember, they were short of at the time. Unfortunately, after the war when Galtieri and the junta were brought to account and the records of certain army officers were examined, it came to light that Behan had also been an enthusiastic warrior in the so-called dirty war against left-wing elements. Torture sessions and massacres were attributed to Señor Behan. Not only that, there were rumours of some rather nasty sexual deviations that found a convenient outlet in a number of the female prisoners unfortunate enough to fall into his hands.

Overnight, their editors sensitive to the political changes in Buenos Aires, the very papers that had hailed his exploits in the Malvinas were calling for his head. Behan, typically, had other ideas and had planned ahead. When a warrant was issued for his arrest he shot two military policemen dead and again made a discreet departure.'

Collins paused, sipping his beer and looking to Latimer for some reaction to this colourful curriculum vitae. None was forthcoming and he smiled, determined at all costs to improve the shining hour. 'I think it's only fair to warn you that Behan is generally regarded as being the cuddlier of Campbell-West's chums.'

He placed a second photograph on top of the first, like a card player laying an ace on a king. It was a square picture of a square man: cropped blond hair and gold-rimmed granny-glasses over a body that might have been hewn from granite.

'Henk Groose. Twenty-five years old, five feet six inches tall and two hundred and thirty five pounds. He was, probably still is for that matter, a world-class weightlifter and would have represented the Netherlands in the Moscow

Olympics but for his arrest two months before on a charge of trying to push steroids to his team mates. He's as queer as a nine-bob note and while on remand for the drugs charge was also arraigned for the homosexual rape of a young offender unfortunate enough to be locked up in the same cell. He's a martial arts' fanatic and extremely violent – a real sweetheart. Apart from Behan and Groose, who accompany him everywhere, Campbell-West also has a team of assorted heavies that he can call on at short notice.'

Latimer's eyes straying to the nicotine-stained ceiling, he drummed his fingers in a display of mock-nervousness. Suddenly, the arsenal that Collins had brought along no longer seemed excessive.

'I reckon we've got enough room to mount a couple of Exocets up forward if you knew where we might lay hands on them at short notice.'

As they walked back to the boat yard, all three fell silent, alone with their thoughts. A high, thin cloud had veiled the sun and the stiffening breeze whispered chill about their ears as they entered the run-down yard. With its rotting hulks and rank, weedy smell, it suddenly seemed a strangely sinister place.

What had until then seemed like a grand adventure was now about to begin in earnest and the stark realities of the undertaking began to weigh heavily: a sea voyage of some 1,500 miles in a small boat, an illegal incursion into a foreign state and the kidnapping of an internationally-known criminal who would certainly be surrounded by guards of nightmare proportions. While Collins might, ten years ago, have been classed as a proper fighting man, since then all three had been nothing more than office workers, highly paid office workers it was true, but nothing more. Two pox doctor's clerks and a woman, off to conquer the world. Latimer sensed the gloom settling like a tangible weight and tried to

114

lift it.

'I'd almost forgotten, we've got one other important task to perform before this show gets on the road. Chantelle, if you'll just wait there on the pontoon, I'll get the bubbly.' Hauling in a line that hung down across the boat's transom, he pulled a dripping bottle of Moët from the dark water. Vanishing below, he returned in seconds with three glasses. 'This stuff is too good to waste, so we'll just splash a little on the boat and drink the rest ourselves. Right, Chantelle, I now invite you to name this boat.' He pointed. 'There's her name, on the stern.'

A little bemused at first, Chantelle's gaze ranged down the length of the vessel's white hull. Then she smiled and stepping forward to the pontoon's dipping edge slopped a little of the foaming liquid over the boat's side.

'I name this yacht *Revenge*. May God bless her and all those who sail in her.'

Latimer and Collins responded with a rather ragged three cheers that were carried away on the rising wind. An awkward interlude ensued: too much to say, too little time. Twice Latimer's eyes held Chantelle's then dropped guiltily. Finally, both men, anxious to put the coming farewell behind them, jumped aboard and began singling-up mooring lines, glad of the diversion.

As the boat eased away from the jetty, Chantelle stood on the gently undulating pontoon, waving until they vanished from sight round the curve of the river. Collins at the helm and concentrating on negotiating the narrow channel, was quickly oblivious to the diminishing figure. Latimer, however, kept his hand raised in salute to the last moment.

Back in the warm womb of the Land Rover, Chantelle ran her tongue over lips wet with the fine rain that now fell and recalled the way Latimer had kissed her.

Twelve

By nightfall the occulting light of the Needles lighthouse was well astern and to starboard the necklace of yellow lights along the Bournemouth esplanade showed clearly. Through the binoculars Latimer carried out a careful all-round sweep of the sea. Apart from the lights of a couple of small fishing vessels trawling about a mile to the south, there was little of interest and, engaging the self-steering gear, he went below into the cramped snugness of the saloon. Collins, who was making notes in a spring-bound pad, looked up from the large scale chart of the Azores that he had been studying.

'Anything happening up top, skipper?'

Latimer smiled inwardly, not displeased at the scheme of things implicit in the title. While they were at sea, at least, it appeared that he was accepted as the senior partner. What would happen when they hit the beach was anyone's guess although the gentle art of abduction was, he was well aware, something beyond his experience. His eyes went to the digital compass repeater set in the bulkhead above the chart table. The self-steering gear seemed to be working OK and maintaining the pre-set course.

'No, all quiet. I'll take the middle watch and shake you at four.' He hesitated, not wishing to destroy all the brownie points that, thanks to his moderation, he'd accumulated over

116

the past few weeks, but nevertheless feeling badly in need of a stiffener. What the hell!

'Fancy a tot before you turn in, Dave?' he enquired casually. 'Just the one to keep the cold out?'

Collins didn't hesitate and it came as a relief to Latimer to realise that his crewman was not afflicted by the prissy puritanism of Chantelle.

'Just the one? If we're to get through all that stuff you've got stowed in the grog locker I think we'll have to do a lot better than that.'

Latimer poured out two large jiggers of rum and, after another trip to the cockpit to assure himself there was no shipping in the offing, returned below. Settling himself across the table from Collins, his face etched in shadow under the subdued yellow glow of the solitary light, he grew thoughtful.

'What I've never really understood,' he said, by way of opening the conversation, 'is how CW got wind that the authorities were on to him. How was it that he did his disappearing trick just before they were about to feel his collar?'

Collins stared down at the dark liquid in his glass.

'Well I'm only guessing, but I suspect that the brethren of the rolled-up trouser brigade had something to do with it.'

Latimer raised an eyebrow. He knew what Collins was getting at. Campbell-West had never made any secret of his masonic links, indeed he had on more than one occasion intimated that, should either of them feel inclined to join the order – the craft as he always called it – he would ensure that their applications were given sympathetic consideration. What he meant in effect was that, with him proposing them, they were as good as accepted. In the event, and perhaps with the benefit of hindsight, unfortunately, neither had felt the inclination at the time. To them, like most young men, freemasonry had always carried a slightly absurd image:

middle-aged bank managers and insurance brokers exchanging secret handshakes. Now, too late, they began to have some inkling of its prevalence and influence.

'There aren't many career coppers in the City of London force who aren't Freemasons. My guess is that he would have been kept well informed about how the investigation was proceeding and, once things reached a stage where they had no option but to arrest him, he would have been given a head start. Remember how he travelled abroad more and more during the year leading up to his disappearance. I guess he was setting himself up in preparation for the day he said farewell to old England for ever. He would have had to let Enriques in on the secret so that funds could be transferred from BdC to other South American countries without setting alarm bells ringing.'

Latimer's features grew hard, his hatred recharged.

'It would be nice if we could wring the names of his informants in the City out of the old bastard. There's nothing I'd like more than to dump this whole heap of pigshit right back in their aproned laps. I'd just love to see those sanctimonious bastards, all those holier-than-thou sons of bitches who were calling for a return to Victorian values when we were thrown to the wolves, have to face up to the fact that the place is rotten from the top down.'

Both men fell silent, listening to the steady thump thump of the waves against the hull, as *Revenge*, on a beam reach and making a steady five knots, punched determinedly into the tide. Occasionally the VHF would crackle into life as vessels, large and small, out in the darkness beyond, passed routine communications between themselves and the shore. In the main, however, it was the sounds of the sea that filled their ears.

At a little after midnight Collins, unzipping his sleeping bag and punching his pillow into submission, indicated that he was ready for his bunk, while Latimer returned to the cockpit and settled down for the long middle watch. They were out in the main shipping channel now and about them little clusters of red, white, and green navigation lights blinked in the night, revealing the presence of otherwise invisible vessels plying up and down the Channel. Latimer breathed in the tangy air, feeling for the first time in a long while totally at peace with himself. He had a purpose in life once more.

The following morning, having been relieved on watch as planned by Collins, Latimer set about preparing breakfast, singing softly to himself as he clattered noisily about the galley. By the time he handed Collins the plate of eggs and bacon it was growing light and he saw that, in the hour or so since he had taken over at the helm, the ex-marine had not been idle. Mackerel spinners were now streamed out astern and a couple of the silver fish lay on the deck, already gutted.

'They'll do for lunch,' Collins said, wolfing down the food Latimer had prepared. He smiled. 'There's just one thing. I don't want to be a nuisance but I usually swim in the mornings. Any chance of us slowing down so I can take a dip?'

Latimer looked doubtfully at the sea, hammered glass stretching grey and empty away to a dawn that was ragged gunmetal cloud and yellow banners. It was far from rough although he knew that at that time of year it was sure to be very cold; but the wind had dropped away so it was not likely to be a dangerous undertaking. He shrugged.

'If you're sure it's what you want, I'll heave to. But it's going to be bloody freezing you know.'

His warnings were clearly falling on deaf ears as, under his jaundiced gaze, Collins quickly stripped and was soon standing naked on the transom, apparently oblivious to the keen wind. Latimer hove to, backing the jib and lashing the helm to leeward, bringing the boat to a standstill almost immediately. When all headway was off the boat and she lolloped idly among the little slapping waves, he looked to the other, to his mind almost certainly deranged man and nodded. Without a moment's hesitation Collins launched himself into a shallow dive that took him several yards away from the stern before he surfaced, gasping with the cold and shaking the water away from his face. With a wave to the boat to indicate that all was well, he proceeded to swim powerfully in a wide circle around the wallowing *Revenge*.

After about twenty minutes he hauled himself over the side and proceeded to towel himself down vigorously. As he pulled on his clothes his eyes met Latimer's, the old challenging glint appearing. For a second Latimer hesitated, but that was all. He knew what was required of him. Before the other man had a chance to speak he had stripped and, with an ungainly leap, arms and legs splayed, was soon gasping for breath alongside the boat, looking up at the laughing Collins.

'You're a pervert, Collins,' he choked. 'A bloody pervert.' However, despite his protestations, he took the opportunity to make a point by swimming further from the boat than had his silent tormentor and then, to doubly underline the fact that he wasn't just along for the ride, spent an agonising ten minutes longer in the freezing water. When he climbed back on board, Collins was performing press-ups, biceps flexing in rhythmic thrusts. He sighed audibly and, dropping to the deck beside him, began to count. Latimer collapsed at twenty-five while Collins went on to fifty, even then barely breathing any harder than normal. Even so, it was clear he appreciated that Latimer was becoming a physical force to be reckoned with.

'By the time we reach the Azores, John, you'll be able to do fifty, no trouble. Now,' he said, rolling onto his back, 'let's see how you are on the sit-ups.'

At midday, with the sun breaking through strongly, Latimer brought his sextant on deck and took a sun sight, nodding approvingly when his calculations produced a position that tallied sufficiently closely with those of the Decca

120

automatic navigator to give grounds for some faith in their accuracy. Despite the stop for swimming they had, since midnight, covered over eighty miles and *Revenge* was still bowling merrily along. At this rate they would reach the Azores inside a fortnight. In addition to taking sun sights, the passing of the sun through its zenith was to be the occasion for another nautical ritual as Collins passed two large tots of rum out into the cockpit.

'The Queen, God bless her,' he said, proposing the old naval toast.

As the rum filtered into the bloodstream and a comfortable feeling of wellbeing settled upon them, both men stretched out in the cockpit. The sun was warm on their faces now and Latimer dozed under its benign kiss while Collins busied himself with his lines, hooking another three mackerel before reeling in the spinners, his fishing finished for the day. During the early part of the dogwatches they took the helm off the auto pilot and steered manually for an hour or so, conserving the batteries for the night hours when automatic steering meant that the man on watch could spend more time in the shelter of the cabin. Sooner or later they would have to run the engine to charge up the batteries but to break the gentle, somnolent spell of the afternoon was unthinkable. At a little after 5.30 Latimer stirred and, blinking, looked around him, his eyes instinctively sweeping the horizon for any sign of shipping. There was none.

'Do you ever miss the City, John?' Collins asked absently, gazing away into the distance, his arm draped lazily over the tiller. 'I know it used to mean a lot to me when we both worked there, but that was only for a couple of years. You were there for how long?'

'Over eight years. Yes, I miss it. It's a fascinating place – a world in itself. It's hard to explain but, in some ways, it was almost like a village, so parochial in its relationships and atmosphere; after a while you seemed to get to know everyone who mattered. Yet at the same time it was so sophisticated in its operations. I used to love it. I can remember thinking that the streets used to buzz whenever I was putting a really big deal together; I could actually hear the excitement inside me.

I used to like the social side too. The wine bars and restaurants at lunchtime, the pubs in the evening after work – and all those gorgeous women as well. You were never certain whether you were working or playing, it was all such fun – and we seemed to make a lot of money at the same time.' He hardened up on the jib sheet, the wind was backing, and hauled in the mainsheet. It wasn't really necessary but, aware of his tendency to become effusive on the subject under discussion, he took the opportunity to check himself temporarily.

'It's all changed, of course, too many scandals in too short a period. Lloyd's, the Stock Exchange, not to mention our own little hiatus. The days of the financial privateers are over for the time being, too many top people caught with their fingers in the till. It was inevitable I suppose, but the mandarins are in control now, grey faceless men with the official stamp of Whitehall on their foreheads and computers for hearts. Look!'

He pointed ahead of the boat where a dozen bottle-nosed dolphins had suddenly broken surface and now sped ahead of them in gleaming echelon, plunging through the waves, disappearing and reappearing in the modest bow wave *Revenge* pushed up before her. For maybe five minutes they sported about the boat, sometimes coming in so close that, with their friendly eyes and crooked grins, they seemed to be inviting the men in the cockpit to join them in their sport. Eventually they peeled off and swam away to the north in search of other entertainment.

'Do you think you'll ever go back?' Collins asked, as if nothing had interrupted their conversation. 'Work in the City again, I mean?'

122

'That depends. I'd like to, but things would have to be very different from when I was chucked out. If we manage to bring Campbell-West back to face the music, I might consider it I suppose. But that's the main thing, nothing else matters so far as I'm concerned. I want to make all those mealy-mouthed shits who raised their hands in horror, and who were quite happy to see us take the rap for something we had no part in, deal with having the real culprit handed to them on a plate. I want him delivered up to the Guildhall magistrates, among whose illustrious ranks, you will remember, he himself was numbered at one time, and then watch them agonise over having to pass judgement on a man who will no doubt have something pretty juicy on each and every one of them. I want to see them squirm the way they made me squirm.'

As he looked up at the great white bellying of the sails and the gently rolling masthead that traced invisible curlicues on the high cirrus, Collins said softly.

'Instead of a personal revenge, would you consider settling for something more tangible?'

'Such as what?'

'A financial settlement – give CW the chance to buy us off?'

'No. Why do you ask?'

'Well, it occurs to me that Campbell-West is setting up a pretty big deal down there in the Azores. It also occurred to me that we might be able to skim a little off for ourselves if we played our cards right.'

'I thought we agreed that we didn't want to get involved with Chang. That we'd be out of our depth in that sort of company – as though we weren't already.'

'Yes, I know all about that but just supposing we grabbed CW and the heroin. We'd be in a position to offer Chang an alternative cash deal. He could keep the nightsights, they're a very saleable commodity which he'd have no trouble whatsoever in disposing of elsewhere, and we would sell him the drugs at half the agreed price, say ten million. Chang's a businessman. I know he'd be interested if we approached him along those lines. We could really clean up. The South Africans would never dare admit to dealing in drugs and, even if they did turn nasty, no one would ever associate us with that sort of thing. We'd be long gone before they knew what was going on.'

Latimer shook his head definitely.

'No. We shouldn't get sidetracked from our original plan. So far as I'm concerned we're here to take Campbell-West and that's all. Anyway, we don't want to get involved in drugs, Dave – it stinks.'

Collins looked at him hard and Latimer realised that, momentarily, they were eyeballing each other in earnest. Then the cropped blond head nodded in acceptance and he gave an easy throwaway smile.

'OK. It was just an idea. I guess you're right, we'll have enough on our plate as it is without trying to be too clever.'

Later, as the night was shouldering up over the eastern horizon and the oily aroma of the frying mackerel hung over the boat. Collins took one of the self loading rifles from its case, together with a couple of clips of ammunition, and went on deck. Half a dozen empty beer cans were tossed over the side at regular intervals, the most distant some thirty yards away by the time he assumed the firing position. Latimer stood at his shoulder as he fired away, in single shots or short disciplined bursts, at the bobbing marks. He was very accurate, none of his shots falling more than a couple of inches either side of the cans, which jumped about briefly on the water before sinking from sight. Slipping another magazine home, he handed the weapon to Latimer.

'Right, John, let's see how good a shot you are.'

In the event Latimer proved to be a more than passable marksman, choosing not to reveal that he had won a blue at Oxford for small bore shooting, representing his college at Bisley on a number of occasions. It was with some satisfaction that he handed back the gun with the magazine still not empty and all his targets on their way to the sea bed. Later, Collins gave him instruction in the use of the machine-pistols and the grenades. By the end of their first full day at sea they were, it seemed to him, developing into a fairly well-trained team.

As night fell they sat below in the cramped cabin, listening to a wind that had backed round to the west and into which *Revenge* was now punching her way with a short and uncomfortable motion. The boat's working caused the water in the bilges beneath their feet to slop about in a disconcerting manner and the stores in the lockers to roll, first to one side and then the other, with a rhythmic, ponderous thudding.

'What does Chantelle think about all this?' Latimer asked, lowering his voice as he added: 'She told me about losing the baby.'

Collins didn't answer at first and it was clear, as he rubbed his face in his hands before replying, that it was a matter that troubled him more than a little.

'It's a bit of a problem actually. Chantelle hates Campbell-West with every fibre of her being. You and I hate him I know, but she wants him dead. It's something we are going to have to watch out for when we actually make contact. For her own sake as much as his, I don't want her to get too close to CW when we snatch him. You'll have to take care of that, John, you're going to have to keep an eye on her.

She had a breakdown, shortly after the miscarriage. Her family took care of her while I was in jail and by the time I was released she seemed back to normal. Since then she's had bouts of near suicidal depression and at times I've feared for her sanity. It's only since we've put this scheme together that she's got back to anything like her old self. It's been like therapy for her and she's put her whole being into it. I'm just scared about what'll happen when she eventually confronts him for the first time.'

At three in the morning the wind was gusting up to force

nine and, reluctantly, they went on deck to put a double reef in the main sail and to replace the working foresail with the storm jib. The main was reefed down with comparative ease, but fighting the flapping canvas of the jib into submission as it flogged about in the howling wind was another matter. The deck ran green and treacherous beneath the assault of regular, explosive torrents as it plunged and rose like a bucking bronco beneath them. By the time they had got the storm jib hoisted and set to Latimer's satisfaction both men were soaked to the skin and breathing hard. However, under reduced sail *Revenge* rode more easily into the gale than before and, as they set about stripping off their dripping foul-weather gear, things seemed to have settled down sufficiently for Latimer to produce the rum 'just to keep the cold out'.

As Collins, his hair plastered to his head, towelled his body down vigorously, attempting to induce some warmth into freezing limbs, he grew thoughtful.

'What I was saying earlier, about Chantelle and Campbell-West, it was only because of her that I suggested we might try for a negotiated settlement. I wouldn't have anything to do with drugs otherwise. I hope you understand that.'

Latimer looked at him closely. 'Sure, Dave. I know that.'

Thirteen

Ponta Delgado, São Miguel, The Azores

With a grunt of relief Chantelle dropped her case and looked around the deserted reception area. It was clean, yet with an air of slightly wistful neglect. In the sunlight that fell between the heavy curtains motes of dust danced in swirling confusion on the breeze of her entrance. Behind the desk a row of brass hooks bore heavy iron keys, each with a numbered plastic tag. The bank of deep pigeon-holes affixed to the wall next to them seemed significantly bare of mail: the Hotel Miramar, it seemed, was not oversubscribed. Shaking off the drowsy spell of the place she brought the palm of her hand down firmly on the tarnished chromium dome of the desk bell. Her reward was the deadest, most unbell-like, of clicks; like much else at the Miramar, as she was later to discover, it had seen better days.

'Hallo,' she called tentatively, 'anyone around?'

From beyond the door marked 'Manager' came the sound of a chair being scraped across the floor and, shortly afterwards, a tall dark youth, dressed in jeans and a stained tee shirt, appeared.

'Hi,' she said brightly, 'do you have any rooms available?'

At first the boy – he was little more – stared uncomprehendingly at her then he smiled, revealing a row of yellow, equine teeth.

'American?'

'Yes. Do you have any rooms?'

'Si. We have rooms.' From the flatness of his tone, question and response were not related, but she was aware of his eyes running over her body.

'Can I have a single room? I guess I'll want it for a week – maybe two.'

He considered the matter, then nodded.

'Sure. I show you.'

He led the way up the worn carpeted stairs, leaving her to struggle with the dead weight of her case, past gloomy engravings of Christ, the Madonna and various lachrymose martyrs. On the first floor, halfway along the dark corridor, he halted before a door that bore a crazed ceramic plaque numbered 13. As, standing back to let her pass, he pushed the door inwards, Chantelle fancied she glimpsed something small, black and shiny scurrying for cover beneath the bed.

While the youth hesitated awkwardly in the doorway she walked around the cramped perimeter of the room, her eyes critical. Despite the likelihood of exotic wildlife lurking beneath the bed it was, if shabby, clean enough, and the sheets on the bed had been crisply ironed. Best of all, in the corner stood a curtained shower unit. After two days travelling, the prospect of a proper shower would have made a king cobra an acceptable room mate.

'I'll take it.'

'You have passport?' the youth asked, quick to explain as he saw the question in her eyes: 'Is regulations – I return it tomorrow.'

'OK.' She delved in her shoulder bag and handed it to him. Having made this concession she was determined to re-establish her position. 'I'm going to take a shower first then I'd like something to eat. Any chance of getting a drink?'

'Sure. We got whisky, Bacardi, tequila.' She would, she decided, be difficult.

'Gin?'

'Sure, we got gin.'

When he had gone she locked the door and went to the window, intent on drawing the flimsy, faded curtains. The window overlooked a small courtyard, paved with uneven red tiles, at the centre of which stood a solid-looking fountain, filled with a still pool of greenish water. An empty, half-crushed lager can floated on its scummy surface. On pulling the curtains she found that, since they were no more than narrow strips of fabric, it took a great deal of careful arranging to ensure they provided even the most minimal privacy. Satisfied, she laid her case on the bed and began to unpack.

Beneath the clothes and minimal toiletries she had brought lay the black radio with which she would, hopefully within the week, make contact with the boat. Its presence in the case had caused her to be questioned by customs at Heathrow and again at Lisbon. Thankfully, the rather less stringent security arrangements that applied on São Miguel had allowed her to pass without problem. Also, by way of window dressing she had brought a portable typewriter. Having transferred her things to the low chest of drawers, and laid the typewriter prominently on its cracked varnish top, she carefully relocked the case and slid it under the bed.

Sitting down on the bed she kicked off her shoes and began to unbutton the jacket of the safari suit that she had now worn for nearly forty-eight hours. She warily sniffed a raised arm, her nose wrinkling disapprovingly; even the regular application of deodorants had ceased effectively to mask the warm, slightly acrid musk of her body. Slipping off her jacket and skirt she went to the shower and ran the rather erratic jet of water until it had reached an acceptable temperature. Before she could strip completely there came a soft knocking at the door and, pulling a short silk robe around her, she went to the door and peered round it.

It was the youth, now bearing a small, circular tin tray on

which stood a half-bottle of gin, ice, tonic and a large, fairly clean tumbler. She stepped back, allowing him to pass, and he walked across to the chest of drawers, laying the tray beside the typewriter. She turned the shower off.

'Thanks,' she said, again aware of the way his eyes strayed to her legs. He was, she guessed, about sixteen. Young enough to be hesitant, unsure of himself, yet physically a walking pistol. In a place like Ponta Delgado, with its repressive Catholic morality and provincial strictures, just to find himself in a woman's bedroom would be like manna from heaven. It was an essential part of her role in the scheme of things to make herself conspicuous. Might as well get started. She unstoppered the bottle and, bringing another glass from the washbasin, held it up. 'Drink?'

The boy, torn between the urge to flee and the unimaginable potential of the situation, hesitated. Then he took the glass with a hand that visibly trembled.

'Si, Señora, thank you.'

She poured him a stiff one, coming close so that he might catch a glimpse of shadowy cleavage, then, pushing the door shut, she nodded to the rickety cane chair.

'Take a seat ...?'

'Manolito.'

'Take a seat, Manolito.'

She stretched out on the bed, casually crossing her legs as she sipped the perfumed spirit. Manolito's eyes were devouring her as he stumbled for some words that might cover his confusion. His mouth dry, he nodded at the typewriter.

'You are a writer, Señora?'

'A journalist,' she said airily. Somewhere, trapped between the curtains and window, a fly buzzed sleepily. Chantelle ran a hand through her hair. 'I'm in Ponta Delgado researching an article.' The boy frowned.

'An article on what, Señora?'

'Oh you know, just a travel piece. The Azores today – local

130

issues, the people who live here. That sort of thing.'

'Azores is very boring.' The words were heartfelt.

'Come on, nowhere's that boring. Are there many rich people on São Miguel?' She dipped a finger into her drink and sucked it dry.

'Some. Not many.'

'I saw a very fine house as I came here in the taxi. A few miles to the east. The owner of that must be very rich.'

The boy frowned then smiled, pleased to find himself able to assist.

'It belongs to a Chinaman. He never use it. Maybe once, twice a year he come here. Mainly it empty.'

'Mr Chang?'

The dark-brown eyes narrowed and she wondered if she was perhaps pushing just a bit too hard.

'You know Mr Chang?' There was suspicion in his voice, and fear too. She decided it was time to back-pedal.

'Hell, no. The taxi driver mentioned him on the way here, that's all. I'd sure like to meet him though – living in a big house like that.'

'He not there. Not for long time now.'

Throwing back the best part of her drink and setting it down, she looked at her watch pointedly. At least she had made a start and there was no point in being too obvious. It was time to get rid of the boy. The show was over.

'If you've finished your drink, Manolito, I'd like to take that shower now.'

He was on his feet in a trice, at once disappointed yet relieved to have the responsibility of the encounter taken out of his hands. In the doorway he lingered, sufficiently composed now to risk a slight flirtation. His eyes flashed.

'Welcome to Ponta Delgado, Señora. I hope we shall speak again – it is good I practise my English.'

When he had gone Chantelle relocked the door and set about adjusting the shower once more. She hadn't expected to glean anything of value from the boy but, if Azorean youths were anything like their American counterparts, the story of his visit to her room, inevitably exaggerated, would ensure that within the week her presence would be common knowledge in every corner of the island.

Allowing the robe to slip from her shoulders she stepped out of her flimsy briefs and, unhooking her brassiere, sighed at the sense of freedom her nakedness brought. Running a testing hand under the shower, she smiled. The boy had been quite sweet really. Going to the door she slid the key out of the lock and tossed it onto the bed.

Outside, his eye clamped to the keyhole, Manolito stifled a groan as she vanished into the shower.

That evening, having eaten dinner in her room, Chantelle wandered listlessly about. She was edgy tonight. It was nearly a fortnight since she had waved farewell to Collins and Latimer, and *Revenge* had ghosted from sight down the wind-troubled waters of the Hamble. On the pontoon she had kissed both men. Collins had responded with his usual perfunctory, stiff-upper-lip hug but Latimer had been strangely tense. His lips had lingered, almost imperceptibly, on hers, his eyes troubled, and she could remember exactly the way his hand had caressed her shoulder. She shook her head. God, she was like a bitch on heat. First that pathetic performance for the benefit of the boy and now fantasising like this. What she needed was a drink. Pulling on a pair of jeans and a faded denim jacket she went down to the bar.

It was cramped and crowded, cigarette smoke hanging like a layer of cloud under the low ceiling. On the nicotine-stained walls 1950's style pin-ups, probably regarded as rather risqué in that provincial watering-hole, curled dryly at the edges. Heavens, she thought, one of them's showing a lot of tit.

She was the only woman in the place and, from the way every head turned at her appearance, a lot of those present had come in just for the pleasure of seeing her. 'That Manolito must have a real vivid imagination,' she thought. The few tables all being occupied, she took a tall stool at the bar. The barman, Manolito senior she guessed, smiled welcomingly. His English was good and he beamed with pleasure when she told him as much.

'My name is Pedro, I am for three years chief engineer on a British tramp steamer – the *Cardiff Town*. We go everywhere – America, Australia, South Africa.' He was tall, like his son, with strong leathery features, and could have been any age between forty and sixty. When he spoke next there was a twinkle in his eye that suggested father and son shared everything. 'Gin, Mrs Kolowitz?' She matched his smile.

'Please. With tonic if you have it.'

Since it seemed Azoreans drank neither heavily nor quickly, the job of bartender at the Miramar was not an arduous one, and Pedro spent the next hour giving her leads and ideas for the article she was supposedly researching. With a third of a bottle of gin gone, she came to the crunch.

'I was interested in the big house. Manolito said it was empty.'

His eyes, troubled, flicked round the bar.

'Usually it is, but my wife's sister, she is a maid there, tells me an Englishman arrived two days ago. Flew in from Funchal. Must be a real bigshot – got bodyguards, everything. A real bigshot.'

'Sounds fascinating. Perhaps I'll pay him a visit.'

He lay a cautioning hand on her arm.

'Best not, Mrs Kolowitz. It is a bad place. Dogs, guards. Understand, Ponta Delgado is a very small place, we do not have much crime here. Last year, however, a couple of youngsters, kids not much older than my Manolito, broke into the place. Their bodies were found a week later in Horita Bay. They had both been garroted.'

Chantelle nodded sagely, conveying that his revelations

were more than enough to remove all thoughts of a visit to the house from her schedule.

'Thanks for the tip, Pedro. Perhaps I'll give it a miss after all.' She refilled his glass and slopped another inch into her own. 'It's interesting though, I'd sure like to know who the mysterious Englishman is.' She glanced at her watch. 'Well, I guess it's time to hit the sack.'

'Pleasant dreams, Mrs Kolowitz.'

Leaving the bar, she mounted the darkened stairway, halting in the shadows at the top. A minute later she heard the rattle of the telephone on the reception desk and Pedro's thick tones drifted up to her.

'Si Señor, she has just gone to her room. Yes, twice she has asked about the house. Yes, like you tell me, I say there is an Englishman staying there now. Yes, I will keep an eye on her – it is not an unpleasant task.' In the shadows Chantelle smiled grimly; now everyone was in on the act.

At two in the morning, unable to sleep for the oppressive and unseasonal heat, she kicked the sheets from her bed. Above her, the broad circling paddles of the fan beat listlessly at the heavy air. Swinging her feet to the threadbare carpet she walked naked to the window, drawing back when, lurking like a spider within the black web of the courtyard, she glimpsed the slim figure of Manolito. His eyes were fixed on her window. She smiled to herself. Had the kid really got the hots for her, or was he out there spying for Campbell-West? In the darkened room her hand found the neck of the gin bottle and, pouring half a tumblerful, she returned to the crumpled bed. Abandoning all thoughts of sleep she puffed up a pillow against the bedhead and, pressing her back to it, stretched out her legs.

She looked at the drink in her hand disapprovingly. She'd have to cut back on the booze. It was one thing to act the part of a gin-sodden journalist, but she didn't want to end up in the same state as Latimer when she had found him.

This rememberance of Latimer troubled her. Why was it she couldn't forget that farewell kiss? It had been chaste enough, yet with it she knew, she just knew, he had been trying to convey something deeper. It troubled her even more too to find that this vague contemplation of infidelity, the merest mental exercise perhaps, yet infidelity none the less, was indescribably delicious.

Her relationship with Collins, since her miscarriage and subsequent breakdown, had grown less and less physical. They seldom made love these days – her own indifference as much as his – and she knew for a fact that he was finding solace elsewhere. How long was it now? A month? Two? A bead of sweat ran down the curve of her breast to hang, like morning dew on a rose, from the nipple. She brushed it off, her fingers lingering on the moist pink blossom that hardened under her touch.

Would Latimer make his move when this operation was over, she wondered? Or would his friendship with David prove too big an obstacle? She imagined his hard lean body against hers and realised that, for the first time in more than three years, her thoughts were not of vengeance. She sipped at the perfumed spirit thoughtfully, her free hand straying lightly across her stomach to lay limply in the steamy dampness of her crotch. What would he be like in bed she wondered? Reserved and calculating, the way he was in the office, or an animal who would inflict every imaginable perversion on her willing, hungry body?

Setting her drink down, Chantelle closed her eyes, imagining the moment when, after hours of sybaritic foreplay, he would enter her. Her hand curled between the velvety softness of her thighs, probing fingers sliding up into the secret mollusc-like, hotness, searching for the blood-swollen trigger that would bring oblivion. Drawing up her knees, she gasped aloud as, within seconds, she climaxed. Once, twice, three times it hit her like an electrical charge. Her head went back, lips parted, her hips jerking uncontrollably as she rocked to and fro. With a low half-moan, half-sigh, her limbs loosened and she opened her eyes, staring up at the cracked plaster of the ceiling.

'Get a grip, Kolowitz,' she hissed through clenched teeth. 'Let's not forget what we're here for.' Slowly her breathing eased to a regular sigh, the tom-tom beat in her ears fading as Latimer's phantom presence receded and she drifted off into a dreamless sleep.

Half-an-hour later the telephone at her bedside jangled stridently, bringing her jarringly to startled consciousness.

'Hallo?'

'Mrs Kolowitz?'

'Yes.' She recognised the voice immediately: the carefully modulated tone, the precisely rounded vowels.

'Chantelle, my dear, how nice to talk to you after all this time. You must forgive me for calling at this time of night but, once I heard you were in Ponta Delgado, I just had to ring. You can imagine how news travels in a place like this. We must get together.

I've been considering your idea for the definitive book on the Algoan affair. The older I get the more I am inclined to try and put the picture straight. It isn't pleasant to spend one's declining years under a cloud like that. Anyway, with Brazilian citizenship on the horizon I have nothing to fear. What's more, I might be useful in finding a publisher. Can we get together for lunch later this week?'

Chantelle did not hesitate. 'That's what I'm here for.'

'Splendid. I'll send a car to collect you.'

She put the phone down slowly and thoughtfully. Then she got up, pulling on a robe against a night grown cold. The courtyard was deserted now, white moonlight fretting down through the black filigree of the trees.

She wished John and David were there. Suddenly she was afraid.

Fourteen

'Exactly what,' asked Collins, as he sat cross-legged in the sun among the spread out components of the rifle he was meticulously cleaning, 'do you know about the Azores?'

Latimer looked skyward with an air of mock concentration.

'Since you mention it, apart from the fact that the big chunk of rock over there is one of them – São Miguel, if my navigation isn't totally up the spout – my knowledge of the Azores amounts to little more than the square root of bugger all.'

In fact this was not totally true, but he preferred to see what the other man knew first before making his own contribution.

With deft, economical movements Collins reassembled the rifle in a matter of seconds and brought it to his shoulder, the muzzle following the low effortless flight of a passing shearwater. Squeezing the trigger he brought the firing pin down on an empty magazine with a dry metallic click. He could, as he had demonstrated more than once in the ten days they had been at sea, carry out this task with his eyes closed just as swiftly. Smiling as the dark bird went skimming fast and low on its way, hugging the contours of the long restless swell, oblivious to the threat to its existence, he lay the weapon aside and proceeded to deliver his lecture.

'The Açores, as the Portuguese call them, is an archipelago of nine major islands dispersed in three widely scattered groups and lying approximately 1,000 miles west of Lisbon. Colonisation began in about 1450, initially by the Portuguese but later augmented by large numbers of Flemings, mainly political malcontents, sent here to keep them gainfully occupied and out of the way. The ethnic mixture, and the natural environment, produced a race of superb seamen – they still hunt whales from open boats in some of the islands, you know. Columbus came here in 1493 on his way back to announce that he'd found America, and Vasco da Gama looked in some six years later. The islands are part of a volcanic chain, mildly active in some parts, rising almost sheer out of the sea which is about two and half miles deep all around ...'

'Although the earliest map to show them is a Genoese chart dated 1351,' interrupted Latimer with some satisfaction, 'it is thought that Arab travellers knew of their existence and the discovery of Carthaginian coins on Corvo, the most westerly of the group, suggests they visited that island at least, sometime during the fourth century BC. There is a legend that the islands are all that is left of the lost continent of Atlantis.' He examined his fingernails modestly. The hour spent reading up in Southampton public library, a couple of days prior to their departure, had been repaid a thousand times over by Collins' expression. Latimer continued.

'The major exports of the islands are pineapples, mainly grown under glass, dairy products, hides and fish. The name Açores means the islands of hawks and was a reference to the buzzards that used to abound here. There is a NATO airbase on Terceira and the main centre of population is Ponta Delgado with approximately 23,000 inhabitants. Ponta Delgado is on the far side of São Miguel, the aforementioned chunk of rock now lying on our port bow and largest island in the group. More significantly from our point of view, because of the geological formation of the islands the only natural harbour worthy of the name in the whole group is on Faial, some 150 miles west of here. The others are – and here I'm quoting no less an authority than a prep-school geography book abandoned by my eldest son – little more than open roadsteads, unsafe for vessels to anchor in at all times of the year. Southwesterly winds especially, make navigation around the islands extremely dangerous.'

'I was coming to that.' Collins smiled ruefully. 'I was aware of this lack of decent anchorages. There have been a few yacht marinas built in recent years but we can't use any of them without risk of losing the element of surprise. Especially we can't go into Ponta Delgado which is the only decent harbour on São Miguel. We'd be too obvious and that's where the meeting between Campbell-West and Chang, according to the last information I had, is scheduled to be held. However, on the chart I noticed there are a couple of fishing villages marked on the north side of the island where we might be able to anchor.'

Latimer brought over the large-scale chart of São Miguel, running a finger along the northern coastline of the island. There were indeed several small villages marked, but offshore the fathom lines depicting the topography of the sea bed were tightly packed showing that the bottom dropped away sharply, and that to anchor there was clearly not going to be feasible. It would be especially dangerous in the northwesterlies that had prevailed for the past week or so and which had carried them so speedily to their destination. Presumably the fishermen of these places beached their boats, not a practical proposition for *Revenge* with her deep keel. To the western end, however, there was a small inlet with about three fathoms of water shown, which Latimer felt might just be possible.

'We'll try there,' he said, folding up the chart. 'It should

139

be OK, otherwise we might just have to stay at sea and operate from the boat. We should be there in an hour or so. Who knows, we might even get a run ashore today, there's a village a mile or so away. Think of it, Dave, a bottle of wine and, if we strike lucky, a quick leg over with one of the local beauties. What a lovely prospect.'

Collins smiled, clearly finding the prospect attractive, but shook his head firmly.

'No. Not tonight. I want to make contact with Chantelle first. She's been in Ponta Delgado for a while now, I must let her know that we've arrived and where we'll be anchored. Because of the height of the mountains inland, I doubt if the boat's VHF will be any good from this side so we'll need to go right round the island, making sure we are off Ponta Delgado after dark. She's got a pretty powerful CB with her and she'll have been keeping a listening watch for the last few days. We'll just give her the details and arrange a rendezvous for tomorrow, then we'll have a look at the anchorage at first light.'

Latimer put the helm over, gybing *Revenge* smoothly round onto a southeasterly course that would take her well clear of the sharply rising cliffs marking the eastern end of São Miguel. Clearly Collins had thought very carefully about this coming phase of the operation and he saw that, now the crunch point was approaching, it was apparently considered an accepted fact that it would be he who would be calling the shots. Latimer didn't mind. What he had seen of this square set ex-marine suggested that, despite the odds against them and the enormity of what they were about to do, nothing would be left to chance and no unnecessary risks would be countenanced.

At about eight that night, the Milky Way brilliant above them in a cloudless sky and a thankfully gentle, almost balmy breeze carrying them smoothly on, the lights of Ponta Delgado were clearly visible on the starboard bow. To Latimer, at the helm and keeping a wary eye on the bobbing lights of the flotilla of small fishing boats scattered on the velvety darkness around them, came the even, practised voice of Collins from the cabin below as he began transmitting.

'Eagle, Eagle, this is Lion One, Lion One,' he repeated every five minutes. 'Eagle, Eagle, this is Lion One, Lion One.' It was a code they had agreed in England. Chantelle was Eagle, Collins was Lion One, and Latimer Lion Two.

For twenty minutes he went through this prearranged routine until, just as Latimer began to fear that all was not well ashore, came the awaited response, half lost in the hiss of static at first but then becoming clearer as Collins adjusted the set. 'Lion One, Lion One, this is Eagle, Eagle. Switch to channel 72.' Latimer relaxed. Somewhere, over there among the twinkling lights of the little town, Chantelle was very much in business. He listened as Collins briefly exchanged greetings and then, in what he assumed to be a prearranged code, jotted down her instructions for the rendezvous on the following day. The whole transmission took less than a minute. 'Lion One, Lion One,' she drawled, 'this is Eagle, Eagle. Out.'

Collins was silent when he came into the cockpit, staring thoughtfully at the fast receding town for several minutes until, sensing things were not quite what they seemed, Latimer felt obliged to ask if all was well. The other man shook his head.

'No, something's not right, though exactly what I'm not quite sure, at the moment,' he said, stroking his chin. 'I can't think they're on to us, but they're certainly paying enough attention to Chantelle to make her careful. They may just have bugged her room – she'll be able to deal with that alright – but for safety's sake we must act on the worst possible assumption which is that they are actually holding her and that her message was transmitted under their control.'

'How can you be sure?' Latimer stared, appalled that they

should find themselves considering a setback of this magnitude so early on.

'We had a prearranged agreement that, if everything was OK on the island, we would communicate on channel 67. If not, she would instruct me to switch to channel 72.'

'Which she did?'

'Yes. It may just be a minor hiccup, perhaps to warn us they were also listening out. That wouldn't be too big a problem since her message was coded, but we had better draw up our plans for tomorrow on the basis of their being ready for us. She wants us to meet tomorrow, at a disused quarry up in the north of the island. We're to be there at eleven. She's given me the coordinates so it shouldn't be too difficult to find. Since we do now have this question mark hanging over us, I want to be at the meeting point at least two hours beforehand so that we can pre-empt whatever, if any, reception they are planning. How soon will we be at the anchorage?'

'Three or four in the morning I guess, but I'd really prefer to take her in in daylight. I've never sailed in these waters before and the chart may well be inaccurate. There's not going to be a lot of room in there you know,' he added defensively.

'We haven't got that sort of time to waste I'm afraid,' said Collins flatly, 'I've had a look at the maps and we've a two or three-hour march over rough country to the rendezvous so you'll have to take her straight in. You take the boat for the next couple of hours and give me a shake around midnight. We'd better get as much sleep as possible while we can, I've a feeling we're going to be busy over the next couple of days.'

With that he was gone, leaving an uneasy Latimer contemplating the somewhat disconcerting prospect of a night entry into an unlit and restricted anchorage in pursuit of a quest that might already have been compromised beyond recall.

As he sat at the helm, ruminating on these latest disturbing developments, one of the fleet of little fishing boats came chugging out of the night ahead sliding, less than twenty yards away, down *Revenge's* starboard side. In the stern stood three men, all dressed in rough sea jerseys, staring unsmilingly across the intervening water, the dancing yellow flare of the kerosene lamp that burned above the wheelhouse playing eerily upon their thin, weatherbeaten faces. He waved, aware that, deliberately so, *Revenge* was showing no lights, his gesture drawing no response from the other vessel. He guessed it was the lack of lights that had brought them to investigate, her Azorean crew clearly disapproving of such unprofessional behaviour.

The boat melted into the darkness astern until only the feeble flickering of her lights was visible and Latimer knew ruefully that by tomorrow morning the whole of Ponta Delgado would probably be aware that a strange yacht, showing no lights, had passed south of the island that night. His only comfort was that they had, day and night for the past week, been flying the French tricolour. At least the Frogs would get the blame for this appalling display of poor seamanship. Returning his attention to the chart spread out on his knees, he turned to the more pressing matter of locating the anchorage.

In fact, it was nearly five in the morning before they had rounded the western headland and the entrance to the anchorage was definitely identified. It was little more than a semicircle of low lying, weed-covered rocks, set beneath beetling cliffs that rose vertically to a height of some eighty feet. By this time there was just enough light for Latimer to make the approach with reasonable confidence. At dead slow, with Collins standing in the bow prepared to let go the anchor, and alert for any uncharted rocks that might appear in their path, *Revenge* edged her way into the tiny bay, her anchor rattling out as she finally came to rest in a comfortable two fathoms of water. With a brief burst of engine astern to help the anchor bite into the pumice and weed-strewn sea bed, he put the engine to neutral and she swung elegantly round, coming head to wind.

Even as Latimer lingered at the helm, keeping the engine ticking over until he felt confident that the anchor had dug well in and was not likely to drag, Collins was manhandling the crates of ammunition up from below. By the time the engine was finally cut he had inflated the Gemini and was loading it up with a minor arsenal of offensive materials. As, with a single effortless pull, Collins brought the outboard growling to life, he indicated to Latimer that he was to bring the remainder of the weapons up on deck while he ferried this first load ashore.

Within half-an-hour they had transferred most of the weapons from the boat, burying the majority well above the the high-water mark in the dark volcanic sand that fringed the cliffs. For the coming link-up with Chantelle, entailing as it would a march across rough country, they retained two of the machine-pistols and as much ammunition as they could conveniently distribute in the voluminous pockets of the camouflaged combat jackets they now wore. Collins had also stored a couple of grenades about his person.

'We'll take the Gemini down the coast and see if we can find a break in the cliffs. Failing that I'm afraid we'll have to climb,' he said, slinging his weapon on his shoulder and clearly eager to be moving off, while Latimer made a final check that everything was properly snugged down on the boat. They climbed into the inflatable, Collins half-lying in the bow, scanning the seemingly impregnable wall of cliffs that stretched away to the east, while Latimer at the helm cast off. The Gemini cut a wide arc of expanding wave across the still waters of the anchorage as, with a buzz like an angry bee, they made for the gap in the circling rocks and the open sea beyond.

Fifteen

It took half an hour of spine jarring pounding through the long Atlantic swell before they eventually found a suitable landing point, a short stretch of steep pebble beach that led up to a narrow cleft in the otherwise near vertical cliffs. There ensued several anxious moments as the sea surged powerfully beneath the inflatable, lifting it like a leaf and carrying it headlong towards the shore, Latimer fighting with the outboard's throttle as he repeatedly burst the engine astern. Time after time only his skilful boat-handling averted disaster, sometimes by inches, hauling them away from the jagged rocks that rose and disappeared like malevolent sea monsters in the growling surf all around.

The moment was critical, one error of judgement and the buoyancy chambers of the flimsy craft would be ripped wide open, taking its heavy load to the bottom. Latimer glanced anxiously over his shoulder as the next roller came roaring in from astern, hoisting them like a toy up towards its overhanging crest before breaking with a thunderous bellow upon them, swamping the inflatable. Slitting his eyes against the stinging salt water and deafened by the crashing surf, he killed the engine and swung the propellor of the outboard clear of the water. Both men clung on for grim death as with one final, irresistible thrust, the Gemini was hurled up onto the hissing, tumbling shingle. Soaked to the skin they leapt out, up to their knees in the water, desperately struggling to keep their footing in the savage undertow as they dragged the dead weight of the Gemini up the beach before the fickle sea might change its mind and the next wave pluck them out again.

Hammering a metal spike deep into the shingle to ensure a secure mooring, Collins quickly set about camouflaging the inflatable with rocks and seaweed. In minutes it was invisible, even from a few yards away and, confident that their presence was unlikely to be detected, he took up his bulky backpack and slung the machine-pistol on his shoulder, setting off up the ravine with Latimer bringing up the rear as they moved swiftly upwards.

It was a steep climb, not dangerous but physically demanding, over crags of crumbling volcanic rock. By the time they stood on the rim of the cliff Latimer's thigh muscles were burning. Breathing hard, he turned away with studied unconcern to take in the view behind him, glad of the rest but not prepared to reveal his physical distress to the other man who seemed impervious to any discomfort. A miasma of steam rose gracefully skyward from his drenched clothes as his heart beat began to slacken and his breathing became less laboured. The respite was to be brief, however, for after making a summary examination of the map and carefully refolding it into its original creases, Collins glanced at the marching compass slung round his neck and set off at a steady jog trot. Southwards they went into the harsh, rugged landscape, under a sun that was gaining strength by the second.

The rendezvous was, as Chantelle's message had indicated, a disused quarry, a natural amphitheatre cut into a barren hillside and open to the south from whence a dusty, unmade road led to Ponta Delgado. A long-abandoned corrugated iron shack, its fabric rusted to a dry russet wafer in places, the sun-bleached door hanging open, stood at the entrance.

146

On the slope away to their left a couple of emaciated goats grazed on what sparse foliage could find sustenance in that arid bowl, their bleating small and hollow, the occasional clatter of their hooves as they moved among the loose rocks breaking clear and sharp in the oppressive silence.

For fifteen minutes they lay motionless in the dust, the sweat trickling down their necks and faces, staring down into the quarry, until Collins was satisfied that no one was there lying in ambush for them. He handed the binoculars to Latimer, rolling onto his back as he spoke, careful not to let his form break the natural skyline.

'Right. I'm going down there. You stay here, John, and watch the road. If you see anyone coming before I'm ready give me a shout. I'm going to lay low. At the first sight of anyone who looks as though they've come from Ponta Delgado, go down and meet them, try to get them right in the centre of the quarry where I can get a good look at them. Even if it's Chantelle, and even if she appears to be alone, you must act as though you're on your own – they mustn't know I'm here. Keep as clear of her as you can. She may well be being followed so tell her that I'm waiting on the boat and then head off eastward.' He pointed. 'That way, away from the Gemini. I'll follow up and pick off anybody trying to tail you. Whatever happens, they mustn't locate the boat.'

Before he went, Collins paused and they shook hands. He nodded at the machine-pistol that Latimer held. 'I should load up now, John, and remember, if things start getting lively don't hesitate to use it – they won't.'

As Collins picked his way down the steep incline below him, Latimer scanned the distant road through the binoculars, a dusty thread that broke up in the marbling heat haze. Then he turned the binoculars onto the figure below and frowned. Collins had stripped to the waist and was now digging into the quarry floor with a trenching tool, a small low cloud of yellow dust floating about him. He worked steadily and methodically and within twenty minutes or so had scooped out a hollow, perhaps a little over three feet deep and twice that in length. He then stretched a sheet of heavy gauge polythene across the hole, pulling it taut and pinioning it down with rocks. Next he began shovelling the yellowish dust evenly over his hide until it merged imperceptibly into the landscape. This done he spent a good ten minutes examining his work in great detail from every angle. He moved thoughtfully around, rearranging rocks and casting random handfuls of dust about to erase all sign of his footprints until, apparently satisfied with his hide's invisibility, he gave a quick thumbs-up to Latimer and slid under the sheet.

Once the dust had settled Latimer turned his attention to the road down which Chantelle must come. It was nearly ten; an hour to go. As the sun gained strength, he discarded his combat jacket and, recalling Collins' words, slipped a clip of ammunition into the magazine of his machine-pistol. He was sweating profusely and wondered how the other man was coping in the claustrophobic confines of his hide. At five to eleven, far down the road, a small white speck danced and jinked in the distant, heat-crazed air, its image solidifying and sharpening as it drew closer.

Latimer cursed as the car, a big Peugeot estate, its driver clearly intent on making life difficult from the outset, drew to a halt about 100 yards short of the quarry entrance. It was dispiritingly clear that already things were not going according to plan for he could see that it was not Chantelle at the wheel but a square face behind small wire-rimmed glasses – Groose. In the shadowy rear seat he fancied he could see a pale face and blonde hair. Shit. They had been blown. Worse, Collins could have no idea what was going on from his hide unless they actually came into the quarry. It would be up to him to tempt Groose in closer. Pushing the machine-pistol away from him and hurriedly emptying the spare ammunition from his pockets he stood up slowly and then, so that there could be no doubt as to the peaceful nature of his intentions, carefully and deliberately picked his way down towards the quarry floor, praying as he went that his movement into the open would indicate to Collins that all was not well. Loose rocks rolled from under his feet as he descended unsteadily, racking his ankles, and black pumice dust floated about his knees.

When he reached the centre of the quarry he stopped, arms hanging loosely at his sides, waiting for some response from the car. Clearly the man was in no great rush for it was perhaps three or four minutes before the driver's door opened and the squat, almost dwarflike figure of Groose eased itself out into the sunlight, standing, legs straddled, staring directly at him. He appeared to be unarmed yet there was something about his lack of wariness, the confident slant of the chin, that instinctively told Latimer that here was a man who considered he held all the aces. He was quickly to find out why. Turning, Groose curled a forefinger, beckoning to the woman in the back to get out.

Chantelle looked pale and he was aware of a growing anger as he wondered what sort of treatment she had received at the hands of Campbell-West's nightmare crew. She wore a short, rough-weave poncho draped loosely about her shoulders which, at a grunt from Groose, she let fall to the ground. The Dutchman returned his gaze to Latimer with a smile. Beneath the poncho she was naked save for a pair of the briefest blue cotton shorts and, around her neck, what at first glance Latimer thought, unlikely enough, was a string of fruit.

At a jerk of the head from her captor she moved, barefooted, slowly forward, coming to within ten yards and thankfully into Collins' field of vision, before at another grunt she halted. He saw now that what she wore around her neck was in fact a necklace of five phosphorous grenades. To the pin of the centre grenade was attached a length of fine steel wire that glinted like gossamer in the sunlight. Groose, following cautiously another thirty yards in her wake and to one side, held the other end taut across her shoulder. The first solid tug on the wire would detonate the grenade which, in turn, would detonate the others. Not that the others would have anything to do, since the first would reduce the lovely body to a burning mass of liquefied flesh in an instant.

The situation was clear: one false move on his part and Chantelle paid the ultimate penalty. Latimer became aware that his right leg was shaking uncontrollably and cursed his own weakness as he made a conscious effort to still its treacherous rebellion. At the same time he struggled to find some words that would get the dialogue going. In the event it was Groose who spoke first, the smile never fading although his eyes flitted about him and up the sides of the quarry, fearing deception.

'Where's Latimer?' he demanded thickly, clearly assuming that Collins would be dealing with the negotiations and that it was he who now stood before him. How this mistake might be turned to their advantage Latimer couldn't really say, although if the Dutchman felt that he had the more dangerous of the two of them hors de combat it might lull him into a false sense of security.

'Back at the boat.'

Groose stared closely at him, suspicion plainly written on the flat, almost oriental features. 'Kneel,' he barked, and Chantelle dropped to her knees in the dust while he strutted in a wide arc round the woman who knelt in silence between them, her eyes cast down. Keeping the long tripwire taut, and intent on demonstrating just how strong a hand he held, he executed a casual backhand flick of his wrist, sending a visible tremor running down the wire. Its strength was spent by the time it had snaked along to the deadly necklace but it was still strong enough to make the woman gasp in fear. The smile broadened a fraction.

'Where is the boat?' His English was good, with only the

slightest accent apparent.

'A couple of miles northeast of here.' Latimer lied, his eyes fixed on Chantelle's who returned his gaze without emotion.

Again the Dutchman's eyes narrowed as this lie was assessed. Latimer prayed the real position of the anchorage hadn't already been detected, but then the monstrous shoulders shrugged indifferently; apparently, the whereabouts of the boat was not something that Groose considered of great moment.

'You go to the car.' The head went to one side enquiringly, as though inviting Latimer to make some foolish move that would justify his pulling the tripwire. 'You go now – we follow. You go or else ...' Again the wrist snapped and Chantelle closed her eyes tightly as again a tremor whipped along the line between them.

'OK, OK, I'm going.' Latimer raised his hands in a token of submission as he started towards the car. 'Just take those things off her. I'm not going to make any trouble.' He thought quickly, trying anything to allay the man's doubts: 'For Christ's sake, it's only a bloody book we're talking about.'

Groose, nodded approvingly, winding in the slack on the wire around his hand as he came closer to the woman.

There was, Latimer realised, going to be no opportunity for Collins to intervene so long as the Dutchman retained his hold on the wire. One startled reflex action on his part and Chantelle would die. Their best hope was now for he, himself, to go along with things, until Collins could somehow regain the initiative. At the car he was ordered to stop. Here the Dutchman produced a pistol from the glove compartment and, with this at her head, a pair of handcuffs were handed to Chantelle which, at Groose's command, she snapped over Latimer's wrists. Groose then placed a pair of similar cuffs on her before removing the tripwire and unbuckling the grenades from about her neck. He tossed the deadly collar

151

onto the front seat before indicating they were to get in the back of the car. There was a strong steel grill between the front and rear seats as though the car might have been used to transport dogs at some time or another.

With studied disinterest Groose pulled the poncho over Chantelle's nakedness, presumably to avoid attracting the attention of any locals they might encounter on the road, before slamming the doors on the pair of them. As, in a cloud of ochre dust, the Peugeot swung round and headed south Groose regarded them contemptuously in the driving mirror.

'They said you were tough, Mr Collins. A real hard case. You know what? I gotta sister back in Vlissingen is tougher.' He laughed hugely at his joke. So far as he was concerned, it was over. Mission accomplished.

Sixteen

Not a word had passed between Latimer and Chantelle since they left the quarry. Both were afraid of betraying the fact that Collins was still at large and, in so doing, compromising their only remaining hope of rescue. Whenever their eyes met, however, her features seemed so completely devoid of life that he began to fear he was not completely au fait with the whole situation and that things were even worse, if that were possible, than they appeared. Occasionally he would smile encouragingly, but her response was so half-hearted that he eventually turned his attention to the topography outside, memorising landmarks that might be useful in the event of their having to find their way back to the boat.

This, the southern side of the island, was more fertile than the region where they had made their landfall, with coppices of lush green vegetation nestling between the black volcanic mountains. As they sped onwards they passed through small villages and low whitewashed farm buildings.

One thing that did cheer him was to see that, in the dust of the unmade roads they followed, the treadmarks left by the car's tyres were clearly visible. Providing it did not rain or the wind get up, Collins should have no trouble in following them. Obscured by the Dutchman's massive shoulder, he could not see the mileometer on the car's dashboard but estimated they had travelled no more than fifteen miles from the quarry. Even on foot Collins would cover that in a couple of hours although, knowing the man, he would most probably wait for dark before making any move. Until then there was little that could be achieved by fretting. They would have to convince their captors of their lack of malicious intent and develop the story of carrying out research for a book that would clear their names. Whether Campbell-West would be taken in by such a story he couldn't be sure, but it represented their only chance of getting out of this situation and into one where they could effect their true purpose – the abduction of the man.

Despite the unforeseen reversal in their fortunes Latimer realised with a certain satisfaction that, mentally he still felt as though they were on the offensive; he was still thinking aggressively. Collins would have approved. Soon they would be face to face with their quarry; while they might be his prisoners he would be within their reach.

The house was set into the hillside, a two-storey building overlooking a wide bay and lying a couple of miles to the east of Ponta Delgado. A high wall marked the perimeter of the surrounding grounds, its newly painted whiteness almost hurting the eyes as they approached. At each corner stood crenellated towers with arrow slit windows that gave the appearance of a Moorish fortress.

At the entrance two surly, moustachioed thugs, shotguns under their arms, peered into the car, dark eyes lingering on the woman before, without a word, opening the wrought-iron gates to let them pass. Inside was another world, a world of green gardens where sprinklers played on perfect lawns and peacocks strutted beneath orange trees that were just beginning to blossom.

As the Peugeot crunched easily up the long gravel drive that led from the gateway to the elegantly colonnaded facade of the house Latimer made a note of the tripwire alarms, discreetly sited among the rose beds and security cameras that followed their passing like cybernetic birds perched in the trees. Away to his left another guard patrolled the outer wall, a slavering Doberman tugging the man forward as it strained at its leash. The place didn't just look like a fortress. It was one.

As the Peugeot drew to a halt in front of the house a huge figure, wearing only a pair of faded jeans and ornately tooled cowboy boots, came out of the shadowy entrance, waiting watchfully in the shade of the colonnaded entrance. Groose unlocked the car and, with an eloquent flourish of his revolver, indicated they were to get out. There could be no doubt as to the newcomer's identity – Luis Behan in the flesh was infinitely more menacing than even his pictures had suggested.

'You go up there,' Groose said, waving his pistol towards the giant in the doorway. As they mounted the steps Latimer was aware of the car being driven off behind them.

Behan smiled at their approach, twirling the solid-looking Colt .44 on his index finger, cowboy fashion, as though it were no more than a toy. He was huge, his muscular torso and arms covered with tattoos: one said 'Malvinas Argentinos'. Latimer was a fraction over six feet yet against this man he felt dwarfed.

Slipping an arm around Chantelle's shoulders, the giant pulled her diminutive, unresisting form against his as, with a sharp jab of his pistol to the kidneys, he indicated that Latimer should lead on. Whatever had or had not occurred between them previously, he was clearly pleased to have her back.

'You miss me, honey?' His English was of the American TV tough guy variety. 'I bet you don't get no fun with that fruit Groose eh? You wait till Mistuh Campbell-West come back and we have time to get better acquainted. I show you some real smart tricks.' Chantelle made no reply and Latimer, if unenthusiastic about tangling with the man, felt honour bound to attempt to take some of the pressure off her.

'And just when will Campbell-West be back?' he enquired briskly over his shoulder. 'I want to get this thing cleared up. I know he may not like us following him around, but there's no need for this sort of behaviour. I intend to report the whole matter to the British Consul at the first opportunity.' Behan, clearly, was not greatly impressed with his modest display of self-righteous outrage.

'Shut your trap and keep walking, limey. I do the talking here, ain't that right, honey?' Again his banter drew no response from Chantelle but a low chuckle and rustling suggested that the Argentinian's hands were busy under her poncho. 'Sorry, honey, but I gotta search you – can't trust that fruit Groose to do anything right.'

At the head of a curving flight of wide, much waxed stairs they came to a halt before a solid looking door, its dark oak decorated with iron studding. With a casual kick Behan pushed it inwards, removing their handcuffs while still carefully covering them with his automatic. He leered down at Chantelle, caressing her hair with the back of his huge hand: 'I'm afraid I gotta leave you now, honey, but I'll be back just as soon as I can – we'll have a ball then.' He turned to Latimer. 'Oh yeah, Mistuh Campbell-West has left you a message on the TV.'

The door slammed shut on them and Chantelle, slumping down into a wicker chair, forcibly expelled a long hissing breath.

'Jesus Christ, what have we let ourselves in for?'

He put a finger to his lips, pointing to the door. Then he indicated himself, mouthing 'David'. Her quickness of mind had not deserted her. 'And where's John anyway?' she continued without a moment's hesitation. 'I thought he was supposed to be providing back up on this. How can you produce a properly researched book if one of the authors is permanently pissed?'

He smiled at her warmly, for she clearly understood precisely where their best chance of survival now lay and had, assuming the room was bugged, added significantly to their credibility in a single sentence.

'He didn't like the way we were going about this operation and chickened out. He's talking about producing his own book. We're better off without him. But I'm absolutely serious about going to the British Consul once we get away from here. Campbell-West really has gone too far this time.' For the first time that day she grinned as though she meant it, and he felt they were still in the game with a chance.

Their prison was at least comfortable. A large double bedroom with a stylishly furbished en suite bathroom. There was one large window, across which ornate wrought-iron leafwork provided total security with some suggestion of style, and which afforded a view of a large cerulean marble pool fringed by palms and umbrellas.

All their immediate needs had been provided for. There was a wide range of expensive toiletries in the bathroom cabinet and a selection of stylish clothes, both male and female, hanging in the fitted wardrobes. A bowl of fruit stood on the bedside table along with a carafe of red wine and another of orange juice. Pouring himself a glass of wine, Latimer moved casually about the room, carrying out a quick survey of this very comfortable prison. He found the inevitable bug behind a bad copy of Monet's *Water Lilies*, plus a sneaky back-up lurking among the spray of dried grasses on the windowsill. Leaving both intact he sat down and stared out of the window considering what, if anything, their next move should be. As Chantelle headed for the bathroom, intent on washing the grime of the day away, she hesitated, speaking distinctly and slowly for the benefit of their unseen listeners.

'Tell me, David, what do you think that cretin meant when he said CW had left us a message on the TV?'

Cursing himself for his slowness Latimer went to the television, pressing the 'on' button and waiting patiently while an electronic snowscreen blipped across the screen before settling down to an acceptable image of Sir Peter Campbell-West's sleek, smiling features. The sound quality was not perfect yet sufficiently true to the original to conjure echoes of board meetings of the past. Smooth, courteous and totally in command, it made Latimer's hackles rise. Chantelle, all thoughts of bathing deferred, sat down beside him on the bed, staring at the screen.

'My dear friends, I greet you well. Please accept my apologies for not being available to meet you on arrival, I hope to join you for dinner this evening until which time I beg you to make, within the necessary constraints of the situation, full use of the house and its facilities.

When I made this video I was not sure exactly how many of you I would be addressing. Certainly you will be watching, Chantelle. Groose's suggestion of using the phosphorous grenades to ensure your good behaviour and David's total compliance, seemed an inspired idea and one certain to guarantee that the pair of you at least will be present at our little get together. I do hope you are there too, John, although, if not, I am confident it can have little impact on matters. My informants tell me that you have taken to drink and, despite your colleagues' rash attempts to involve you in their mad schemes, remain something of a broken reed. Be that as it may, I look forward to seeing you all tonight. I do hope also that, when we finally meet, you will do me the courtesy of not pursuing the line about researching a book. I know exactly why you are here and intend to deal with you accordingly. In three days at the most I shall be safely back in Brazil. Where you are at that time depends entirely on how you behave in the intervening period. Please believe me, despite the circumstances that we meet in, I am delighted to be able to entertain you all and look forward to reminiscing about old times.'

With a faint hiss the screen reverted to its original blizzard image and Latimer switched it off, experiencing something outside the understood meaning of malevolence. Staring at the blank screen, the old hatred burned anew. 'Broken reed' Campbell-West had called him – a name that carried all the hateful connotations of 'nodding donkey', and he longed for the coming meeting. Whatever fate awaited him personally, he welcomed the coming opportunity to face his tormentor over dinner. He hoped there might be a sufficiently weighty blunt instrument to hand. Chantelle, sensing his anger, laid her hand, cool and calming, on his and he came out of his malignant reverie.

'Don't let the bastard get to you,' she whispered, aware they were being overheard, continuing in much louder tones. 'Come into the bathroom and help me with my clothes.' He raised his eyebrows questioningly, then smiled as he realised that, once the taps were running, it would effectively confuse any bugs that may have been planted. At the bathroom door, however, he placed a hand on her shoulder and, pulling her to him in a passionate embrace, he softly mouthed into her ear.

'Watch out for the mirror, it may be a two-way job.'

Initially taken aback at this display of passion, she smiled, nodding to indicate that she understood his warning and then returned his kiss with a warmth that made him stare wonderingly.

The problem of the mirror, a large, bevelled-edge square set into the mushroom tiles above the washbasin, was quickly dealt with as Chantelle, a towel wrapped about her, sprayed it liberally with deodorant and then proceded to stick strip after strip of toilet paper on it until it was totally obscured. Rapping sharply on the glass she screamed a shrill admonishment to whoever, if anyone, stood beyond.

'Fuck off, you pathetic perverts. Go and play with yourselves!' Latimer imagined he heard the muffled sound of discomfited movement from behind the mirror, as smiling, she ran both taps and then drew him into the inner sanctum of the glass shower cubicle. 'Where's David?' she asked. 'I thought he would be at the quarry with you.'

'He was, I thought Groose was going to step on him at one stage. He couldn't do anything with you strapped up with those grenades like that. I guess he'll follow us here. We'll just have to be ready to move when he makes his play, although he'll have the devil's own job getting through the security arrangements in this place. We'll have to see if there's any way we can set up a diversion of some sort. But what the hell went wrong? David suspected you'd been rumbled from our first contact on the VHF. But how did they get onto us?'

She shook her head, testing the steaming jet that ran into the bath with a tentative hand before selecting a bath oil from the well-stocked cabinet; she poured the thick yellow liquid on the swirling water.

'I don't really know, but I had no sooner checked into my hotel than there was a call from Campbell-West saying he had reconsidered my previous requests for an interview and felt that, since his application for Brazilian citizenship was going through smoothly, he would very soon have no reason to fear extradition; perhaps the time had come for him to tell his story to the world. What could I do? If I had refused his offer to see me after dragging my arse all the way to these godforsaken islands it would have looked distinctly odd. So, last night, shortly after speaking to you on the VHF, a car arrived to bring me here. It was lucky you made such good time getting here, one day is quite enough in the company of CW's pet gorillas.

Of course, when I arrived here Campbell-West was no-where to be seen and I ended up spending a very unpleasant evening with Groose and Behan. Luckily Groose, as we

160

know, isn't into women, so that keeps Behan on a short rein although I'd hate to be left alone with that one. CW obviously knows his men's personal traits very well since it had been clearly stipulated beforehand that Groose was to accompany me to the meeting. I expect CW will put his cards on the table at dinner this evening.' She kissed him lightly on the cheek. 'Now, be a darling and let me use what time we have to make myself as desirable as the circumstances will allow.' She winked cheekily. 'It's not vanity – that ape Behan has got the hots for me – or I'm no judge of men – and that may come in very useful if things turn nasty.'

Leaving her to complete her toilette, Latimer returned to the bedroom and re-ran the tape of CW, gaining nothing of further value in listening to the man's self-satisfied address other than an additional boost to his hatred. Switching off, he looked around him, surprised to see that while he had watched the video a card had been slipped under the door. It was a formal invitation to dinner. Sir Peter Campbell- West MC requested the pleasure of Mr David Collins and Mrs Chantelle Kolowitz for dinner at eight that evening. Dress was black tie.

Chantelle appeared, a towel tucked around her, looking pink and freshly scrubbed, and he showed her the gold trimmed card. She was not over-impressed.

'Pompous old shit. Doesn't he realise he's nothing more than a goddamn thief? You'd think he was still a City of London bigshot.' She explored the contents of the wardrobes, examining and rejecting a number of dresses before finally selecting a simple silk number in sapphire blue which she held up against her and then, approvingly, laid aside on the bed. 'I'll say one thing, apart from her choice of men, Miss Israel certainly has good taste.'

'Speaking of whom,' he took her arm and led her to the window, taking care to keep well back and out of the sunlight, 'look who else is here.'

At the poolside, on a yellow sun lounger, lay Sarah Mendelsohn. She wore 50 per cent of the briefest of bikinis, the upper half having been discarded and lying draped across the table. She was tanned to a deep bronze, oiled and gleaming in the afternoon sunlight. By her side stood a bottle of mineral water and a plastic sun oil dispenser. Latimer gripped Chantelle's arm softly.

'Doesn't look much like a mother-to-be, does she?'

Even as he spoke he regretted his unnecessary observation and she turned towards him frowning, as though she hadn't understood his words, her head to one side.

'What?'

Instantly he recalled Collins' words as to her mental state, and wondered whether it had been altogether wise to disclose Sarah's condition. It was too late now, however, and he continued, his tone casual.

'She's pregnant, only a couple of months as I understand it, but definitely pregnant. The old goat's trying to get a divorce from poor old Victoria Campbell-West so that he can bestow an element of respectability on the kid when it eventually arrives.'

Chantelle stared silently down at the figure below, as Sarah rolled languorously onto her back as if to flaunt the, as yet, undistorted lines of her stomach to their gaze.

'Well, what do you know? Miss Israel is in the club, is she? How nice for them both.' Her words were barely audible, as though they were for her ears only, but there was a malignant gleam in the narrowed eyes that made Latimer curse his thoughtless lack of discretion.

'Come on,' he said lightly, hoping to divert her thoughts, 'we've got to get ourselves looking spick-and-span for to-night.' He took a tuxedo that looked as though it might fit, from the wardrobe and held it up in front of him. 'What do you think, does it suit me?'

She appeared not to hear, still standing at the window,

162

looking down at the unsuspecting figure below. A maid appeared at the poolside pointing to her watch and Sarah, collecting up her towel, strode regally into the house. Chantelle continued to stare at the now empty lounger.

'Well,' she whispered, 'isn't that just dandy for everyone.'

Seventeen

The sun fell warm on Groose's cheek as he wound down the window of the car and looked up into the fresh features of the young beachbum. He smiled, almost pleasantly.

'Yes?'

'Nothing. Didn't mean to be rude, mister. Just admiring your car is all.' The boy was slim and Californian-tanned. He wore faded, cut-down jeans and flip-flops. 'You sure do keep it polished. Must be just about the best kept vehicle on the whole damn island. Is it yours?'

Groose considered the question.

'No, a friend's.'

The boy extended a bony hand.

'Wayne LeFarge from Santa Barbara. Dropped out of university last year – I'm working my way round the world.' The boy's eyes ran approvingly over the massive body behind the wheel, 'I guess you must be a bodyguard of some sort – uh? You sure look fit.'

'That's right.'

'I work out myself when I get the chance. But since I came to this fly-shit island – no offence, I hope you're not a local – I've done nothing but work my ass off.'

'No, I'm not a local, Wayne. What sort of work do you do?'

'Oh, just about anything, I guess. Once I've got the fare together I'm moving on to Europe.' His eyes lingered on the Dutchman's. 'I've got a room down by the harbour – it's not far.'

Groose looked at his watch. If past experience was anything to go by he would be kicking his heels here for another hour at least. His job was to wait until the doctor had examined his precious ward and then to return her to the safety of the house. If Campbell-West ever found out he was enjoying himself on company time he could end up in a lot of trouble. Still, this was a nice-looking youngster. The boy, sensing he was making progress, turned the pressure up a notch.

'I sure would like to ride in a car like this.'

Groose leant over and pushed the door open.

'I take you for a ride, then you show me your room maybe?'

The boy assessed the situation. The Englishman, whom he guessed would be watching the proceedings, had already given him $50 to pick up this fearsome-looking man but, what the hell, he might as well make a little extra if he could. He nodded.

'OK, it'll cost you fifty though. That understood?'

Groose smiled, at least they were speaking the same language.

'Sure, fifty's fine – but, believe me, you'll earn every fucking cent of it.'

The boy slipped into the seat beside him. He was nervous now, overawed by the sheer bulk of his client.

'You ain't a sado, are you?'

Groose smiled blandly as he pressed the central locking and brought the windows shut.

'That's for me to know and you to find out.'

Sarah was waiting at the kerbside when Groose returned, pacing impatiently up and down in the cooling evening. It would mean trouble when they got back to the house, he knew, but it had been worth it.

'Where the hell have you been?' Her eyes blazed. A fifteen-minute wait was an insufferable imposition.

'I had to get fuel.' He got out of the car and went round to open the door for her. She ignored the gesture, determined to make the most of her self-righteous high dudgeon.

'I shall drive,' she said firmly.

Groose shrugged and got in. Over the last couple of years he had seen enough of the woman's tantrums to be in no doubt that his shortcomings would be reported back to Campbell-West. Still, the boy, if stupid, had been good. He looked down at his hands. The knuckles were skinned and bloody. The fool should have known better than to try and up the price though. Fifty had been the agreed price and fifty was what he got. Fifty would have put him on a flight to Lisbon. Now it should just cover his doctor's bill.

He looked at the woman out of the corner of his eye. He despised her. She had silver spoon written all over her; never done a real day's work in her life. Why the hell she'd come on this trip in the first place he couldn't understand. Perhaps she was afraid that Campbell-West might find himself another piece of tail while he was out of the country. He wouldn't put it past the old goat.

Groose had a certain amount of respect for the man. When he had been down on his luck, and with a prison record, Campbell-West had given him a job. At first it had been menial but, as he won his master's confidence, things became more serious and better rewarded. He had, so far as he could recall, killed three men on Campbell-West's orders. How many he had permanently maimed, he couldn't even begin to guess. As a result he now had nearly $100,000 in the bank and, once this job was over, would be able to think about going back to Rotterdam and picking up where he had left off.

It was Groose's dream to open a health centre. Not one of those fashionable meat markets where pampered whores played about on chromed equipment and drank carrot juice, but a no-nonsense gym where guys could come to work out. He still had plenty of contacts back home and the market for steroids was as hot as ever. He closed his eyes, smiling to himself as Sarah crunched remorselessly through the gears as they left the outskirts of Ponta Delgado behind.

Dozing, he recalled the boy again. The little punk had been no different from dozens of others he had met. Selling themselves to anyone, man or woman, who could come up with the price of a drink or a fix. Groose had seen, and used them, all around the world. He had been willing and inventive in his lovemaking, however, and, in being foolish enough to try to rip his client off, had provided the perfect excuse for the kind of orgiastic violence that gave Groose the ultimate thrill.

'Sir Peter doesn't pay you to go off sightseeing,' she snapped, resenting the feeling of wellbeing he exuded and keen to dispel it. 'I don't like being kept hanging about.' Christ, he'd seen her annoyed before but today, all that day now he thought about it, she had been like a bear with a sore head. He bit his tongue.

'I went for fuel.'

'Then how is it the tank's still half-empty?'

'Garage closed.' Groose said disinterestedly. Acting as chauffeur to this bitch was the worst part of the job. Give him a nice knee-capping assignment anytime. He took some small comfort from the knowledge that this should be the last time he would need to perform this distasteful chore. Tomorrow, assuming everything went to plan, they would be heading back to Rio. Apart from the boy, and the unforgiveable sin of keeping this stupid, over-privileged cow waiting, the whole thing had gone very well.

Campbell-West had been full of praise for his work thus far. For it had been he, Groose, who had picked up the radio transmission from *Revenge* and who had then come up with the inspired idea of using Chantelle and the grenades as the bait to capture Collins. He had handled the situation at the quarry that morning with a cool professionalism that was sure to raise his value in Campbell-West's eyes. Whatever tales Sarah told out of school, he was sure of a fat bonus once the deal was settled.

It would put that moron Behan in his place too. Behan, who taunted him mercilessly for his lack of interest in women, and who had tried to embarrass him in front of their American prisoner. The previous night, after the pair of them had picked up Chantelle and taken her back to the house, Behan's needling had brought Groose to boiling point.

In the cool bodega where they had held her he had, all evening, delighted in humiliating the bound and blindfolded woman. Among the ceiling height wine racks he had whispered obscenities in her ear and pawed at her unresisting body, inviting the Dutchman to do the same.

'Come on and feel,' he had said, 'she's got a real nice body.'

At first Groose had feigned indifference, concentrating hard on the bodybuilding magazine he was reading, but when Behan began to unfasten buttons he could stand by no longer. The son of a Calvinist pastor he had been appalled at the prospect of looking on a woman's breast. There were limits to what was acceptable.

'Stop that – animal.'

Behan had withdrawn his hands instantly, his eyes growing hard.

'What did you say?'

'I said stop that.' Groose, sensing trouble, laid the magazine aside. He stood up, legs astride, massive arms held wide of his body. 'You behave like an animal.'

Behan came forward cautiously. He towered over the other man yet it was the squat Groose who held the moral high ground. For several seconds neither blinked, then the

Argentinian's hand had strayed towards the big pistol he wore at his hip. He patted the holster.

'One day we will see who is an animal – fruit.' Behan spat the final word.

'If you hope to leave this island alive, Behan, I suggest you stand exactly where you are.'

Campbell-West, dressed in a crimson, silk dressing-gown, had entered the room unnoticed and now stood in the doorway, snub-nosed 38 aimed directly at the man's head. Despite the evenness of his tone there could be no doubt that he was furious. As the tension between the two guards eased, he lowered the gun, nodding towards their prisoner.

'Untie her, you cretin, and take that blindfold off,' he barked. 'You're not living in a police state now.' As Chantelle blinked and rubbed the circulation back into her wrists, Campbell-West apologised effusively for Behan's lack of chivalry. 'I'm so sorry you have been treated in this disgraceful manner, my dear. I'm afraid my men are selected for qualities other than their gallantry.'

'You can say that again.' She fastened the buttons of her shirt. 'What the hell is this, Campbell-West? I thought you wanted me here to talk about the Algoan scam. I come along in all good faith and your gorillas behave like this.'

He shook his head rather ruefully. He was disappointed in her.

'In all good faith? My dear Chantelle, I'd hardly say anyone with a radio under their bed and planning heaven knows what kind of illegal activities could be said to be acting in all good faith, would you?'

Somewhat at a loss, Chantelle fell silent and, accepting this as an admission of guilt, Campbell-West briskly issued orders to her guardians.

'Right, lock her in here. She can't escape. You, Behan, will stand guard outside.' His eyes narrowed dangerously. 'Outside, you understand.' He turned his gaze on her. 'I'm afraid you will have to stay here tonight but tomorrow, when we have rounded up your fellow conspirators, I hope to be able to offer you rather more comfortable surroundings. Right, Groose, you come with me. We must make our plans.'

As they closed the door on the woman, Groose had smiled sweetly at the scowling Behan. The recollection of his triumph brought a satisfied smile, his pleasure heavily reinforced by Sarah's continuing attempts to change gear without benefit of clutchwork. Seldom required to drive, she was becoming increasingly cross at her own ineptitude, aware of the unspoken contempt of the man next to her.

'You want me to drive?'

She pulled over to the side of the road. They had climbed several hundred feet since leaving the town and here the narrow, meandering road skirted a deep ravine that fell sharply away to their right.

'Yes, I think you should. God knows, you're not much use for anything else.' She climbed out and stalked around the car, waiting for him to move over behind the wheel and allow her to get in. 'Come on,' she snapped, as he proved slow to move. 'We haven't got all day. I want to get home.'

Pulling the door open impatiently she watched, frozen into shocked disbelief, as the man slumped to one side, his desperate eyes on hers. He was trying to say something but the dark blood that bubbled between his lips muffled his words into a choking death rattle. She recoiled in horror as he reached out towards her, entreating her aid when, in truth, he was far beyond all help. The crescent wound slashed across his throat dripped richly into the yellow dust as the pale eyes glazed. A hand to her mouth, Sarah shook her head uncomprehendingly as Groose, still croaking the most obscene gutteral noises, slipped helplessly from the car to lie at her feet, failing fingers clawing feebly at the earth.

Without a word Collins climbed from the rear of the car, the stained stiletto still in his hand. Taking the rasping, jerking figure by the heels, he dragged it to the edge of the precipice with one quick tug and sent it tumbling down into the boulder-strewn ravine, watching as it rolled and bounced between the rocks until eventually it was lost to sight. He looked up and down the deserted road then began to kick fresh dust over the bloody earth. Satisfied, he turned to the terrified woman who, supporting herself with a steadying hand against the car, gasped to gain her breath, wide-eyed and shocked beyond words by what she had just witnessed.

Collins took her face in a powerful hand and turned it towards him. He stared into the frightened brown eyes.

'Right then, Sarah Mendelsohn, I think it's time you and I had a little talk.'

Eighteen

At 7.30pm, with the last rays of the sun slanting down the geometric groves of orange trees and only the occasional wild lamenting cries of the peacocks disturbing the evening peace, a sharp rapping on the door heralded the appearance of Behan. Intent on escorting them down to dinner he wore an evening suit that had been tailored for a much smaller man and, had he not remained so inherently menacing, would have been positively risible. The seams of his jacket were stretched almost to bursting point over the massive biceps and shoulders, while the cuffs of his trousers ended before his socks began. Apparently unaware of his own sartorial shortcomings, he was however, patently appreciative of Chantelle's efforts to dress up to the occasion, leering down at her as she stood in the doorway.

'Hey doll, you look a million dollars.' He nodded contemptuously towards Latimer. 'A pity you only got that limey faggot in there with you – a real waste of space.' Half-hidden from sight by the intervening door jamb, Latimer raised a single insolent middle finger in response, while Chantelle, seeing an opportunity to ingratiate herself, smiled ingenuously, almost purring her pleasure.

'Why thank you, Mr Behan. A girl always likes to feel appreciated,' she cooed, slipping her arm through his. 'Perhaps you'd care to escort me down?'

He beamed, it had been a long time since any woman had willingly encouraged his clumsy advances and he led her down to dinner with as much grace as his shambling bulk would permit, Latimer going on before them. His feelings of gratification were soon to be dealt a shattering blow.

Campbell-West stood, posed would be a better word, in the window, a glass in his hand, staring thoughtfully out at the evening and Latimer was instantly taken back to another evening. He recalled the occasion, ten years before, back in the City of London, when they had first set up the Algoan deal and the long trail of deceit and treachery that had brought them here, had begun. He spoke softly, before the other had time to turn and face them, keen to let this sleek headed thief know he still had problems.

'Hallo CW, you're looking well – all things considered.'

The older man swung round sharply, the satisfied smile he had prepared so carefully for their discomfiture crumbling to nothing in an instant. His eyes, hard as flints, went to Behan.

'What's this? Where's Collins?'

The Argentinian blinked stupidly, jerking his head towards Latimer.

'There, boss.'

With an effort, Campbell-West controlled his anger, speaking between clenched teeth.

'That's not Collins, you damned fool, it's Latimer.' He spoke quietly yet his words were clearly being taken on board by Behan who let Chantelle's arm drop and stood, almost to attention, as his master spelt out the situation. 'I thought I had made it crystal clear that Collins is the chief danger to our plans. You were supposed to take him at all costs. Where the hell is he?'

Behan shrugged.

'On the boat they came on, I guess, that's where this guy said he was when Groose picked him up.'

Campbell-West shook his head in disbelief.

'No. If I know Collins, at this very moment he's not more than a mile or two from here and possibly a great deal closer than that.' He looked to the window. 'I want all the guards doubled tonight and let the dogs out. I want you down in the control room monitoring all the surveillance equipment. Anything in the least suspicious, I want to know instantly. When Groose gets back I want a party out looking for the boat they came on. It must be up on the north coast somewhere. Tell him to find it and report back to me.'

Behan, angered to find himself upbraided for what had, after all, been Groose's mistake, and keen to regain credibility, took a menacing step in Latimer's direction.

'Give me ten minutes alone with this fruit and we'll know where the boat is soon enough.' Latimer smiled sweetly into the brutish features as Campbell-West sighed at such an unseemly suggestion.

'You really have no idea, do you? You're dealing with gentlemen now, Behan, not revolutionary scum. There are things a gentleman will not countenance.' He almost spat out his final words. 'You're bloody incompetent, the pair of you. I'm not even sure we can afford you on the payroll much longer.' He might have been speaking to a Martin & Nicholson wages clerk who had been found wanting, and Latimer was amused to watch this brute of a man, who had made a lifetime's profession of killing, take his dressing down without a response. With a terse, 'Get out,' to send him on his way, Behan quit the room, leaving the three of them alone, although Latimer guessed CW would be unlikely to leave himself exposed to their wrath and that there would, almost certainly, be a guard outside.

Recovering his poise and attempting to minimise the previous display of waspish irritation, he smoothly reverted to the role of considerate host, waving them into the large leather bound chairs ranged in a wide semi-circle about a log fire that burned fitfully in the hearth, despite an evening that was far from cold. The room was low and long with white-washed walls of rough plaster. Furnishings, cabinets and bookcases, were of dark oak and almost medieval in their solid construction.

Campbell-West looked fit and well, a little greyer at the temples and perhaps slightly thicker at the waist yet at sixty, immaculate in dinner jacket and broad scarlet cummerbund, he looked no more than forty-five.

'My dear Chantelle and John, this is a rare, though to be honest not totally unexpected, pleasure. I do so miss all the old faces. I'm afraid dinner may be a little delayed, Groose has yet to return from Ponta Delgado with Sarah.' He smiled proudly. 'I insist that she consults the doctor once a week and during our stay here this has meant going into town.' He looked towards the window again. 'She's expecting our child, you know.'

'Yes, so I hear. Congratulations CW, you must be delighted.' If Chantelle intended her words to be ironic, it was evidently lost on him.

'Thank you. Yes, let's drink to that, then we can decide what is to be done about the situation we find ourselves in. I had hoped that David might have joined us but I'm sure he'll be with us in spirit.' He poured out three glasses of dark red wine, his eyes again straying to the window, perhaps finding the thought of Collins prowling out there somewhere in the night unsettling. Handing them their drinks he slumped down into a chair, his face serious but not menacing: he might have been about to warn them of the dangers of inflation to the economy.

'Now, let's get one thing straight before we start. I know exactly why you are here, so please spare me any nonsense about researching a book. Unfortunately for you, Mr Chang became aware of Collins' interest in our activities during his last visit to Vancouver. He passed such information as he possessed to me and I, being a naturally cautious man, have had you watched ever since. I know all about your visit to Poole, Chantelle, to enlist John's help, and have a tape of your conversation at the Savoy.' He smiled blandly, thoroughly enjoying himself. 'Wine waiters can be so treacherous – I do hope you didn't tip him, he was already being paid well enough.' He glanced at his watch. 'Anyway, to get to the point. Despite your unfriendly intentions towards me, I have no desire to complicate things by compounding your clumsy plans.

It's very simple. Providing you give me no further trouble, I am prepared to disregard your foolish desire to bring me to justice. Within a month or so I shall be a citizen of what Kipling called, 'a Just Republic' and therefore safe from the petty vengeance of the British Government or freelancers like yourselves. The deal with Chang is set for tomorrow morning and I intend to be away from the Azores by the afternoon. It is my sincerest hope that this will be my last evening on these somewhat dismal islands. It will be pleasant to spend it in the company of old colleagues. As I say, providing you behave, you will merely be detained here until we are safely away and then released. Cause me any problems, however, and I will not hesitate to hand you over to Behan and Groose.'

Campbell-West, eager that they should fall in with his conciliatory mood, refilled their glasses, unaware that Latimer had poured his first drink into the pot of one of the huge yucca plants that lined the walls. As he returned to the fire, there came the distant double toot of a car horn and he achieved a credible smile for the first time that evening.

'Ah, no doubt that will be Sarah and Groose. Another five minutes and we can dine. Until then, you must tell me how you have been getting on. We all have so much to discuss.'

For five minutes, relaxed now that Sarah was once more within the safety of the laager, he kept the conversation going on a series of platitudes until, from outside, came the clatter of hurried footsteps on the stairs. Campbell-West's gaze went to the door, the embryonic smile fading as it swung inwards to reveal, not Sarah, but Behan standing there, his eyes troubled.

'What is it, Behan?' he snapped, sensing that all was not well. 'Wasn't that the car I heard just now?'

'Sure it was the car.'

'Well?'

'It was empty. No Miss Sarah, no Groose. Only …' he hesitated, then dropped a tangled bundle onto the low table that stood between them. 'Only this.'

Campbell-West reached forward tentatively, as though there might be something here that bit or stung. Gently he teased out three separate objects, laying these in front of him and peering down at them as a seer might examine the entrails of a sacrificial chicken.

The first was a pair of wire-rimmed spectacles, Groose's spectacles. The gold frames glinted in the subdued light as CW twisted them in his hands, silently trying to divine the tidings implicit in this enigma. For Latimer the message was plain and clear: both lenses had been shattered. Cracked across, the shards of glass were held together only by the retaining frames; tiny vitreous crystals fell like snow onto the dark-grained oak of the table top. Groose, he suspected, had looked his last on the world.

The next object he took up was a pair of flimsy yellow briefs, a translucent wisp of satin which had, that very day, undoubtedly graced the glorious pudendum of Sarah Mendelsohn. The crotch gusset was liberally daubed with dark blood and Campbell-West stared in silence at the scrap of silk in his hand, appalled at its implications. For a second Latimer almost felt sorry for this man who seemed to have aged visibly in a few seconds. Collins was clearly a master of psychological warfare. Between the shattered spectacles and the bloody briefs lay an audio cassette.

At a barked instruction Behan disappeared, returning after

177

a few moments with a battered tape deck which he set down between them. Campbell-West's hands were shaking as he slotted the cassette home with an unsteady rattle. Chantelle took up her wine and stretched back in her chair, smiling triumphantly across at Latimer, both of them luxuriating in this unexpected turn of fortune as he set the tape rolling. Collins' words came distant but clear.

'Good evening CW. I'm sorry I can't be with you tonight but, as you will be aware by now, I have a guest of my own I have to look after.' Collins' voice, mildly goading, now became brisk and businesslike.

'Thus far, Sarah is perfectly safe. However, since your treatment of Chantelle this morning was rather less than chivalrous, let me assure you that I feel perfectly at liberty to return the compliment should you not obey my instructions to the letter. I want Chantelle and John delivered, unharmed, to the quarry by 9 tomorrow morning. There's something else. In view of the fact that I lost my entire personal fortune as a result of your Algoan scam I am, unlike my colleagues, also looking for compensation of a fiscal as well as a personal nature. Together with the pleasure of nailing your arse to a tree I want the heroin too. Have it packed into rucksacks for easy carrying. I shall be watching every move you make, so any tricks will have immediate and unpleasant repercussions for Sarah – and your son and heir.'

There was a pause, just sufficient to allow the full implications of his words to sink in.

'I'm afraid your Mr Groose had some rather antisocial habits, Peter. I found some packets of white powder on him. I suspect he has been making free with your stock-in-trade. Anyway, seeing how valuable the stuff is, it would be a shame to waste it. It's very simple, the least deviation from my instructions and Sarah will begin a course of injections that will lead to all sorts of unpleasant results.

It's a funny sort of drug, heroin. As a matter of fact I've

been doing a bit of reading on the subject. Apparently it's unlikely that Sarah will become addicted – good self image, too strong willed – but you never know, four or five shots of high grade stuff in fairly rapid succession and you just might have a junkie on your hands. Be that as it may, what scientific research has shown beyond all doubt is that even quite small quantities can have a significant effect on children during the foetal stage, as well as increasing the risk of a miscarriage.'

Another pause ensued.

'Another thought that occurs to me is the fact that the only hypodermic I have available is the one used by the late Mr Groose. Everything I've heard about the man suggests that he was not only a drug user but also as queer as a clockwork orange. You've probably read about AIDS and its spread among gays and junkies – a nasty business. Anyway, all this is pure speculation, I'm sure you're absolutely aware of what might happen were you to put a foot wrong.'

The tape hissed and for a moment it seemed as if that was the end of the message. Then came Sarah's voice, small and frightened.

'Hallo darling. I'm alright, but you must do what David says. He's utterly ruthless – he slashed Groose's throat. He'll kill me if you don't follow his instructions.'

His voice flat and uncompromising, Collins signed off.

'I expect Chantelle, John and the heroin to be delivered to the quarry at 9. You'll receive further instructions after that.'

For several seconds the tape rolled silently on before Campbell-West stopped its progress with the jab of a mani-cured forefinger. He had, initially, clearly been taken aback by the swift turn of events but, while he might remain concerned about Sarah's well being, Latimer sensed that he had not accepted Collins' mastery yet. He was, even now, still looking for a loophole. Drawing Behan to one side he whis-pered terse instructions before returning his attention to his guests.

179

'An interesting situation,' he mused, 'and one fraught with all sorts of possibilities.' He looked at his watch and smiled wryly. 'Since it appears that Sarah will not be joining us after all perhaps we should go in to dinner.'

As the meal progressed Latimer became more and more convinced that, despite the strong hand held by Collins, Campbell-West felt he still had a few trumps. He barely mentioned the tape or Sarah's abduction but talked at length of the old days in London; indeed at times his apparent lack of concern brought an air of unreality to the occasion. At 10, wiping his mouth with his napkin, he indicated that the audience was at an end.

'Time for bed I think,' he said. 'You will want to look your best when I return you to David on the morrow.'

They were escorted back to the bedroom by a guard, although of Behan there had been no sign all evening. Another indication, Latimer thought, that some kind of subterfuge was being planned.

'I don't like it,' he said, as they lay fully dressed on the bed, both aware that the coming day might as easily bring oblivion as freedom. 'Why has David brought the drugs into this? That was no part of the deal. With Chang flying in tomorrow Campbell-West can't let those go, no matter how badly he wants Sarah back. He could have set up a meeting and then snatched CW. That was the plan.'

'I don't know, but we've got to trust him. He's our only hope. Like you I get the feeling that Campbell-West is planning a double-cross anyway, so we'll have to keep on our toes.'

He fidgeted awkwardly, his hand going down to his sock. Her somewhat mystified gaze turned to a grin as he produced a wooden hafted steak knife. He tucked the serrated sliver of steel under his pillow with a satisfied smile.

'Picked that up while CW was waffling on about the old days. I hope they're not the kind of people who count the silver.'

In an unexpected show of affection she snuggled close, planting an approving kiss on his cheek.

'Know something, Latimer? Despite everything, I think we might just come out of this thing ahead of the game.'

Slipping his arm about her shoulders, he stared into her eyes. In spite of Campbell-West's claret making him bold, his words were even and serious.

'In normal circumstances, being locked in a bedroom with you would have been as close to paradise as I expect to get.'

'When this thing is over, I guess that's something we'll have to talk about.'

Nineteen

The following morning they were woken early with coffee, croissants and fresh orange juice, the maid pointedly leaving the door to their room unlocked. From the window Latimer could see that the car that had brought them to the house again stood in the forecourt, presumably to return them to the quarry. Around it stood several armed men who, by their appearance, were locally recruited. Whether they fully understood what was going on he had no way of knowing.

While Chantelle showered, he made his personal gesture to sartorial considerations by running an electric razor over his chin, remembering, as a final touch, to slide the steak knife down his sock. Hopefully there would be no need for it, but still, there was no harm in taking precautions.

At 8.30 they were escorted out into the bright morning. As he greeted them Campbell-West seemed rather less sanguine about the situation than he had the previous evening. Unshaven and with dark circles under his eyes, he looked as though he had not slept and Latimer wondered whether this would have been because of his concern for Sarah or as the result of a night spent scheming. Knowing the man, he favoured the latter explanation. Having supervised the loading of the heroin-packed rucksacks into the car, CW drew Latimer to one side.

'Please, I beg you,' he entreated, 'don't let anything happen to Sarah. I have kept my side of the bargain to the letter. You have the stuff and, for what it's worth, you have had your revenge. Once it becomes known that I have allowed myself to be tricked out of £20 million worth of heroin, I will be a marked man. My principals will certainly have a contract out on me before the week is up as, if I am any judge, will Mr Chang once he finds the deal is off. What more can you ask? All I ask is that no harm befalls Sarah.'

Despite the apparent earnestness of his plea, Latimer still had a niggling feeling that things were not quite what they appeared. For a start, Behan was nowhere to be seen and, although they had been allowed to inspect the rucksacks to confirm that they did indeed contain heroin, and to supervise the loading of the truck, so far as he was concerned the majority of the packages might just as easily have been filled with flour or some such substance. While he was convinced that Campbell-West would be loath to take any risks with his beloved Sarah and her precious cargo, nevertheless everything seemed to be going just a trifle too smoothly. As they prepared to depart Campbell-West, reinforcing the sense of unreality that prevailed, held out his hand.

'Good luck to you both. Despite everything, I wish you well. Believe me, I have always had the highest admiration for you all. Give my regards to David.' His voice cracked touchingly. 'And send Sarah back to me soon – please.'

As Latimer eased the car away from the house and the main gate yawned wide to let them pass, Chantelle voiced her own fears.

'I don't like it, John. Something's wrong. We've been let off the hook too easily.'

'Yes, I know what you mean, but until we actually link up with David I don't see what else we can do but go along with it. I reckon Behan will be trying to follow us; we must keep our eyes open.'

They reached the rendezvous on time and without sight of

the dreaded Behan, despite twice stopping on side roads to ensure that they were not being tailed. The quarry was apparently deserted, although Latimer was aware that Collins might well be lying in hiding, less than twenty yards away, in the dugout he had previously constructed. Since the rugged terrain that lay between the quarry and the coast meant that moving on foot was the only practical option, he unloaded the rucksacks from the car, dragging them into the shelter of the tumbledown shack, out of the sun. There were three, all made of a uniform synthetic material and all a drab khaki in colour. One had a small Portuguese national flag embroidered on its flap.

Satisfied that the valuable, albeit to him thoroughly distasteful, load was safely out of the increasingly fierce sunlight, he returned to the car, climbing in next to Chantelle who sat listening to the radio. A local station churned out a non-stop selection of pop records; impatiently, she switched from channel to channel as the time dragged slowly by and the temperature in the car soared. For three hours nothing moved in the quarry apart from the tiny sand lizards that darted among the rocks or sunned themselves in the now brazen noonday sun. Switching the radio off Chantelle, the sweat beading her face and arms, closed her eyes.

'Come on for Christ's sake, David, do something,' she hissed through clenched jaws.

Latimer laid a hand on her arm, trying to ease her tension.

'He won't break cover until he's 100 per cent sure that everything is OK. Don't worry – he's watching us right now. I'm certain of it.'

Almost as he spoke there came a low whistle from away to their left and Chantelle gasped as the earth appeared to open and Collins, dust-caked, climbed from his hide into the open like a man resurrected from the grave. Leaning down he lifted the semi-conscious Sarah out, keeping her close as his eyes ranged warily along the circling crest. Quitting the car,

Latimer ran across to them, relieving the other man of the dead weight of the fainting girl and handing him a water bottle. His eyes were slits in the mask and as he grinned, tiny fissures appeared around his mouth and eyes. Taking only the smallest of sips from the water bottle, he poured a little onto Sarah's lips then splashed more of the precious liquid around her face. The wide brown eyes opened and, as she recovered a little, Latimer lowered her carefully to the ground where she squatted for a second or two until, shaking her head, she was able to gain her feet again. Chantelle came running up.

'Did you know he was there all the time?' she demanded with mock belligerence. Latimer grinned.

'I suspected as much, but thought it was best I said nothing – just in case you gave the game away. Sorry, but I felt it was the best thing in the circumstances.' He felt a little guilty at this display of lack of trust but, to his surprise, she smiled approvingly.

'You're a sly dog, John. I expect as much from David, but you continue to surprise.'

Collins looked towards Sarah, his manner surprisingly gentle considering the range and standard of threats he had made against her in his taped message to Campbell-West.

'How are you feeling now?' he enquired softly. Despite her ordeal she seemed strangely unresentful in her reply.

'Better, thank you. It was the heat I guess.'

Collins' eyes again swept the crest of the surrounding crags.

'Right, let's pick up the stuff and get back to the boat. We'll take a rucksack each. Keep close together – Sarah will stay in the middle of the group as a disincentive to anyone feeling inclined to take a pot shot at us. Once we're safely on *Revenge* we'll discuss exactly what we're going to do with her.'

This suggestion caused Latimer to frown. What was there

185

to discuss? Sarah came back to England, under threat of death or worse, and wasn't released until Campbell-West was in the hands of the British police. He prayed that Collins, now he had possession of the heroin, wasn't going to move the goal posts. It was, however, neither the time nor place for lengthy debate and he fell in alongside Chantelle as they began to climb the steep quarry wall.

Each rucksack weighed about 40 pounds and they took regular rests, mainly for Chantelle's benefit, although at no time did she flag or complain. Indeed, as he watched her negotiate the rocky ravine down to where they had hidden the Gemini, Latimer was aware that he was growing ever more fond of this diminutive, resilient American who, no matter what befell them, always came back for more.

On the beach Collins, ever practical, quickly threw up an improvised barricade of rocks and driftwood at the bottom of the ravine. From cover of this, with the machine-pistols and grenades, they could hold their bridgehead against a small army and, if anybody had managed to follow them – a possibility that seemed unlikely – they would be able to cover their withdrawal with comparative ease. Collins handed his machine-pistol to Chantelle.

'You watch the ravine,' he instructed her tersely, 'while John and I get the Gemini ready. There's not room enough for us all to get back in one trip so I suggest that you, John, take Chantelle and one load of the stuff back first. Then come back for Sarah and another load and then, finally, for me and the last rucksack. That way we will be covering all points where we may run into trouble, someone's always keeping an eye on Sarah and, by dividing the heroin up into three separate loads, we reduce the risk of losing all of it should the Gemini get swamped for any reason.'

While he couldn't argue with the tactical sense of Collins' thinking, Latimer was nevertheless distinctly unhappy with the whole idea of taking the drugs on board *Revenge*. He would dearly have liked to thrash the matter out there and then, making his general disapproval of Collins' unilateral change of direction patently clear. However, aware that now was hardly a propitious moment, he decided to bide his time and set about launching the inflatable.

It was the work of a few minutes to clear away the camouflaging rocks and to make the outboard ready; this done, he and Chantelle dragged the clumsy craft between them down to the water's edge. There was still a heavy swell running, although departing from the beach presented less of a problem than landing. As a selected wave began to retreat, they shoved the blunt bow of the Gemini into the sea, bringing the outboard to life and applying full throttle before the next roller could dump them, high and dry, back up the beach again.

Once Chantelle had clambered aboard *Revenge* and secured the Gemini to the guard rail, Latimer handed her the first rucksack. As she hauled it aboard she echoed his own thoughts.

'Jesus, John,' she grunted, dropping it heavily to the deck with patent distaste, 'I don't know what we're doing messing with this shit. I thought it was Campbell-West we were after, not a load of crap like this.'

He looked directly at her, his own repressed anger coming close to the surface.

'I know. I'm going to have it out with David the moment we're away from this place. I want no part of it – I'll dump it over the side if I have to.'

As he untied the painter and prepared to return to the beach, she reached down and stroked his cheek, the tenderness of her touch taking him by surprise.

'Take care,' she said softly.

Back at the beach, playing the throttle to keep her on station, he held the Gemini a few yards off while Sarah, the second rucksack slung on her shoulder, waded thigh deep to where he waited. Climbing with some difficulty over the slippery rubberised gunwale she slid inelegantly into the bottom of the boat. Pivoting the outboard sharply, he swung the boat about, bringing its head directly into the next incoming roller and, bursting through its ragged crest, was quickly clear of the beach and bound for *Revenge* once more.

As they hammered down the coast Latimer watched Sarah as, oblivious of his gaze, she scooped up a handful of sea water and began to wash away the dust of what had been, for all concerned but her especially, a very traumatic twenty four hours. Effective, essential in fact, though Collins' ploy to kidnap her had been, Latimer regretted that she had been put through such an ordeal. His hatred had always been solely reserved for Campbell-West and, although she had certainly benefited handsomely from her lover's thieving ways, he had always regarded her part in the matter as a secondary one.

'I'm sorry you got involved in this, Sarah,' he said flatly, not wanting to appear too apologetic, yet hoping to allay her worse fears. 'It's CW we want – not you. I know David made some pretty nasty threats but that was only to force CW to release us. You'll have to come back to England with us on *Revenge*, of course, but the moment CW gives himself up to the police you'll be free to go, I promise.'

For a second she stared at him then, to his surprise, she laughed. A deep, liquid chuckle.

'Oh I know that, John. David and I had a great time putting that tape together. I was pretty scared at first, of course – my God, the way he dealt with Groose was terrifying!'

'What happened?'

'I don't know exactly, he must have been watching the house and followed us when we left for Ponta Delgado. He was hiding in the car. We left the doctor's surgery at about five. I was driving and Groose was sitting beside me. About

188

twenty minutes later, just as we came off the main road, Groose gave out the most awful choking sound and the next thing I knew there was blood everywhere. David had slit his throat. The poor man, I mean, I know he was a sadistic brute and all that, but to die like that, barely knowing what was happening to him. It was horrible.'

She didn't, he reflected, sound in the least embittered by her experiences or resentful of their malevolent intent towards her lover. Perhaps his doubts showed in his eyes for she laughed again.

'You don't know, do you?'

'Know what?'

'My God, David certainly plays his cards close to his chest.' She sluiced a handful of water down one bronzed thigh before continuing, her eyes growing serious as she gathered her thoughts. 'I'm in this thing with you. I'm the one who told David about Chang and the deal with CW. If it wasn't for me, none of you would be here at all.'

Latimer grew cautious, his eyes narrowing. This was just a bit too much to accept. He mustn't lower his guard.

'How come?'

'Last year I went to Switzerland to see a gynaecologist. After eleven years of failing to get me pregnant, CW decided that I should see a specialist. The best man was in Basle, so to Basle I was duly sent. Anyway, I was out shopping one day when who should I bump into but David. He was over there trying to trace some of the money that had gone missing from BdC – a fair bit of it went into numbered accounts, but by that time most of it had been moved elsewhere.

Of course, at first, he didn't tell me about that or that he was going after CW, and subsequently we saw each other socially on a number of occasions during the time I was over there. I guess he soon suspected I was becoming disenchanted with things and so, eventually, he came clean. He told me what he and Chantelle were planning – I don't think

189

they had contacted you at that time – and invited me to become involved.

Helping to bring a crook like Peter to justice would, he said, ensure me a warm welcome if and when I decided to return to the UK.' She continued to wash her legs and feet with smooth caressing motions, while Latimer struggled to adapt his thinking to these latest revelations. With the mast of *Revenge* now visible round the headland, she apparently became inclined to explain further.

'The fact is, John, I have no desire to become a permanent resident of Brazil. It's a great place but it's not home. Furthermore, neither do I have any desire to spend the rest of my life looking over my shoulder. While my association with Peter might have led to me being tarred with the same brush in the eyes of the press, whatever you, or the world in general, may think of me, I have done nothing wrong. Like you, I wasn't involved in the Algoan swindle in any way. It wasn't until the evening after we were due to leave Amsterdam, en route, as I believed, for Algoa, that he told me everything. I had a choice he said, I could go with him and live a life of ease and luxury in the sun, or I could stay and face the music. He gave a pretty accurate forecast of how you would all fare, once the excrement achieved lift off. Anyway, I was in love with him in those days so it wasn't a difficult choice to make. But all that was nearly four years ago and things change. There are no warrants out for my arrest. I am a British citizen and I want to go home.'

'But what about the baby? Campbell-West is talking wedding bells and living happily ever after.'

'Well, it's been a useful lever, I have to admit, but it's not his baby. For all the thousands of escudos, dollars and francs he paid out for gynaecologists to have the privilege of examining my reproductive equipment, none of them ever came up with the right answer. I suppose they were afraid that if he suspected the fault lay with him he would stop signing their cheques. He was always such a monumentally vain man that the idea he might be sterile would never have occurred to him.' She smiled slyly. 'Makes you wonder how Victoria Campbell-West managed to produce those lovely girls, doesn't it?'

'Whose child is it then?'

Her gaze strayed over his shoulder, back down the coast.

'Let's just say that, for the time being at least, it's better Chantelle continues to think it's Peter's. She'll have to know eventually, of course, but I don't think this is quite the moment for domestic dramas do you?'

By the time he had transferred her to *Revenge* and was heading back for the final pick-up, the sea had built up into a positively dangerous state with a howling westerly wind that threatened on occasion to flip the Gemini over onto her back like a tossed pancake. It took all of Latimer's concentration to pick his way through the peaks that towered above the fragile little craft.

In a sense he was glad of the diversion, but at the back of his mind, he was becoming increasingly unhappy. If Sarah really was carrying David's child, what did that make the heroin? Some dreadful satanic dowry that she had brought with her so that they could set themselves up for life, or purely another means of bringing pressure to bear on Campbell-West? And what about Chantelle, how would she take all this? Did they really intend to tell her about the baby? The entire web of relationships had become a potential mine-field. One thing was sure, once they were all aboard *Revenge* and safely out to sea, there was going to be some pretty straight talking all round.

Taking care not to be thrown up the beach and stranded, he held the inflatable steady a short distance offshore as Collins shouldered the final rucksack and came down the shingle slope towards him at the trot.

As he played the throttle, Latimer became aware of a

movement on the cliff top and his head jerked up. There could be no mistaking the huge figure standing there, black against the sky. In his hand he carried what, at first appearances, seemed to be a gun.

'Run, Dave, it's Behan. The bastards have found us.'

As Collins reached the water, Latimer tried to come in closer but was foiled by the powerful undertow from a receding wave that dragged the Gemini twenty yards to seaward, out and away from the wading man. As he was only to realise later, the freak wave that took him was to save his life.

In a blinding flash the rucksack and the man carrying it dissolved in a searing fireball before his eyes, torn into white hot shreds that scoured and blistered his face, and bloody tatters that streaked his cheeks and hands. For several seconds Latimer was paralysed, gasping and shaking with fear and shock, oblivious of the scraps of charred flesh and clothing that fell gracefully into the sea around him. A red veil dropped over his eyes and he blinked it away, his hand going fearfully to the gash in his forehead where a spent fragment of one of the grenades Collins had carried had buried itself. Instinctively he swung the boat to seaward, still unable to breath properly for the vomit that rose in his throat, and gunned the engine up to a screaming pitch.

It was half a mile down the coast, and with something approaching cogent thought returning, that, glancing down at his feet, he found himself staring at half of Collins' left hand, the bloody fingers lacking several joints. Seizing it up, he hurled it away from him in a paroxysm of horror.

Then he retched and retched.

Twenty

By the time he was approaching the boat Latimer's head had cleared sufficiently for him to form a fairly clear idea as to what had happened back at the beach and what, if he didn't act quickly, might well happen again. As he came up to the stern of *Revenge* the women were waiting for him. They had heard the explosion and the pall of smoke that now hung in the sky along the coast bore grim witness to some catastrophe. His own bloody appearance spoke volumes.

Before they had time to ask what had happened he was in the cockpit, seizing the astonished Sarah by a handful of hair and half-dragging her, gasping in pain, along the deck. Her feet slid from under her and her skull cracked solidly against the boom as he hauled her to her feet, slamming her bodily against the mast and pinioning her there, his forearm across her chest.

Unclipping the main halyard he wound it round her body several times, the final turn going about her throat, binding her so tightly to the mast that she could barely breath. Her eyes reflected fear and resentment, but were also questioning, confused by the erratic behaviour in one she thought she had won over, yet too taken aback by his violence to voice her outrage.

'I guess you weren't expecting to see me again, you two-faced bitch.'

Returning hurriedly to the cockpit he next brought the two rucksacks forward, setting them at the gasping woman's feet and binding the straps to the mast. If these were booby trapped Behan was unlikely to detonate them now he reckoned.

Back in the cockpit he turned to Chantelle who stood watching fearfully. His breath was laboured from his exertions and his hands still trembled as he slumped down. Once he was sufficiently composed his eyes, full of sorrow and concern, came up and locked onto hers.

'David's dead,' he said simply, knowing there was no time for easing the blow and that she would not want the thing dressed up. 'They booby-trapped the rucksacks. It was very quick – he wouldn't have felt a thing.'

She sighed, brushing a hand across her face, then, eyes welling, she turned away, her shoulders slumping in acceptance.

'Oh my God,' she said softly. 'I guessed as much when I saw you coming back alone. How did it happen?' Latimer put an arm about her shoulders. It was a purely protective gesture.

'Behan triggered the device from the cliff top with some sort of radio transmitter. He was trying to kill both of us, I think, but he got it wrong. I guess they'll turn up here pretty soon so we best be away.' He glanced with some satisfaction towards the woman lashed to the mast. 'They won't use the bombs, not while we've got Sarah trussed up like that, but they'll probably have firearms so the sooner we're out of range the better. It would only take one lucky hit on the engine or the rudder and we could be stuck here.'

He started the engine, leaving it idling while he went forward to winch up the anchor. As they edged slowly out of the confined waters of the anchorage, Chantelle's eyes went to the cliff top where a four-wheel-drive Datsun, a square black shadow against the sun, screeched to a halt. Behan, the transmitter that had triggered the first blast still in his hand, stood motionless on the cliff edge, frustration coming from him like a tangible odour. Seconds later the unmistakable figure of Campbell-West, visibly panting, stood at his side, hands on hips in enforced resignation as he viewed the scene below.

'For fuck's sake keep low,' he shouted, as Chantelle, deaf to his warnings, stood up in the cockpit, a machine-pistol up to her shoulder, blazing away at the tiny figures on the cliff top. Both targets dropped, instinctively, to their knees, despite the fact that such a short range weapon would surely fail to reach the shore. She threw the gun aside in disgust.

'Next time, you bastards,' she snarled, 'next time.'

As they came out of the shelter of their anchorage into the open sea *Revenge* began to roll, slowly at first but with mounting momentum as they became increasingly exposed to the long irresistible Atlantic swell. It was a sea that came growling in onto her port bow, sluicing across the foredeck, seething green and ankle deep about the woman lashed to the mast. It struck them in regular explosive torrents that broke in stinging cascades then ran, hissing venomously, down three-quarters of the length of *Revenge's* port side. Sarah looked over her shoulder anxiously, rising and plunging with the motion of the boat; she was already thoroughly soaked, the flimsy dress, plastered to the contours of her body. Chantelle, either from compassion or for the more practical reason that a dead hostage was useless, looked at him enquiringly.

'What about her? We can't leave her up there like that. She'll be dead in a couple of hours.'

He studied her tear-streaked, yet still defiant, features, choosing his words carefully, aware that he ran the risk of opening a new and extremely virulent can of worms by introducing the subject of Sarah's supposed role in the affair. Less than half-an-hour ago David had been murdered and

195

now he, Latimer, was about to lay something very heavy indeed on her.

'When I was coming back with her in the Gemini, she claimed that she was on our side in this, that she had been in contact with David several times over the past year or so. She even claimed that it was her who gave him the information about the deal with Chang.' As he spoke he raised one questioning eyebrow. 'Does that seem likely to you?'

'Not a chance,' she said, perhaps a shade too definitely. 'This has been my operation from the start and I know every one of our sources personally. If Dave had made contact with her he would have told me. She's playing for time, John, we'll have to watch her like hawks. But we can't leave her up there – as long as she's fit and well she's our best chance of coming out of this thing alive.'

So absolute was her rejection of the suggestion that Latimer felt inclined to think she was right in her assessment of Sarah's place in the scheme of things. Nevertheless, being a realist, he was also aware that, if David had been having an affair with their beautiful hostage, he would hardly have been disposed to be frank with Chantelle. Whatever the truth of the matter, Chantelle was right in saying Sarah couldn't stay where she was.

They were perhaps a mile offshore now and it was unlikely that Behan would risk detonating the remaining explosives, even assuming that the transmitter had that sort of range. Setting the automatic pilot for a northeasterly course he went forward to release Sarah, telling Chantelle to keep an eye open for pursuing ships. Sarah was shivering violently as he untied her, strands of wet dark hair sticking to her cheeks.

'We've discussed the matter and decided you're a hostile,' he said, keeping his voice low. 'Behave, and you may come out of this alive. One false step and we won't hesitate to throw you over the side. David is dead – so we'll never know whose side you're on.'

196

The dark eyes, disbelief and dismay clearly written there, stared up at him and for a moment there was the suspicion of tears. Tears for a dead lover, he wondered, or because she had been discovered in her lying? Whatever her thoughts, she took hold of the low safety rail and, struggling to maintain her footing on the slippery, sea-sluiced deck, made her way back to the cockpit without comment while he prepared to hoist the mainsail on the halyard that had, until then, served to restrain her.

Latimer, for the first time able to take stock of the situation, looked about him and, at a single glance, took in the sea state, weather conditions and the pleasing absence of other vessels. Great rolling peaks of cumulus were piling up to the east, advancing towards them like an army on the march, darker patches between sea and cloud marking the violent line squalls that, he guessed, would be upon them before nightfall. He put a double reef in the mainsail, not because he thought the coming weather would be excessively rough but because he preferred a smaller sail to present a weaker radar image. To the same end he finally settled on a scrap of storm jib rather than one of the larger, and in the circumstances probably more efficient, genoas.

He knew they would have to come after *Revenge*, it was the only option open to them now, and doubtless they would be in a powerful work boat that could overhaul *Revenge* with consummate ease once spotted. He knew they had little chance of outrunning their adversary; their only hope lay in avoiding discovery.

Checking the log he was pleased to see that, even under the minimal sail they now carried, *Revenge* was making a steady five knots. Assuming that it would take Campbell-West quite some time to find a suitable vessel and crew, they should be well out of coastal waters before he came in pursuit. Better still, it would be dark in a couple of hours so there was little likelihood of their being troubled until morning. Tomorrow, however, as somebody had said before, was another day.

As he went below, the first spots of rain were rapping on the deck above his head and *Revenge* was beating into a sharp northeaster, her bow slamming into the waves with a regular hollow thudding. Chantelle was boiling a kettle in preparation for his return and pointed forcefully to the bench seat.

'Sit down,' she said, in a no-nonsense sort of way, dabbing a swab of cotton wool into a bowl of pungent yellow disinfectant. 'Christ, you look a mess, Latimer.' She cleaned the wound on his forehead and then, with a pair of cosmetic tweezers, removed several small fragments of metal, dropping them into the bowl. Covering the wound with a large plaster, she then washed his face with fresh water, standing back to admire her work before planting a kiss on his cheek. 'There,' she said, 'that looks a lot better.'

He smiled gratefully. Her ability to deal with situations that, to him, seemed fraught with stress and danger, was amazing. Whether the full impact of David's death would reveal itself later he couldn't tell. Perhaps, he mused, half in hope, they had not been as close as he had once supposed. Certainly David had always had an eye for the ladies and, to his knowledge, had successfully pursued several during his regular visits to London while Chantelle had been keeping an eye on the Algoan office.

'Right, what we have to do now is decide what our next moves are going to be, but first ...,' he produced a bottle of 100 per cent proof rum, 'I think we could all do with a drink.' He poured three stiff ones, handing theirs to the women. Sarah, now warmly dressed in a spare pair of jeans and a thick white jersey, and looking much revived, sniffed at the thick spirit cautiously. There was an awkward silence as, for the first time that day, each had a moment to reflect on their circumstances. Truth to tell, they had precious little to celebrate but, intent on nipping any defeatism in the bud, Latimer raised his glass.

'Here's to David – wherever he is.'

Chantelle raised her glass in silent salute while Sarah hesitated and then, in a voice that faltered, echoed the toast.

'To David,' she whispered and, in the instant, Latimer sensed an almost electric tension between the women that, until that moment, had not existed. He attempted to break the spell by concentrating their minds on the harsh realities of their position.

'Within a few hours, certainly by tomorrow morning, I imagine Campbell-West will have ships and aircraft out searching for us. Hopefully we will have put a good distance between us and them by then and, if we are lucky, this weather will worsen and so make their job that much harder. We've got about 1,500 miles to cover before we get back to the UK, and that's assuming we elect to steer a direct course, which we most certainly won't. Alternatively, we could make a run for the Portuguese coast, it's a lot closer, but I reckon they'll be expecting us to try that and will start searching to the east first. What we've got to do is to follow the least likely course of action. Once it's dark we'll set a heading for Ireland and follow that until we enter the western approaches then we'll head up the Channel and lose ourselves amongst the shipping. Until then ...', reaching across the chart table, he switched on the VHF bringing a ruby bead aglow, 'we have to keep our eyes and ears open.'

Throughout the night, while the women slept fitfully below, Latimer kept a constant look out as *Revenge* hammered into the northeasterly wind that howled about them. To be doubly safe, still fearing treachery from Sarah, he set a course that was virtually due north and that would take them well to the west of Ireland if they maintained it. He would stay on this heading for at least two days, he thought, and then turn onto a more direct heading for home. Apart from the extra sea room it would give them, it would also serve to mislead her as to their intentions. He still harboured misgivings about her and feared that when he took to his bunk and slept, she might find some way of betraying their position.

As well as the hours spent staring out into the blackness he regularly switched through all the channels on the VHF. Assuming that Campbell-West would have more than one vessel out looking for them, they would have to communicate by this means. If, and admittedly it was a big if, he could pick up their conversations, it might give some indication of their position and intentions. As he clicked the tuner through the silent radio channels for the umpteenth time that night, Chantelle's hand touched his shoulder.

'Why don't you get some sleep?' she said softly. 'I'll keep watch until daybreak then I'll shake you. You'll have to tell me what I'm supposed to be doing first though – the last boat I was on was in Central Park.'

He rubbed his eyes, feeling the weariness settling like a weight.

'OK. We're on a beam reach which means that the wind's coming from a right angle to the way we're going so, unless it suddenly goes round, you won't have to do anything with the sails. The automatic steering is set to take us due north so all you have to do is watch the compass.' He pointed to the dully glowing hemisphere of the cockpit binnacle. 'In these seas we're making anything between three five zero and zero one zero degrees; unless it varies much outside that range we're alright. Have an all-round look every ten minutes or so and if you see any lights at all shake me. While you're down below you can keep a listening watch on the VHF although I doubt we'll hear anything until tomorrow. We're well out of the main shipping channels so the only thing you're likely to pick up is local fishermen or Campbell-West's men.'

He looked at his watch. It was two-thirty. 'Shake me at five if I haven't surfaced by then.' For maybe twenty seconds he lay in the protective darkness of his bunk, listening to the regular wreathing hiss of the sea along the hull, then he drifted into oblivion.

In fact it was nine before she shook him, a cup of steaming coffee in her hand. Blinking, he looked around him, running a hand through his hair.

'What's happening?'

'Not much. There's been no sign of any other ships and the only transmissions on the VHF have been regular stuff so far as I can make out.'

'Where's Sarah?' he asked, swinging his legs to the deck and taking the proffered coffee gratefully. Chantelle smiled bitterly.

'Getting a suntan, would you believe?' He would have laughed had the implications not been so ominous.

The morning sun was flooding down the hatchway and, looking up, he could see a patch of cloudless sky. The wind had dropped away to nothing. This was bad news, indeed. He stepped up into the cockpit, looking away as Sarah, raising her head at his appearance, made a token gesture to the niceties and laid a modest arm across her oiled breasts. In other circumstances he might have been interested in this display but now it was the sky that won his gaze.

The threatening conditions of the previous evening had been thoroughly dispersed. There were a few wisps of feathery cirrus away to the west but, that apart, the sky was clear and visibility as good, or in these circumstances as bad, as anyone could have wished. The sea, too, was much abated from the previous night and, although there was still just sufficient wind to keep *Revenge* ghosting along, they were making little more than three knots.

'I'm afraid you're going to work for your living on this trip,' he snapped ungallantly at the reclining woman, his sudden irritability springing from the vulnerability of their situation. 'There's food down below, perhaps you'd like to get breakfast on the go. The fridge has got bacon and there's bread in the locker under your bunk. Bacon sarnies and coffee all round. OK?'

He expected some show of resentment at being allocated such menial work and in such peremptory manner but, turning her back on him, she pulled a skimpy blouse about her shoulders and, knotting it under her bust, went below without comment. Soon the smell of frying bacon came floating up to him. Chantelle had settled herself into a corner of the cockpit and, now that he was once more on deck and in command, slept peacefully, the sound of gentle breathing coming from below the battered straw sunhat she had pulled over her eyes.

Standing, bare-footed, on the boom to gain extra height Latimer scanned the horizon regularly. He knew that if they succeeded in escaping detection during the next twelve hours they would most probably be alright; he was equally well aware that everything would depend on how effectively CW organised his search and how many craft he had at his disposal. If, a not unreasonable assumption, Campbell-West anticipated that they would try to make a run for Portugal, and so deployed his resources to the east to intercept them, then they might just get away with it. If not ...

During the forenoon Latimer, having put the moment off until then, accepted that he had to do something with the rucksacks and their deadly contents. But what exactly? They still lay on the foredeck, a mute and daunting challenge that he had deferred thus far but which could wait no longer.

It would, he told himself, be a simple matter to toss them over the side and be rid of them for ever. However, he had no idea how much, if any, heroin had been used to conceal the explosives. If sufficient of the drug had been sacrificed in the cause of making the whole set-up look convincing the rucksacks might be valuable enough to use as a bargaining tool. He woke Chantelle gently and then called Sarah, who had returned to working on her tan, back into the cockpit.

202

'I'm going to have a look in the rucksacks,' he said in an as matter-of-fact voice as he could muster. 'I'm sure there's no real chance of them blowing up but just to be safe you two should go down to the after cabin. If anything goes bang, come up and see how bad things are. Even if the worst has happened still stay on board – don't leave the yacht unless you positively have to. If you find yourselves sinking there are red flares in the locker under the chart table, instructions are printed on the side of each one.' Contemplating a situation where they would be reduced to attracting their pursuer's attention brought a bitter smile. 'One thing's certain – you won't be left out here for long. There's a self-inflating life raft on the transom and the Gemini will stay afloat as well. As I say, I'm sure nothing will go wrong, so don't worry.'

He watched as they trooped obediently below and then went forward, sitting at the foot of the mast with the first bag between his knees. During their escape from the island both bags had been thoroughly soaked although now the canvas was stiffly dry. The heroin would, he guessed, have been hermetically sealed and the Semtex, or whatever plastic explosive they had used, would not have been affected. What bothered him most was that the triggering circuit, attacked by the corrosive sea water, might well have been rendered unstable. Unstrapping the bag gingerly he peered inside.

The top layers were the small polythene bags of white powder that he had been shown when CW had released them. He reached in, his hand sliding between the cool waxiness of the bags until it touched something solid and angular in shape.

Carefully, he pushed aside the layers of bags until he could see that the lower section of the rucksack, maybe a third of its total depth and hidden by a roughly sewn-in false bottom, held a square cardboard box that was, unhappily to his mind, still limply damp. Ironically, it had, according to the printing on its sides, originally held nothing more lethal than cartons of orange juice; clearly Behan was a master of improvisation. Lifting it out into the sunshine and setting it on the deck, Latimer pulled back the flaps, aware of a tightness around his chest and fingers that had grown strangely awkward.

The device was constructed in two parts. There was a bulky wad, perhaps fifteen pounds in weight, of a yellowish material that might have been marzipan but which he knew was Semtex, and there was a small brown electrical switch, powered by batteries, that clearly could be operated by remote control. The two separate elements were attached by a pair of thin wires, one brown, one blue, that disappeared into the plastic explosive. His pulse accelerating, Latimer carefully pulled the wires away from the Semtex. As the deadly umbilical cord came clear he sighed audibly. Put together in a hurry and of the most basic design, it was a bomb such as this, he reflected, that had blasted David to pieces. Once it was disconnected he took a certain venomous pleasure in hurling the switch far out over the side and set about making the second bag harmless.

Calling the women up on deck he pointed to the heap of polythene bags that lay in a low, insecure pyramid on the cockpit sole.

'Would either of you know how to tell if that is real heroin or not? I'm afraid I wouldn't know where to start.'

Chantelle shrugged, her mouth turning down, but Sarah didn't hesitate, stooping to take up one of the sachets. Pulling the soft plastic of the bag open, she dipped a cautious little finger into the powder, dabbing it onto the end of her tongue. She smiled triumphantly.

'Take it from one who knows,' she said, 'that's the real McCoy. CW wouldn't skimp on details. I'm not up on the financial side of the drugs scene, but I'd guess you've got about £50,000 worth of the stuff there. West End junkies would kill each other for one per cent of that stuff, yet I doubt Mr Chang will even know it's gone.'

He looked towards Chantelle, seeking some intimation of her thoughts on the subject, but she remained impassive. In the madness of the past twenty-four hours he had forgotten all about Mr Chang. The deal had probably been completed by now and CW was free to pursue them with all the concerted malevolence he had been infamous for when he was a wheeler-dealer in the City of London. Sarah broke into his troubled thoughts, her voice, in contrast to her thus far submissive approach, now sharply assertive.

'Look, I know you both have good reasons to doubt me but, I promise you, David and I did meet in Switzerland and it was me who gave him the details of the Chang deal.' Her haughty gaze, and the gauntlet it threw down, settled on Chantelle. 'Do you deny he was in Basle last year? June and July and then again in December? He stayed at The Presidentio in the summer and The Carlton in the winter. Fact is, Chantelle, for all your snooping, I don't think you would have even heard of Chang had I not told David, far less the meeting in Ponta Delgado.' Perhaps feeling she was playing an unbeatable hand, her insistence grew. 'Tell me, where did the information come from as far as you were concerned?' For once Chantelle appeared less confident.

'He said he'd been advised by one of our contacts in Brazil that the deal was on.'

'And you had no reason to question that?' Sarah's voice had taken a slightly snide edge and Latimer began to wish he could stop this conversation here and now. They had problems enough without David's extramural sexual activities being brought into question.

'None,' snapped Chantelle, yet even in her emphatic rejection of the suggestion he sensed that the seeds of doubt had been sown and watered. Her eyes locked firmly on Latimer's, Sarah took a deep breath before renewing her attack and he knew she was about to repeat the story she had told him in the Gemini. He was certain, too, that this time she would include the allegations about the baby's parentage.

'Shut up,' he snapped, the ferocity of his words bringing them both sharply to heel, staring at him as though he had taken leave of his senses. Then they realised what was happening. Still distant, yet its throbbing pulse swelling all the time, came the drone of aircraft engines.

Twenty One

'Keep out of sight.' He ordered, 'I'll go and see what's going on.'

They watched slightly bemused as, before climbing out into the cockpit, he proceeded to strip off his clothes and then, standing naked at the stern, hastily hoisted the French tricolour. Finally, dousing his discarded clothing in the sea he hung it, a convincing line of washing, over the stern, carefully arranged to obscure the vessel's name, so lovingly painted before their departure.

Despite the seriousness of their situation he was aware of a certain amount of restrained hilarity emanating from below. Chantelle and Sarah, torn between modesty and curiosity, smiled as, totally naked save for a pair of sunglasses, he settled himself at the helm and casually set about putting out the fishing lines.

His intentions were simple: if whoever was in the aircraft could be convinced that this was any other boat but *Revenge* they might still gain a few more precious hours. Unable to think of any further deceit he could employ he unhurriedly turned his head towards the sound of the aircraft.

It was still a long way off to the east, apparently carrying out a well-organised track crawl search, flying a series of parallel sweeps that would allow it to cover the search zone in the most efficient manner. Although its search pattern meant that it only approached slowly, he was aware that it was only a matter of time before they were spotted and investigated by the searching aircraft. Sure enough, after some ten minutes the drone of the engines changed pitch and the aircraft came driving directly towards *Revenge*. The brute power of its twin engines vibrated through the sultry air like a wall of solid sound as it closed on them.

'Switch the VHF to channel 16,' he instructed as the crescendo approached, 'but, if and when they make radio contact, let me do the talking. We've got to convince them that I'm the only one on board.'

As the silver Neptune came in low and fast, its flickering shadow in pursuit over the sea below, he stood up and waved his hands, ducking instinctively as it roared over the boat, seemingly only a scant couple of yards above the masthead. Climbing steeply away it banked in the sunlight and Latimer was surprised and not a little relieved to see that it bore the insignia of the United States Air Force. As he continued to wave, the VHF crackled to life and he went below to answer. The voice from the skies was polite and correct to a fault.

'Good morning, sir, this is USAF SAR Neptune kilo foxtrot charlie. Will you identify yourself please?'

Latimer, not sure he could manage a convincing French accent, decreased the squelch suppression on the radio, bringing the level of static interference up a notch, hopefully masking his Inspector Clouseau accent.

'Good morning, foxtrot charlie, this is Mirabelle, Mirabelle. I am on passage for Cherbourg out of Recife.'

'Thank you, Mirabelle, we have had reports of distress flares being sighted in this area. Have you seen anything?'

'No, I have seen nothing.'

There was a pause as the pilot ticked off his check list. 'How many crew are you carrying?'

'Only myself.'

'Thank you, sir.' There was another pause and Latimer

wondered if he had overlooked something which might betray the presence of the women below. He need not have worried for there was amusement rather than suspicion in the pilot's parting observation. 'If I were you, sir, I'd be careful about sunburn. Good luck.'

With a final pass, the Neptune screamed over them again and he stood out in the sun and waved them cheerily on their way as they returned to the search. Apparently deciding they were searching in the wrong sector they now headed further to the east and were soon out of sight. When it seemed safe, Chantelle peered out cautiously.

'So it wasn't CW after all?'

'I'm not so sure. Campbell-West is no fool. He knows that the best way of getting a thorough search put together is to get the authorities to do it for him. It only needs someone to sight red flares, or to say they have, to get a full-blown alert put out. It could be that CW is getting the US Air Force to do his searching for him.'

'But how would that help him?'

'Well, I'm only guessing but it wouldn't surprise me if he had friends at the NATO base on Terceira. I reckon he'll be getting advice of every sighting they make together with its precise position, speed and course. Then he'll check them out one by one. There won't be many yachts of this size in these waters, so even if our American friends are taken in by our lies, anyone checking our course and position will realise it's far too northerly for a landfall in France. I guess we'll get a visit sooner rather than later. We'll go onto a more easterly course and then consider what preparations we can make to repel boarders – just in case.'

Chantelle smiled and, suddenly aware of his nakedness, he blushed. She tried to put him at his ease as he struggled into a pair of cold clammy shorts.

'Don't put it away, John,' she said. 'If that doesn't scare them off, nothing will.'

An inventory of what little remained of the arsenal that David had originally brought on board made him realise that, in their hasty departure from São Miguel, most of their weaponry had been left behind, abandoned unused in the cache that they had set up on their arrival. One machine-pistol, a crate of ammunition and half-a-dozen grenades were all that remained. Considering the opposition it didn't seem an awful lot.

Throughout that long afternoon, the weather remaining bright and hot, they scanned the horizon for sight of any pursuing vessels until the glare made their eyes ache. Only Sarah seemed unconcerned. Since they had rejected her offer of an alliance she seemed content to let things run their course. Apparently, she considered that Latimer's striptease that morning, in the interests of survival or not, was the signal for general nudity to become the norm. She now lay completely naked on the foredeck, annointing herself at regular intervals with sun oil in disconcertingly stylish insouciance.

He could well understand her casual approach to the whole situation. Whichever way things went she wasn't likely to get hurt, at least he imagined, that was the way she probably saw it. Well, he thought grimly, she just might be in for a surprise. She was their only remaining hope of getting to Campbell-West.

Despite the way events had unfolded he still hadn't abandoned his hopes of bringing their prey to justice. If, to achieve that end, pressure had to be brought to bear on a pregnant woman, then so be it. But would he, he wondered, be able to convince her, and the men out searching for them, that he wouldn't hesitate to kill her if the need arose? Only time would tell.

'What made her try that line about David, do you think?' Chantelle asked softly as, through the binoculars, he swept the horizon again and yet again found nothing. He hesitated, keeping the glasses to his eyes, not wanting to meet hers. He felt it was best to appear disinterested in such speculation, to treat it as being neither here nor there. If Chantelle ever thought that the child Sarah carried was David's, he dreaded to consider the consequences.

'Oh, I expect she was frightened and hoped to win our confidence. As she says, she hasn't really done anything illegal. Maybe she's just had enough of CW and wants a free trip home.'

Chantelle fell silent, as though satisfied with his explanation, but on more than one occasion that afternoon he saw her eyes, narrowed and thoughtful, go to the golden body on the foredeck.

By six, with the evening coming in and a full moon on the rise, it looked as though they had succeeded in eluding their pursuers yet again.

There was a feeling of mild elation in the cramped cabin as they sat round the table in the subdued yellow light. Each day they remained undetected meant that the area in which they might be sailing expanded exponentially and made the task of pinpointing them that much more difficult. But as they cleared away the supper things the VHF crackled into life.

'*Revenge*, this is Peter. *Revenge*, this is Peter. Switch to channel 67.' There could be no mistaking the cultured and measured inflection of the words and Latimer felt a thrill that was half fear, half anticipation, as he switched channels and waited. '*Revenge*, this is Peter. Are you receiving me?' Came the call again. Latimer put an unnecessary finger to his lips, indicating the imperative of silence as he took the hand microphone from its bracket on the bulkhead and prepared for the coming dialogue.

He knew he must keep the duration of his transmissions to a minimum. Doubtless CW would have direction-finding equipment and would hope to be able to pinpoint their answer. Even by responding at all it would tell CW that he was almost certainly within twenty miles, the maximum range of a standard VHF in normal atmospheric conditions.

Disturbingly, from the strength and clarity of the incoming signal, Latimer suspected that the scheming bastard was probably a lot closer than that – just over the horizon likely enough. He also knew that the sensible thing would be to observe strict radio silence, yet until they got into negotiations with the opposition the game would remain at a stalemate. Pulling the hatch shut to obscure what little light escaped from the shadowy cabin, he waited for Campbell-West to speak again.

'*Revenge*, this is Peter. Are you receiving me?'

'Receiving you, Peter.' His response was clipped, allowing no time for any direction-finding equipment to get a fix. Campbell-West, a suggestion of relief in his voice, must have been pleased to have made contact and his tone was laid-back and conciliatory, no doubt hoping to encourage Latimer to become talkative.

'John, we must talk. My only interest is getting Sarah back. Believe me, I was as horrified at what happened to David as you must have been. I had no idea Behan would go to such lengths. I promise you he will be punished with the full severity of the law, but you must release Sarah. What do you want? I'll do anything you want to get her back. Please, tell me what your terms are.' He paused, waiting for Latimer's answer. When none was immediately forthcoming, he continued to bait the hook, attempting to wheedle from them some response lengthy enough to betray *Revenge's* position. 'If it's money you want, I'll pay anything to get her back. Please let me talk to her – she is alright, isn't she?' Again he paused, inviting Latimer to take up the conversation. When he realised it was an invitation declined a certain amount of frustration became evident. 'Are you listening to me, John?' he snapped.

Latimer looked to Chantelle. Her eyes were hard as she

listened to this man who, despite his glib protestations of innocence, had undoubtedly ordered David's death. She had, he knew, never wavered from the original plan of bringing CW to justice. For her, as for him, that was the only acceptable outcome. He pressed the transmit button on the handset.

'Keep talking, Peter.'

There was something more than a moment's delay. Doubtless, somewhere in the night, CW was asking his henchmen if they had been able to get a fix on his brief transmission. Unless they had some pretty fancy equipment on board, which he doubted, Latimer knew he would be a very disappointed man.

'Please let me talk to Sarah.' His concern grew more urgent, 'Just a word to assure me she's alive and well.'

'No.'

'Then, for God's sake, what are your terms? Please, I'll do anything. She's pregnant remember, she could lose the baby if you run into bad weather.' A hint of moral outrage crept into his voice, a tone that in the old days had been reserved for striking miners and the like. 'Are you prepared to gamble with the life of an unborn baby?'

'Quite prepared.'

At the other end of the conversation he sensed CW wearying of his fruitless attempts to trap them. His next words came flat and without emotion.

'What must I do?'

Latimer thought quickly, looking out at the gathering dusk. Sooner or later he would have to spell it out but it would do no harm to delay putting his cards on the table until it was dark. It would keep CW on the defensive and give them a chance to put a few more miles on the log.

'Call on this channel. Midnight. Out.'

'Roger, *Revenge*.'

There was silence in the cabin as the set went dead and

Latimer swiftly switched the tuner through all the other working channels. As he had expected, Campbell-West was in earnest conversation with the other vessels in his fleet. He must have had, so far as it was possible to tell, at least three other vessels out searching for them and it was gratifying to hear each skipper reporting his personal failure to get a fix on *Revenge*. Opinion was divided, it appeared, as to whether they had made a run for Portugal or were still hiding out among the islands. Campbell-West, at his most scathing, clearly regarded this lack of certainty as pure incompetence on the part of his subordinates. His final conversation with Behan who was, it seemed, conducting a separate search from one of the other vessels, brought smiles to their faces. Even Sarah was unable to disguise her amusement.

'This may well be our last chance. Make sure everyone is listening in at midnight. If he's going to give me details of whatever he hopes to achieve he will have to be on the air for a few minutes at least. Make sure everyone is ready. I want a definite fix this time.'

'Would you believe it?' asked Chantelle, her eyes widening in mock horror at this evidence of the deceitful side to a member of the British peerage. 'An officer and a gentleman and he goes and does something like that. Next thing someone'll tell me there's no Santa Claus.' She grew serious. 'What do you intend to do about it, John?'

'I think we'll call back in a couple of minutes. Give them time to switch off all their D-F equipment, then spell out our terms.'

'What exactly are they?' Chantelle asked. 'We seem to have been sidetracked, what with Sarah's cock-and-bull story and the drugs. My view is we stick to our original intentions. I say we should settle for nothing less than Campbell-West giving himself up to the authorities – play it hard-nosed. If he doesn't agree to that, we kill her. I want nothing to do with drug trafficking, John. So far as I'm concerned it's CW's balls on the block or nothing.' Perhaps detecting some doubts creeping in, she pointed at Sarah. 'Don't worry about the messy bits. I'll have no problem putting a knife into Miss Israel.'

She sounded totally convincing and Latimer blinked, not sure if she was speaking for effect or whether, if it came to the crunch, she would actually be prepared to kill the woman who sat silently at her elbow. Whatever the case, he knew that it was essential to make Sarah believe that they meant business. If she felt she was among people who would baulk at murder, she would probably not be able to convince Campbell-West of their resolve.

Without further ado he switched to channel 16, the calling channel.

'*Revenge* to Peter, switch to channel 67.'

His eyes were on Sarah as he waited for the reply. She was pale, perhaps at last comprehending that, even if she considered herself innocent, she was among company that didn't give a toss one way or another. After a moment's delay, during which no doubt confusion was rife among the searchers as listening equipment was hurriedly switched back on again, CW's almost urbane tones came to them.

'*Revenge*, this is Peter.'

'Our terms are very simple and not negotiable. You come to London. You buy us lunch at Correlli's. Once you enter the restaurant Sarah will be freed and we will hand you over to the police. Midday two weeks from today. *Revenge* out.'

It had taken less than seven seconds to transmit the message.

'Say again, John.' There was anger and frustration in Campbell-West's words as he realised he had been outsmarted. 'You're very weak, I didn't get the message.'

Latimer returned the VHF microphone to its bracket and, reaching down into the locker, produced the rum bottle again. It was almost empty.

'A toast,' he said. 'Confusion to our enemies.'

At midnight CW tried to make contact again but, although continuing to monitor the messages that passed between the searching vessels, Latimer declined to make any response. From the exchanges between CW and Behan it seemed certain that, despite his protestations, Campbell-West had received their message loud and clear.

'If I go I shall be arrested; if not, they will kill Sarah. What can I do?' he asked despairingly. The Argentinian's replies – he was clearly not of a sentimental disposition – suggested that, if the problem were his, Sarah's lifetime expectancy would not be overlong.

At about three in the morning, as Latimer dozed at the chart table, he once again caught Behan's thickly accented voice over the VHF and turned up the volume, the better to hear. At first he thought the Argentinian was calling up another searching ship but then his heart sank as, with a start, he realised the message was for them.

'Hallo, *Revenge*, this is *Estrella*. You can speak freely now, Señor Latimer, we have a visual contact on you. If you like to look out to the west you will see our lights. We are coming to get you, little ones. We have you on radar too, so we cannot lose you.' Chantelle appeared from the aft cabin where she had been sleeping. Woken by the unexpected transmission she sat by him, her face serious as Behan continued. 'I suggest you stop and wait for us. Is the lovely lady listening? I shall be there soon, my darling. As for you, Señor, I fear you must soon be food for the fishes. Why not give up?'

Switching off the light Latimer slid back the hatch, peering into the darkness to westward. At first he could see nothing but then, with a shudder, he picked out a flickering spark on the horizon, a firefly that danced and died upon his retina, then danced again. They had been found. Bringing the engine to life, he put the helm hard over and headed into the false dawn.

They had no option now but to make a run for it.

Twenty Two

When the sun came up, a great bloody eye in a cloudless sky, the distance between the two vessels had been cut down to a mile or so. *Revenge* was making seven knots and Latimer estimated that *Estrella*, clearly no greyhound of the seas, was probably making rather less than ten. Through the binoculars he could clearly make out Behan standing in the bows of the battered work boat. Stripped to the waist, and with a twist of rag tied round his head as a sweat band, he looked for all the world like a latter-day pirate, his pale eyes seeming to bore directly through the lenses into Latimer's. Occasionally he would look over his shoulder to the wheelhouse, as though exhorting the helmsman to increase speed.

With the Volvo's temperature gauge already hovering close to the red sector, Latimer dared not increase his own speed for fear of overheating the engine. He suspected that the skipper of the pursuing boat was equally aware of this possibility, hence the time it had taken them to get this close. Nevertheless, it was now only a matter of half an hour or so before they were overhauled and the light machine-gun, clearly visible on the roof of the pursuing vessel's wheelhouse, opened-up in earnest.

'Bring Sarah up into the cockpit and tie her hands. Keep her between us and them. Hopefully that will dissuade them from trying to shoot directly at us.' He knew, however, that this was unlikely to be a tactic they would employ and, most probably, they would be quite happy simply to cruise along-side the boat and shoot it up, bit by bit, until either the engine or the steering was put out of action. Then they would, successfully no doubt in view of the *Estrella's* eight-man crew, try to board *Revenge*. Even as he considered the possi-bilities the first faint crackle of gun fire came to them and all three ducked their heads, although at that range the chances of a hit were minimal. It had been purely a ranging shot and Behan, stretched out behind the machine gun, waved cheer-ily across to them. He had all the time in the world the gesture said, while Latimer knew that for them, on the other hand, time was running out. If he was going to make a move it would have to be soon.

'Take the helm, Chantelle, I'm going up forward.'

Both women stared as, keeping low, he went up to where the two canoes which Collins had insisted they bring but, in the event had never used, were secured. In his hand he carried a thick hank of rope, perhaps fifty feet of light bouyant line, neatly coiled.

Tying one end to the carrying toggle at the stern of the first canoe he brought the other end of the line back to the cockpit, running it outside the shrouds and backstay before taking it back to the second canoe and securing it in the same way. He then carefully flaked the rope down in the floor of the cockpit so that it would pay out easily when required. Next he took the explosive charges that had been intended to bring them all to grief, thrusting one package into the stern of each canoe.

Without the original radio-triggering device he knew he would have to improvise some alternative means of setting them off and, to this end, he taped the remaining fragmen-tation grenades, six in all, to each deadly pack, setting the fuses, as Collins had instructed him, to their maximum delay – approximately ten seconds. Even as he put the final touches to his work he was grimly aware that its chances of success

218

were minimal.

As Latimer worked he glanced repeatedly over his shoulder to where the other boat now lay less than 100 yards astern and closing rapidly. He had, he knew, to assess accurately the best range at which to launch his hastily put-together secret weapon. Too soon, and the pursuing helmsman might spot it and take evasive action. Too late and they could all be blown to kingdom come.

Chantelle, her eyes anxious as she crouched in the cockpit, stared up at him as another burst of gunfire came to their ears, the bullets passing over their heads through the standing rigging, one ricocheting off the aluminium mast with a murderous whine, ploughing a ragged furrow in the silver metal a scant few feet above his head. He could see Behan's head come up as the man tried to assess the effect of his fire and to see if, as he doubtless intended, it would encourage them to abandon their futile flight. When he saw *Revenge* maintaining her speed and course he loosed off another short sharp burst, this time into the sea just astern. The gap was down to less than 50 yards by this time and Latimer knew it was now or never.

Pulling the pins from the grenades he lifted the canoe on the starboard side over the guard rail and dropped it, pancaking with a solid smack, into the sea and then, with all the speed he could muster, launched the other over the port side, all the while maintaining his grip on the line. Swiftly making his way back to the cockpit he carefully played out the rope that now towed the bobbing canoes astern in a widening vee configuration as they drifted off and outwards on the spreading bow wave.

Puzzled, Behan quit the machine-gun and came forward, leaning over the guard rail as he tried to make out what was going on. The canoes were now streamed, evenly spaced, on either quarter of *Revenge* and almost level with *Estrella's* bow as Latimer played them out like a pair of horses on a long rein, trying to jockey them into a position where they were equidistant from the pursuing *Estrella*. As he paid out the line he counted ... five, six ... Then he released the rope.

Behan, suddenly aware that there was danger here, gesticulated wildly to the helmsman to change course. It was too late. *Estrella's* bow ploughed directly onward into the connecting rope and, as the slack was taken up, both canoes swung sharply inwards until they lay amidships, hard alongside the work boat, rapping against her sides. Latimer prayed the joining rope wouldn't pass right under her keel and away. Eight, nine.

With a low roar the starboard canoe went up first and *Estrella* veered wildly to port as the helmsman was thrown across the wheelhouse by the force of the explosion. Somehow Behan, despite the unexpectedness of their counterattack, retained his grasp of the situation and, by the time the second canoe erupted into a column of fire down the port side, had managed to get under cover.

To Latimer's dismay, as the smoke cleared he saw that *Estrella*, despite the blistered paintwork and buckled plates she had sustained on either side, was still able to maintain her course and speed, and continued to close rapidly. What was worse, the Argentinian had reappeared and was setting up the toppled machine-gun. Reaching down, Latimer pushed the throttle forward and brought *Revenge's* engine screaming up to maximum revolutions. Although pleased to see the gap opening slightly he knew that, despite this, they had played their last ace and it had been trumped. Then Chantelle pointed.

As Behan, in a berserker rage at these treacherous attempts to thwart his plans for them, and Campbell-West's orders regarding Sarah's safety clearly forgotten, continued to blaze away, the other crewmen were abandoning ship. Leaping into the sea in the wake of a rapidly launched life raft, that inflated like a fat shining porpoise with a serpent hiss, they were soon hauling themselves gratefully over its bobbing gunwale.

'What's happening?' she said, her eyes narrowing.

Then they saw the black smoke billowing from the engine room hatch at *Estrella's* stern, petals of orange flame blossoming in the folds of the acrid moleskin billows. The second blast, not strong enough to break through the work boat's steel hull, had, nevertheless, been sufficiently powerful to rupture a fuel line. Petrol was leaking into the bilges and the flames would, he guessed, eventually reach the main fuel tanks. Sure enough, with a low muffled bellow a fireball mushroomed gracefully into the air above the battered hulk of the *Estrella* and Behan, realising that in seconds she would be ablaze from stem to stern, quit the machine-gun and dived gracefully into the sea, swimming with powerful strokes towards the life raft. The flimsy raft dipped deep in the water under his bulk as he pulled himself on board and, once safe, he turned, pure venom written on his features, to stare balefully at them.

Easing the throttle back Latimer put the helm over and took *Revenge* in a wide, wary circle round the raft. Chantelle came to stand at his side.

'Run the bastard down, John,' she hissed. 'He killed David – now it's his turn.'

Latimer shook his head. He felt totally calm now, his thinking clear and collected.

'No, there's others in the raft. I'm not going to have them on my conscience. At the moment we haven't, unless you count taking Sarah as kidnapping, broken any laws. Anyway, he was acting on CW's orders, remember, and he's the one we're after.'

She glared at him and for a moment he thought she might attempt to seize the tiller and ram the raft herself. Then she turned away with a shrug and, sitting in the stern, stared at Behan who waited, less than a line cast away probably uncomfortably aware of what was being said. He stood up, balancing precariously in the wallowing life raft; despite his discomfiture he was still capable of flashing a smile.

'Hasta la vista, Señora,' he called out. 'A great pity we cannot get closer. Another time perhaps.'

Realising that CW and other boats were probably already converging on the spot Latimer, eager to be away, headed to the west on the assumption that Behan had been instructed to carry out his search from that direction while the others would cover the east. Certainly, the life raft that now housed Behan and the crew of the *Estrella* would have been equipped with a homing device that transmitted a Mayday the moment the raft hit the water. As the raft and the burning wreck of *Estrella* fell astern, red flares soared aloft.

It was time to be moving. Easing the throttle back, Latimer watched the temperature gauge until the needle relented and began to drop back towards the green. Then he slipped an arm round Chantelle's unresponsive shoulders and watched until both boat and life raft were no more than specks on the skyline.

'David was a professional, remember,' he said softly. 'He wouldn't want us to get sidetracked into personal vendettas. We're after Campbell-West and to achieve that we've got to get him back to London by using Sarah. It can still work. You've seen him – he's absolutely besotted with her and the prospect of becoming a father again, so he's sure to follow wherever we go, especially now that Behan has been taken out of the game.'

She didn't answer but later, when all that could be seen was a faint smudge of smoke on the horizon, she returned to the cockpit and sat beside him at the helm. Taking his hand, she laid her head on his shoulder.

'That was pretty quick thinking back there, John, I thought they had us for sure.' She hesitated, 'I guess you were right about not killing that scumbag Behan too.' Now that

222

the immediate threat had been removed he relaxed. Ever since their meeting in Poole he had grown increasingly aware of the allure of her full figure, more importantly he had developed a great deal of respect for her toughness and determination. Appreciating her conciliatory approach he kissed her softly on the mouth. She neither responded nor pulled away from his touch but looked up into his eyes as though seeking some message written there. Not a bad start, he thought, but it would be wrong to push things too hard, she had been through a lot and, anyway, for the time being they had other, more important, matters to consider.

'What we've got to do is to work out what's going to happen once we get back to the UK. It's going to be another week or so before we make a landfall and then we'll have to lie low until the meeting with Campbell-West. Once we're back, if word gets out too soon, we could well find ourselves charged with kidnapping and worse. Unless we hand CW over as a quid pro quo, we'll not get any favours from the British authorities.' The conversation coming onto a subject she felt qualified to comment on, Sarah, once more in her usual state of total nakedness, lifted herself onto one elbow and smiled.

'You see, even if we get back, you are going to need me to get you off the hook with the authorities. I really wish you would accept me as an ally. I can give you a lot of stuff on CW quite apart from the Algoan affair. He's had a finger in just about every sort of crooked deal you can imagine. Drugs, arms, extortion, prostitution – I'm talking high-class stuff here, not streetwalkers – and he's never baulked at murder either.

He's still got friends in high places you know, government ministers and the like in Brazil, Argentina – Europe too. Not only can you bring him within grasp of the long arm of the law and get your own personal revenge, I reckon I can make a few thousand pounds selling my story to the papers – a story which, incidentally, will do you two no harm at all in ensuring that CW, if and when he comes to trial, won't have a hope in hell of getting a sympathetic hearing. By the time I've thrown in a few spicy details about his sexual proclivities, his reputation will be destroyed forever.' Lying back, she closed her eyes, not expecting any response, apparently feeling, perhaps with good reason, that this was an offer they would not be able to refuse. Blandly indifferent, she applied a further generous palmful of sun oil to the magnificent breasts.

Latimer was, as he had been from the beginning, still inclined to consider her story genuine and he was also very aware that if, on top of delivering CW up to the City of London Police, a really juicy exposé on the man and his tawdry twilight world was to break in the nationals, it would go a long way towards ensuring that both their own popularity and his disgrace were enhanced. All the more satisfying would be the opportunity to name some of the big City financiers who had connived to assist his escape and who, presumably, were still prepared to fund many of his overseas deals.

It would be simple enough to set up. He had the necessary contacts in Fleet Street. McColl, for instance, would give his eyeteeth to write the story and he still carried enough clout in the right circles to guarantee its appearing in print. There was an element of risk, though. What he wanted more than anything, however, was to shield Chantelle from the knowledge or, since no one would ever now be able to confirm or deny it, the suspicion that David was the father of the child Sarah carried. He considered that in this scenario Sarah, avaricious bitch that she was, would prefer CW to be recognised as the father, adding as it would another sensational angle to an already lurid story, rather than score a few cheap points over Chantelle.

Later that day when the sun had gone and only a spider's touch of orange sky on the horizon betrayed its departing presence, he sat in the stern, steering by hand and watching the specks of phosphorescence that drifted by on the black waters. He had hoisted the spinnaker and, with the moderate southwesterly lifting them smoothly onwards, he sipped at a can of beer and wondered where they should lie low once they made landfall. He thought that somewhere in the west country would be safest, not too near the floating shanty towns of the Solent and its inquisitive crowds. Cornwall had a lot going for it. Not over-populated by the sailing fraternity and with good railway links to London, it would be a convenient base from which to operate, pending the showdown with Campbell-West. Maybe they would slip into one of the creeks of the River Fal, waters he knew well, and lie at anchor there. He would phone McColl the moment they arrived and hope he was available at short notice to write the piece. But all this was a week off and 1,000 sea miles distant. He dearly would have loved to talk to Sarah in confidence, hopefully to clear up the ambivalence of her place in the scheme of things, but the cramped conditions on *Revenge* made that virtually impossible.

As he steered on through the night his thoughts went more and more often to Chantelle. In a scant few days, their relationship had changed completely, yet he was still far from certain how she felt about him. Sooner or later he knew he would have to push things to a head but just now he felt it best simply to let matters take their course.

He could see her sitting below at the chart table, her back towards him, the single light by which she read diffusing into a pale halo through the ash-blonde hair. She was flicking through the pages of some paperback or other. As he watched he felt an urge to kiss the offered nape of her neck. She turned, catching his gaze, and, as if reading his thoughts, smiled, put the book down and climbed into the cockpit beside him. The fragrance of soap came to him.

'Are you going to stay out here all night?' she enquired, her arms going about his neck. 'Now that we've got rid of all the weaponry, the aft cabin seems to be going spare. Sarah's sleeping up forward so I thought we might take advantage.'

He knew instantly what she was offering.

'Give me a couple of minutes to get the spinnaker down. I'll put a working jib up, then if we get a sudden wind shift we won't end up with a problem – I've always had aesthetic objections to coitus interruptus.' He kissed her and this time she responded, the mouth opening up like a scarlet orchid, her hot tongue probing his mouth like an insistent serpent as she crushed her body into his.

'You've got five minutes,' she whispered. Then, giving his genitals a friendly squeeze, she disappeared below.

Twenty Three

Hamble Village, Hampshire

Latimer was busy in the cellar when the phone rang. Pottering about among the dusty bottles and other abandoned detritus of former occupants. Since his return to the cottage two days previously, he had spent most of his time getting it into some sort of order, aware that he was likely to have visitors in the near future. Laying down his spade he sprinted up the rickety stairs, snatching the phone from the wall, his heart pounding. It was, as he had expected, Campbell-West and the man was clearly worried.

'I want a meeting, Latimer – soon. We can work this thing out but I must see Sarah before I agree to anything. I need to be certain she's alright.'

'No deals. You come to London next week and we'll have a talk about old times. I'll introduce you to a very nice policeman who's just dying to meet you. Then, and only then, Sarah goes free. If you don't turn up, you'll never see her again. And don't think we don't mean what we say. Remember, Campbell-West, it's not just up to me any more. You know what women are like – after what happened to David, Chantelle is just itching to arrange a messy accident.'

'For God's sake, man, Sarah had no part in the Algoan affair. Please, tell me where she is.'

Latimer smiled to himself. The man didn't miss a trick.

Even now he was trying to glean what information he could.

'Not here, so don't try anything silly. She's being very well looked after. Shackled hand and foot, gagged and blindfolded, in a darkened room. We've still got the heroin and Groose's needle. One false move and she starts a course of injections that'll just blow her mind. When the police find her she'll simply be another anonymous junkie who overdosed in a London squat.'

Latimer felt no remorse at torturing the man at the other end of the line like this. In fact, Sarah was aboard *Revenge*, anchored in an idyllic creek of the Fal and spilling the beans to McColl. However, it would do no harm at all to apply the screw another turn or so.

'She wasn't very well yesterday though, pains in the abdomen. I don't imagine it's anything too serious though.'

'I don't believe I'm hearing this,' Campbell-West's tone was of moral outrage. 'Don't you understand? She's pregnant, it could be anything. You'll kill them both.'

'That depends on you.'

'Let me talk to her then.'

'No.'

Pulling the net curtain aside fractionally he stared through the flyblown window. Just above the low privet hedge that marked the boundary of the long front garden, the red top of a car was visible. This was the second time he had seen it that morning. His voice took on a rather schoolmasterish tone.

'This seems to be turning into a rather negative sort of discussion, CW. You know what you have to do. We'll see you next week at Correlli's – your treat. Oh, and do try to get a corner table, will you? We'll have a lot to talk about and I wouldn't want strangers eavesdropping.' He rang off and after five minutes returned once more to the window, pulling the curtain cautiously aside. The red car had gone.

The call, he was sure, had been made from within the UK so Campbell-West was back in the country and, if he had discovered the phone number, would certainly have no trouble locating the cottage. The way Latimer saw it, in CW's position the only possible means of attack remaining to him was to seize Latimer and then try to bargain with Chantelle for the release of Sarah in an exchange of hostages. However, he suspected they would not be likely to rush matters for fear of triggering Chantelle into wreaking a bloody revenge. In the time left to Campbell-West, before the meeting next week, he guessed they would concentrate on trying to locate Sarah. If they failed in that then they would be left with no choice but to grab him.

It was unlikely that CW would come out into the open of his own volition since he had entered the country illegally, already a wanted man, and faced instant arrest if his presence came to the attention of the police. Even assuming that Behan had been picked up from the life raft he, too, was a wanted man although, with the current state of relations between London and Buenos Aires, his status was anyone's guess. Most likely Campbell-West would recruit local talent to do his dirty work, initially at least; perhaps Behan would be brought on for the coup de grâce. He would have to keep on his toes.

He returned to the cellar and, in the cobwebbed gloom, set about putting the finishing touches to his interrupted work. Satisfied, he washed, shaved and put on a fresh set of clothes. Finally he checked that his wallet, the only luggage he would be carrying, contained all his credit cards and driving licence, together with enough cash to keep him going for a day or two. Thrusting the wallet into his back pocket he cast an unsentimental glance around him. The place was an absolute pigsty; he was glad he wouldn't be coming back.

Before departing he took a last cautious look out of the windows, both to the front and rear. Outside, all seemed quiet. The house stood a little way back from the road, surrounded by a largish garden that had long since gone to weeds. Breast high in places, nettles and thistles, cow parsley and dandelion were just starting their annual advance on to the narrow path that led down to the road. Never a keen gardener, Latimer liked it that way.

Pulling the door closed behind him he walked out into the spring sunlight, his jacket slung over his shoulder, and sauntered off in the direction of the village. The last thing he wanted was for anyone who might be watching to think that he was going somewhere in particular.

About 100 yards down the narrow lane, parked a little off the road in the deeply rutted entrance to a field, he became aware of a small red car, a Fiat he thought. His heart began to thump as he drew near, his shoulders tensing as, keeping his eyes firmly to the front, he passed with as good a show of indifference as he could muster. If they meant to seize him they would never get a better chance than right now. His fears were to prove unwarranted for he was allowed to pass unhindered although, after he had walked some distance, he fancied he heard the distant slamming of doors. His mouth was dry – he could use a drink.

Aware that his standing in the Jolly Sailor would probably remain at a low ebb well into the next century, and despite the fact that his appearance – fit, clean-shaven and bronzed – would probably have meant he would have passed unrecognised anyway, he elected to walk the extra half mile or so to the King's Arms. Here he had been an infrequent visitor and his reputation had suffered in direct proportion. At just after eleven, the place was almost empty.

The last time he had been here had been the day they had departed for the Azores. He looked at the window seat where he had sat with David and Chantelle and where they had told him, like parents warning a child about the bogie man, of Behan and Groose. It seemed a lifetime away, yet how long was it since they had blithely embarked on their deadly crusade? Three weeks? Putting all these distracting thoughts out of mind he ordered a pint of bitter and sat himself down in a corner seat that gave a good view of the door.

Within five minutes they came in, two youngish men, maybe thirty years old or so. Both were bulky individuals; one, slightly the taller and with features and hair that hinted at negro blood, took the room in at one smooth glance. The other, blond and beefy with heavily tattooed forearms that publicised the man's undying support for Tottenham Hotspur, went straight to the bar and ordered two pints of lager. As they lounged nonchalently at the bar Latimer was aware that, although they were looking away from him, their eyes followed his every move in the big Victorian mirror that backed the rows of bottles beyond.

Was this just a reconnaissance party, he wondered, or would these be the ones designated to snatch him? Outside, through the reeded glass of the door, he could make out the blurred outlines of a red car and the head of the driver behind the wheel. Blurred it might have been but it was a blur that could very easily have been Behan. Throwing back his beer he stood up and went to the bar, elbowing his way a little clumsily between the two strangers. If they were put out by his lack of manners it didn't show.

'Same again, please,' he called loudly to the barmaid who was already serving in the other bar and hence slightly miffed at his impatience. At the same time he staggered, tottering slightly against the tattooed man. 'Oops. Sorry, my dear fellow.' The other glared but, again his clumsiness drew no comment. With a dismissive sniff the barmaid set his beer heavily down before him and he returned to his seat.

Well, he thought, they've had a good look at me so they shouldn't be in any doubt as to who I am. Just got to wait for developments now. He hoped his purchase of a fresh pint of beer would be sufficient for them to deduce that he intended to remain there for a while yet and, if they wanted to give the cottage a quick once over, now would be as good a time as any. Leaving their drinks half-finished on the bar, they ambled out and seconds later he saw the blur of the car draw away outside. Presumably they were confident they knew where to find him should they need to do so later.

Sipping his beer he allowed a good five minutes to avoid any connection being made between him and the others and then, draining his glass, stepped outside, heading away from the cottage towards the railway station. He knew there was a train at midday that, providing he made the connection at Exeter on time, would get him to Truro and back on board *Revenge* by that evening. At the station he bought an early edition of the *Hampshire Post* and sat on the platform awaiting the train.

At five to twelve he heard the muffled thunderclap and smiled, folding his paper the better to attack the crossword. Ahead of him, rising above the tops of the intervening trees, a column of acrid black smoke billowed skywards. Down the platform, a couple of kids danced about their mother in delight, pointing excitedly at this unexpected display of pyrotechnics. Latimer felt very gratified. It was amazing what you could do by leaking the contents of ten bottles of propane gas into a cellar with a few matches jammed into an internal door, set to ignite by the friction generated when it was opened. Climbing aboard the near-empty train he slammed the door firmly on the sound of sirens.

Making his connection at Exeter by the skin of his teeth he went directly to the buffet car and ordered dinner. By British Rail standards of cuisine it was one of their better days and, as the train thundered into the gathering dusk, he proceeded to demolish a half bottle of claret, trying to work out what their next move should be.

If, as he suspected, the man in the car outside the King's Arms had been Behan, his elimination in the holocaust at the cottage now left Campbell-West friendless. The manner of his despatch would also go far to underline just how serious they were in their threats to Sarah. He took no pleasure in his success in removing the Argentinian from the game, but equally felt no remorse. Behan had killed Collins, now he had, he hoped, killed Behan. The other two were just unlucky to be standing in the way. Now, with Campbell-West isolated and without allies, it seemed they just had to wait for the showdown the following week.

He had wished it could be sooner, but McColl had been most insistent that he would need at least that period to get the exposé on CW properly written up and ready to go to press. It was essential that news of Campbell-West's arrest and Sarah's story broke simultaneously if it was to have maximum impact. Of their own roles in the affair they had been scrupulously non-communicative, for fear of incriminating themselves. McColl knew nothing of David's death nor would he be told of Latimer's casual incineration of Behan and his henchmen. They had simply offered him a story on the grounds that Sarah wanted to return to the UK and was prepared to dish the dirt on her lover. For a newshound like McColl it had been enough.

Campbell-West had treated her abominably, she told him, and in support of this total fiction had cited imaginary lovers, male and female, famous and obscure, to ensure the story would appeal to the widest possible audience. It had the Fleet Street man slavering for more. Campbell-West had abused her physically, too. He was a pervert, she said, and threw herself into graphic descriptions of humiliation and degradation. More importantly, the political and financial revelations she paraded before him were dynamite. Significantly, unlike some of the more lurid personal aspects, these were totally factual, requiring no exaggeration or invention on her part. The man moved in a world of high-living and intrigue and the story she told was developing into a cocktail of sleaze and power politics that would have the punters fighting for their copies at the news stands. McColl could not believe his luck at finding such a story dropped into his lap.

It was dark by the time Latimer reached Truro and he spent an irritating half-an-hour before finding a cab to take him down to the riverside village of Malpas, the nearest jetty to the creek where *Revenge* was lying at anchor. From there he would have to row the half mile or so downstream. Before that, however, he thought he would fortify himself with a well-deserved couple of quick ones in the Magpie.

As he pushed through the heavy, brass-handled doors it was with some surprise that the first face he saw on entering the noisy, good-humoured atmosphere of the pub, was that of McColl. The sleeves of his shirt were rolled untidily up his arms and his tie hung loosely about his neck. The journalist, clearly well oiled, greeted him like a long lost brother.

'Come and have a drink, old boy,' he bellowed affably. 'Come and celebrate the completion of our Herculean labours.'

Latimer looked around him, he did not want to attract any undue attention to himself. If he was ever implicated in the explosion at the cottage, his story was going to be that he had been on board *Revenge* at the time. At that stage of the proceedings, with the jukebox going full belt, however, no one spared him a second glance.

Taking the proffered drink Latimer stared as McColl, with trembling hand, lit a cigarette, noisily exhaling a wreathing cloud of foul-smelling blue smoke about his head.

'You've finished? I thought you said it would take until next week.'

McColl looked over his shoulder suspiciously, fearful that his scoop might be compromised. Then he tapped his nose conspiratorially.

'Got it all on tape, old boy. Every word of it. It's bloody fantastic, it'll be the biggest thing since the Profumo affair. I've got names in the government, in the City – everywhere.

234

I've written you into it as well; with a bit of luck you'll get a fair crack of the whip now. I reckon you could get monumental compensation if you got yourself a decent lawyer.' Discovering his glass to be empty, McColl's bloodhound eyes ranged desperately down the bar, trying to gain the attention of the beleaguered landlord. His immediate needs satisfied, he continued.

'I'm travelling back to London tonight, I want to drop this little lot on my editor's desk first thing tomorrow. It's terrific stuff. Don't worry, I won't let it break until Campbell-West is in custody – I want pictures of that too. I'll have a photographer outside Correlli's on Wednesday.'

Latimer nodded, it all seemed like good news. There was no point in McColl remaining on board if he had everything he needed: conditions were cramped enough.

'Right then, Sandy, I must be getting back.' He held out his hand and McColl, briefly thrown by the problem of co-ordinating glass and cigarette, shook it warmly. 'There's no love lost between the women. I don't want a cat-fight on my hands at this stage of the proceedings.' He crossed his fingers. 'Oh, I meant to ask, did Sarah say anything about the child?'

'Only that she wanted it to be a British subject and hoped it wouldn't grow up like its father. She wants me to include a quote to the effect that she is only selling her story to ensure the kid gets a proper education.'

'She's all heart that one.'

Rowing back to the boat through the cool blackness of the night, the only sounds the nervous calls of roosting birds uneasy at his shadowy passing, Latimer began to relax. It seemed that the parenthood of the child was not going to become an issue. In five days they would travel up to London and the whole affair would come to its concluding act. His revenge on Campbell-West would be complete, especially if, as McColl had suggested, it meant his credibility in the City being restored – he could consider returning to the world of finance once more.

As he tied the rowing boat to the stern of *Revenge*, Chantelle came out into the cockpit, kissing him warmly on the mouth, moulding her body into his as her arms went round his neck.

'I've missed you,' she whispered as his hands found the heavy warmth of her breasts.

'Me too.' He buried his face in the softness of her hair. 'Me too.'

Later, as they lay in the after cabin, she told him that there had been a report on the six o'clock news about the explosion at the cottage. Three men, all apparently with criminal records, had been badly burned in a mystery explosion at a cottage on the Hamble. Police were treating the case as an attempted burglary that had gone disastrously wrong. They were trying to contact the owner who was believed to be abroad.

As he drifted into sleep Latimer felt a warm glow that he had been able to avenge David's murder so dramatically and yet so elegantly. Although it seemed he had not succeeded in killing the man, he was out of the game now. He prayed that Behan would be scarred for life.

At about two in the morning the sound of clumsy rowing and the solid thump of a boat coming alongside came to him. He wasn't sure, but thought he could also hear the strains of rather unmelodic singing. With a groan, he swung out of the bunk and pulled his trousers on. Chantelle opened her eyes with a sigh.

'What's going on?'

He smiled grimly.

'Bloody McColl has obviously decided to join us after all. I expect he lingered in the bar too long and missed his train. I'd better go and help him aboard, I suppose. We don't want the drunken bastard to drown after all this. You stay there.

I'll be right back.'

His eyes straining into the darkness, he climbed the companionway and stepped towards the tottering figure, now struggling to raise a leg above the level of the guard rail. He smiled.

'I thought we'd seen the last of you, Sandy old son,' he said, stretching out a steadying arm. Fingers grasped his forearm in a grip of steel.

'Oh no, Mistah Latimer, but you're sure going to wish you had.'

The cold button of a pistol muzzle was pressed to the exact centre of his forehead and he dropped his hands to his sides as the figure stood upright.

It was Behan.

Twenty Four

When Latimer regained consciousness he was tied hand and foot, lying propped in a corner of the cabin. How long he had been out, felled by a blow from the Argentinian's pistol, he could only guess. The boat was in darkness, the only light the square of silver moonlight that fell through the hatch, gleaming and fading with the passing clouds. From the other side of the cabin Chantelle, similarly bound, stared at him.

'John, wake up,' she hissed desperately. 'You must wake up.'

He shook his head and, blinking to clear his eyes of the blood that ran from the wound in his scalp, tested the ropes that cut into his wrists. A moment's straining told him he was wasting his time and he lay back.

'Where's Behan?'

'He's gone ashore with Sarah. I think Campbell-West's here to pick her up. They've been gone about twenty minutes so we haven't got long. What we need is a knife to cut these ropes. I've looked everywhere I can think of but he threw all the obvious stuff over the side before he went.'

Ever cautious, the Argentinian had removed all the cutlery from the galley and dumped it into the black waters of the creek. As they hopped and rolled around the confined cabin it soon became clear that nothing even vaguely suitable had been overlooked. Moreover, the distant rhythmic plashing of rowing heralded the return of Behan. Latimer looked about him desperately. Then he remembered.

'The chart table, there's the steak knife in there – the one we took when we had dinner with Campbell-West back on São Miguel. I threw it in there when we made our getaway.'

Standing with some difficulty and with his hands behind him, he lifted the hinged top of the table and reached in, his fingers sliding under the sheaf of charts as the thump of the dinghy at the stern sent a tremor through the boat. As the clatter of oars being unshipped came to him, he finally found the knife, lowering the table-top gently and throwing himself back into his original position in the corner of the cabin and feigning unconsciousness.

As Behan came awkwardly through the narrow companionway his massive bulk seemed to fill the confined area, his vengeful presence permeating every corner of the saloon. He switched on the lights and, after a quick glance about him to ensure that all was as he had left it, smiled down evilly at the inert form of Latimer. He brought his face close, the foetid smell of his breath rank to the apparently insensible man, and patted the lolling cheek.

'Looks like time to say goodbye, limey,' he leered. 'Pity you're not awake to appreciate it – I'm really going to enjoy this.'

Latimer, filled with dread yet, after all this, determined to make some show of defiance, opened his eyes and stared back unblinkingly into the pale, washed-out eyes. Behan's eyebrows were scorched and blackened and the man's face was an unnatural reddish hue. He must have escaped death by inches. Latimer had the knife blade in position against his ropes now but dared not start to saw at his bonds with the man so close. Finding him awake clearly improved the shining hour for Behan.

'Ah, so the limey is with us. Good. Now I start the barbecue.'

'What are you going to do?' asked Chantelle hoarsely, knowing that Latimer would have no chance of freeing himself while he remained the sole subject of Behan's attention. She was successful in diverting his attention for her words caused the giant to move away from Latimer across to the starboard side of the cabin where she lay tightly trussed. Sitting down beside her he ran a bloodstained hand through her hair.

'Ah Señora, I'm afraid this is goodbye for all of us.' His hand went to the buttons of the checked shirt she wore, unfastening them with slow deliberation and pulling the shirt back over her smooth shoulders. His eyes feasted on the full breasts that strained against the clinging silk of her bra. Kissing her unresisting mouth, his tongue probed wetly as he reached behind her, his hand searching for the clasp. Latimer gently began to slice at his ropes.

'Please don't hurt me,' she pleaded, as he clumsily pawed at her now totally exposed breasts. He appeared not to hear. At first he was gentle, but slowly began to increase the pressure of his fingers, pummelling and twisting the smooth flesh like a baker kneading dough, his gaze fixed on her face, luxuriating in her distress as she writhed and shifted under his grasp. It was painful, but Chantelle was well aware that behind the fixed humourless smile the man was becoming aroused by the situation.

And it was true, for he revelled in his total domination of her. There had been other times like this, back in the old days when a soldier's duty had been a straightforward matter of getting results for the people who paid and fed him. Other times when women, women older and uglier than this, had pleaded with him for mercy and when he had permitted them to extend their lifespan by a few minutes in return for gratifying his desires. As Latimer continued to work at his bonds, she laid her head against Behan's massive chest. 'Don't hurt me,' she said faintly. 'I'll do anything you want – anything.'

Behan glanced at his watch. Campbell-West would be growing impatient on the jetty and he was not a man to be kept waiting. On the other hand, this lovely gringo bitch was a great temptation. She sensed his predicament and, fearing he would move before Latimer had time to free himself, lent forward to nuzzle her face into the tautness of his lap. The Argentinian had brought a jerry can of petrol into the cabin and she guessed that they were intended to burn to death. She must try harder.

'Untie me,' she whispered, 'I can't do you any harm. Untie me and I'll show you what I can do.' For a moment she thought she had failed for he stood up as though to leave, then he turned and she saw the big service pistol in his hand. She had won them a little time but Behan remained very much in the saddle.

'Stand up, Señora.' Obediently, she did as he commanded and he deftly removed the ropes from her ankles, although not from her wrists. He then pulled off her jeans and the briefs beneath so that, save for the shirt twisted about her arms, she stood naked before him as his hand went to the buckle of his belt and he pulled his trousers down around his knees, his eyes never leaving hers as he released his stiffening penis.

'Now, Señora,' he glanced at his watch, 'you have five minutes. Show me what you can do. If it pleases me, who knows, I may even take you with me.'

Chantelle knew that if they were to have any chance of survival she must prolong the performance as long as possible; once Behan had been satisfied they were as good as dead. As she dropped to her knees she glanced at Latimer who stared blankly back at her, no indication in his expression as to whether he was making progress on the rope or not. In fact he was, but it was a slow painstaking business for the knife was awkwardly placed between his hands.

As Chantelle knelt before her captor, eyes fixed on the

man's huge and urgent erection, Latimer began to work faster, well aware of what she was trying to do. Several minutes passed, minutes silent save for Behan's occasional low grunt of animal pleasure and the liquid sounds of her mouth. Despite the sounds of approval, however, he was a man in a hurry and Chantelle's efforts were not producing the required effect sufficiently rapidly. Seizing her by the throat, he disengaged himself with a snort of impatience and lifted her gasping to her feet. Picking her up like a doll he threw her, face downwards, spread-eagled across the table. Her chin slammed down on the table with a sickening thud and for a moment she lost consciousness. As she regained her senses his intentions became obvious as, with an effortless thrust, he forced her legs wide with his knees.

'That was very nice, Señora, but I am in something of a hurry. Now let me show you what I can do.' He moved in towards her and, simultaneously, the ropes at Latimer's wrists parted. Careful not to make his move until he had the knife securely in his hand he watched as Behan attempted to penetrate the now wildly struggling Chantelle. 'Hold still, you bitch, or I will kill you now,' he hissed in her ear, crushing her beneath his bulk until finally, exhausted, she lay still and submissive. 'Just hold still, honey,' he grunted, moving back a little, the better to renew his assault on her. 'You won't feel a thing.' Before he could consummate the act, however, Latimer struck.

With his ankles still tied, he was aware that he would get only one chance and that it would have to be decisive. Taking a deep breath he stood up, precariously hobbled, rearing above the locked figures on the table and plunged the knife into Behan's neck, an inch below the right ear. With its slim narrow blade it was not, he was well aware, an ideal stabbing weapon and he feared it might snap if it met bone on its deadly journey. As, with a roar of agony, the giant figure reared up, spine arched like a strung bow, his head crashed solidly into the deckhead.

Fearful that he had missed his target and near to panic, he wrenched the knife free of the grasp of the neck muscle and, with his left arm locked about the man's throat, thrust it savagely into the kidney area several times in rapid succession, fascinated to find how easily it slid in and out of its target, black blood running in a warm, dark rivulet along his arm. Finally, with a crash, the jerking figure toppled to the deck where, after several rictus spasms, it finally lay still, the gouts of blood pumping from the throat and back slowly stemming as the heart eventually failed.

Bending down, Latimer sliced through the ropes on his ankles and, ignoring the pain as the blood began to circulate, went to Chantelle who stood, her arms still bound behind her, looking down at the dead giant at her feet. He could imagine her feelings and slipped a comforting arm about her trembling shoulders.

'Don't let it get to you,' he said softly. 'You saved us both.' She shuddered, then began to sob convulsively and he held her close, gently kissing her tightly closed eyelids. 'It's all over,' he kept repeating. 'It's all over.' Of course, it wasn't.

'He's out there, John,' she said, flatly logical once her nerves had recovered from the ordeal at Behan's hands. She pointed to the awful contorted cadaver at their feet. 'He's out there on the jetty, waiting for this scumbag to submit his report on our deaths. He's the bastard who started all this – who ruined us, who killed David. McColl is dead too – drowned. Behan took great delight in telling me while you were out for the count. Yet another accident to protect Campbell-West – so there's no big story about to break. He's got his precious Sarah back and he's thinking he's going to fly out scot-free.' She spat her words. 'Fuck that, John, we can't turn back now, he's going to pay in full.'

Ten minutes later Latimer rowed the dinghy down the black cathedral of the tree-lined creek as the first bloody flashes of flame flickered like lizard tongues from the hull of the doomed *Revenge*. She had served them well and now was to be sacrificed to provide them with an alibi and Behan with a Viking funeral. They had burned their boats in every sense and Latimer wondered if things would ever be the same again. In the past two days he had killed and maimed like a bloody maniac and yet they still hadn't achieved their objective. The truth of the matter was that he no longer cared about Campbell-West. Chantelle sat silent in the stern as they steadily closed on the low shadowy outline of the jetty and Latimer found himself questioning why, having come so close to being killed, they were going on.

All he wanted was to take Chantelle away somewhere safe and to attempt to bring her back to something close to normality. In the nightmare that had been enacted before his eyes back on the boat all his vitriolic hatred had drained away. He didn't want it anymore – he just wanted to get back to real life. Chantelle, however, seemed never for a moment to doubt what their next move should be.

McColl! Latimer stared into the night. Another death to add to the final tally. Somewhere out there on the ebbing black waters of the Fal the body of the shambolic McColl was drifting out on the tide; he had emptied his last bottle and met his last deadline. The old anger surged again and he pulled the harder at the oars.

As they came beneath the lee of the jetty he could just make out the bulk of a big black limo parked on the road above. Slipping Behan's pistol from his belt he held a finger to his lips and indicated that she was to stay in the boat until he called for her. Crouching low, he mounted the creaking, weed-carpeted wooden steps that led up to the road, briefly pausing behind the low wall as he checked that no one was lying in wait. Campbell-West's car was parked, lights out, about twenty yards down the road and, satisfied there were no traps, Latimer edged carefully forward in the shadows.

In the heat of what clearly was a highly emotional reunion, they had been otherwise occupied as he slipped into the rear seat. Sarah drew back from Campbell-West in a hurry, pulling her skirt down over her knees and brushing her hair into order. Neither gave him a second glance. Assuming Behan had accomplished his mission, Campbell-West didn't even bother to look over his shoulder as he reached to start the car.

'All OK?'

Latimer felt like God.

'Perfect CW. Just perfect.' He pressed the pistol into Sarah's hair. 'Just wait a minute or two and we'll have a full team.'

Ten minutes later, Chantelle covering Sarah with the pistol in the back and the men in the front, they were driving through the darkened streets of Truro.

'I must admit, I'm a little lost for words, John.' Whatever Campbell-West was feeling he didn't let it show and, recalling the Machiavellian twists that had almost dragged them to destruction over the past weeks, Latimer was careful not to let his concentration waver for a second as the man continued. 'I realise it's probably too late to suggest a compromise but, if there is anything I can do that might persuade you to let me go, I'm always ready to deal. What do you want? Money? Property?'

'There's nothing. Just keep driving.'

'Where are we going?'

It was a good question and one that Latimer had been asking himself for some time. It was nearly midnight on Friday and he didn't think that handing Campbell-West over to the City police on a Saturday morning, a day when the City of London was virtually shut down, would have the impact he wanted. Anyway, to ensure that there was no cover-up it was essential that their arrival received maximum publicity; with McColl dead he would need to let the papers know about the return of the prodigal.

'The next phone box you see, pull over. I'll see if I can arrange some suitable accommodation.' As they eventually drew to a halt he looked to Chantelle. 'Keep that gun on her all the time. While I'm phoning you can tell CW all about the baby you lost thanks to his thieving ways. Explain how it has rather jaundiced your whole view of motherhood.'

The phone booth stank of urine and stale cigarette smoke, and he was surprised to find that, even in rural areas, whores still scrawled their numbers on every available space. It took several minutes before he got a response and several more before he had satisfactorily explained the situation.

'We need somewhere to lie low until Monday,' he explained. 'If you don't want to get involved I will quite understand. I just thought you might like to be in on the end of this thing, seeing as how you were part of it. Apart from that we've got nowhere to go.' There was no hesitation at the other end and he smiled. 'Thanks. We should be with you in about three hours I guess.'

Back at the car Campbell-West was beginning to get edgy.

'Where are we going?' he demanded shortly. Latimer indicated that he was to move out of the driver's seat before answering. Adjusting the seat and mirrors he smiled broadly at Campbell-West.

'We're taking you home, Peter. We're going to spend a couple of days at Fairview. Victoria's really looking forward to seeing you again.'

Twenty Five

Inspector Ellis, putting in a row of runner beans when his wife appeared on the patio to advise him there was an urgent call, had not been best pleased to have his weekend disturbed. To be summoned to the depths of Oxfordshire by Latimer, someone whose name and criminal context he had at first barely recollected, was testing his devotion to duty to its limits. However, when the bait was as succulent as that shifty bastard Sir Peter, fucking, Campbell-West, he had little option but to respond.

Memories of twice returning home empty-handed, once from Spain and then, later, from Brazil, when the errant knight's legal advisers had proved too slick for Scotland Yard's best brains, had rather soured Ellis's view of the whole affair. Until Latimer had called he had considered the case closed and even now took a stance that he would believe it when he saw it. Nevertheless, business was business and he certainly didn't want anybody else getting the glory and the television interviews, least of all some country bumpkin.

So, setting aside his honest horticultural toil, he made the necessary arrangements, collected the essential warrants and arrived at Fairview a little after three in the afternoon. He was accompanied by two other officers and, in token of Sarah's presence, a policewoman. As the two unmarked cars

247

drew to a halt on the broad gravel forecourt, Latimer went down to greet them with a certain amount of misgiving.

'Now let me get this straight, sir,' the inspector said when they were all seated around the huge, yet tastefully furnished drawing room. 'You claim to be holding Sir Peter Campbell-West in this house?'

'That's right. We knew there were warrants out for his apprehension so we made a citizen's arrest.' Latimer's tone was throwaway, as though such things happened every day. He was intent on remaining as vague about the details as possible, grimly aware that his own activities over the past few weeks – kidnapping, arson, murder – were sufficient, should they ever become general knowledge, to see him sharing a cell with CW for the next ten years at least.

They had all, CW and Sarah included, discussed and agreed what their story would be but were under no illusion that it would need great care in the telling to avoid incriminating slip-ups. CW, recognising the weakness of his own position, had, it seemed, resigned himself to facing the music over the Algoan affair. In return for this they had agreed not to muddy the waters further by introducing the subject of drugs or the deaths of Collins and McColl. In a counter-concession Campbell-West would conveniently forget the kidnapping of Sarah and the deaths of Groose and Behan. In all, it seemed a fairly evenly balanced equation.

Sarah, perhaps frightened by the summary removal, at Campbell-West's orders, of both David and McColl had remained very tight-lipped and was clearly reluctant to get further embroiled. The tapes of her interviews, it seemed, must have gone into the river with McColl and Latimer could understand that she was unlikely to repeat her story until Campbell-West was safely behind bars. Thus far, he was obviously unaware of her collaboration and, during his temporary imprisonment at Fairview, his overriding concern remained her wellbeing. This manifested itself in a continual stream of messages of reassurance, conveyed via Latimer, from his bedroom prison. To Latimer the whole story seemed like a precarious edifice that might collapse like a house of cards at any moment. However, if all went according to plan...

'Where exactly was this citizen's arrest made?'

Latimer, in no doubt as to the substance of his answer, nevertheless racked his brains for the most appropriate form of words, something that would not overly complicate matters or beg further questions. To his relief, the door swung open and all heads turned as Victoria, bearing a trayful of tea things, advanced towards them. The silver pot, sugar tongs and neatly folded napkins all suggested she was entertaining a meeting of the local WVS rather than the forces of law and order.

'Why, here of course, inspector,' she beamed. 'When Peter told me he was intending to pay me a visit I immediately got on to John and Mrs Kolowitz. We've been waiting here for him to arrive for the last three days. My goodness, I think I've played more whist this week than in the entire preceding year.'

The three days supposedly spent waiting for Campbell-West at Fairview were an important part of the story, distancing Latimer as it did from the savage events at the cottage and on the boat. The inspector, already more concerned about the problems of balancing a cup of scalding tea on one knee and taking notes on the other, seemed to accept this without demur.

'What brought him here? I would have thought that it would have taken wild horses to drag him back, all things considered. He's looking at a ten-stretch minimum, shyster lawyers or no.'

Perhaps gratified to hear of the prospects facing her incarcerated husband Victoria smiled warmly, settling herself cosily beside him on the settee and crossing her long elegant legs before replying.

'True to form he was hoping to organise a divorce and to get rich at the same time, inspector. You see, although we were separated several years ago, we still have a lot of property over here that's registered in our joint names and, greedy as ever, he's very keen to get his hands on as much of it as he can. What he wants is to be able to sell his share in several large arable farms we jointly own in East Anglia. Without my agreement I'm afraid that it could be a very drawn-out procedure.' She giggled, a hand going to her mouth to stifle such wicked utterances.

'I'm afraid I've been rather uncooperative. He's been writing to me on the subject for months now and, since I chose not to answer, he decided he would risk a brief visit to his native land in the hope of changing my mind. I understand that he has severe cash-flow problems and I think he must have felt that things had quietened down sufficiently over here to make it worth the risk. He entered the country from Ireland by the way – flew into Shannon and then came across on the Dublin – Liverpool ferry.'

She laid a confiding hand on Ellis's knee, the gesture causing his teacup to rattle audibly in its saucer. 'He was always such a bully, inspector, that I felt it best that I should have some moral assistance on hand. Of course, John and Chantelle were the natural candidates, seeing how badly they suffered from his swindling ways. The idea of actually arresting him didn't occur to me at first but when they suggested it I saw that they were quite right. It was our civic duty. The man's a criminal and, what's worse, greedy to the point of vulgarity.'

Latimer held his breath, waiting to see how her story would go down with this hard-bitten copper whose appearance on the scene four years ago had marked the beginning of the Campbell-West affair. His fears were unwarranted for, in the presence of such graciousness, the inspector seemed totally disarmed. He had seen a great deal of greed in his time in the Fraud Squad and he was readily inclined to accept this as a credible motive for CW returning home. Truth to tell, hardly able to believe his luck, Ellis was pleased to find that the whole case seemed to be evolving in such a refreshingly straightforward manner. The last thing he wanted at this stage was complications.

'Where is Sir Peter now, Lady Campbell-West?' he asked, putting his notepad down and finishing his tea.

'Upstairs, locked in his bedroom, inspector – and please do call me Victoria.' With a disarming smile she handed him a large brass key and the inspector nodded to the two burly officers.

'Perhaps you'd like to take us up,' he said, a certain amount of grimly pleasurable anticipation evident in his words.

Two hours later they lined up on the broad steps, that led up to the front of the house, like a guard of honour as a hand-cuffed Campbell-West, flanked by the two policemen, was escorted away. As he passed down the line he stopped briefly in front of Latimer and smiled bitterly into his face.

'Looks as though you win after all, Latimer. I'm afraid I underestimated you all down the line. Still, who knows, maybe the game's not over yet.'

He turned away and, as the trio crunched away across the gravel forecourt, Chantelle slipped her arm through Latimer's. Even now, manacled and securely in the hands of the police, the man manifested a tangible presence, a disconcerting ambience of menace.

'What do you think he means by that?' she asked softly. 'Do you think he's told Ellis the story we all agreed, or has he made a full confession?'

'I wouldn't have thought even a vindictive swine like CW would dare go back on our agreement. If the whole tale comes out, even though it would mean a long prison sentence for

251

me, it would be far more damaging to him. We rehearsed him well enough. He knows that, providing he substantiated our tale, we wouldn't drag in unsavoury details like the heroin and the nightsights, or the various bit players, such as Mr Chang, Korean generals and South African intelligence agencies. CW's a pragmatist, he'll do the sensible thing. He'd rather face a fraud charge than get on the wrong side of people like that.

No, he's a wily old bird and I reckon he's counting on his lawyers to drag the thing out. He'll probably have to surrender his passport but if he gets bail he'll be happy enough living over here. On past performance it'll take the Department of Public Prosecutions a year minimum to get all the evidence and witnesses together. That'll give CW's lawyers plenty of time to put together a pretty good case for the defence. No, I don't think he'll go back on his word in this case.' He kissed her forehead and mustered a confident smile. 'Anyway, we'll soon see, here comes Ellis.'

To their relief, the inspector seemed happy enough with the official line and clearly Campbell-West had, in the interests of self-preservation, substantiated the tale.

'I'd like you all to come to Wood Street Police Station on Monday – say around ten o'clock if that's convenient – just to get your statements signed. I expect Sir Peter will be charged at Guildhall Magistrates Court on Monday morning, by the way. You might care to be present, seeing as how you were involved in this from the beginning.' He turned his head to where Sarah hovered uncertainly in the huge doorway. 'I shall be giving Miss Mendelsohn a lift back to London. She's going to stay with her family until matters settle down.' So far as he was concerned Sarah had arrived with Campbell-West from Brazil. No thoughts of drugs, kidnapping or three dead men troubled his mind as he escorted her to the car, notepad already in his hand with a view to preparing his report for the chief as he travelled back to London.

This was better than planting beans any day. As she followed Ellis across the gravel Sarah half-turned and, with a mocking, pouting smile, blew a kiss to Latimer. Chantelle, still smiling, imperceptibly tightened her grip on his arm and growled into his ear.

'Forget it, Latimer – you'd never get bacon for breakfast again.'

As the two police cars pulled away from the house Victoria, enjoying her part in the subterfuge enormously, waved gaily to the inspector who, embarrassed by the antics of this undoubtedly slightly dotty member of the aristocracy, returned the gesture as discreetly as possible.

'Well,' she said, as they disappeared down the drive, 'so far so good. I think we've all earned a drink.' Following in Indian file, they trooped into the house.

It came as a relief to Latimer that Victoria appeared to have accepted Chantelle's presence with good grace and showed no sign of being in the least put out to find her former lover now paying court to another. When they had arrived in the early hours, physically and mentally exhausted from the nightmare episode with Behan and the long drive to Fairview, she had been totally prepared for their appearance. Having taken great pleasure in feeding them royally and then conducting them to their rooms she had, prior to this, delighted in personally locking the door on Campbell-West's bedroom prison.

'It's ironic to think that many a night I've locked myself in there to escape your unwelcome attentions, Peter, and here we are with the roles reversed,' she had said sweetly. 'Sleep tight, darling.'

Now they sat around considering what to do until Monday when Campbell-West would be finally arraigned. Victoria was most pressing in her suggestion that they stay at Fairview and Latimer, aware that his own options for accommodation, both house and boat, were now no longer habitable, would have been more than happy to accept her offer. Chantelle, however, had other ideas.

'It's very kind of you, Victoria, but I think we'd do better to get back to London today. We need to buy some new clothes; remember, practically everything we had went up in flames aboard the boat. If we start now we should get back just before the shops close. David had a flat in Chelsea, friends of ours have got a spare set of keys so we can stay there.' She looked at Victoria with unmistakable concern in her gaze and it slowly dawned on Latimer that perhaps she was more sensitive to the situation than he had imagined and keen not to rub salt into the older woman's wounds.

The fact was, like most affairs, it had been a subject of frequent conversation between Chantelle and Collins and, despite Latimer's fatuous belief in his own discretion, had been equally thoroughly debated among the senior members of M & N, almost from the time it started. No one had disapproved, everyone had been delighted to see Campbell-West being done unto as he had so often done unto others.

'Thanks for everything, Victoria, you've been terrific. If you hadn't given us an alibi we could have been in big trouble.' She held out her hand. 'We'll see you on Monday. I reckon we should go along to the Guildhall to see the old bastard charged and then go out and celebrate.'

Victoria leant forward, rather wistfully Latimer thought, taking her hand and kissing her lightly on the cheek. 'That sounds marvellous, my dear. I shall look forward to it.' She turned to him and, incised in thin shadow by the late afternoon sun, he noticed for the first time the lines at her neck and eyes as she whispered her farewell.

'You're a very lucky man, John – good luck to you both.'

They were back in London by six that evening, stopping off in the West End to buy a few toiletries and essential articles of clothing before heading for the flat. It was raining as they drove along the Embankment and up Flood Street, the darkening streets gleaming under the yellow street lights. While Chantelle went to pick up the key from the neighbours, Latimer drove round into the King's Road to get an *Evening Standard*. On page five an article, a couple of inches inserted by the editor as a useful filler on a slow news day, caught his eye.

Under the headline, "Veteran Newsman Drowned", the piece told how the body of Sandy McColl had been recovered from the River Fal that morning. Mr McColl had been seen drinking heavily in a local public house the previous evening and was believed to have stumbled and fallen into the river while returning to Truro. Foul play was not suspected. It was a story that wouldn't raise any eyebrows among Sandy's colleagues, he knew.

What the police would make of the burnt-out wreck of *Revenge* and the incinerated remains of Behan he didn't know. Certainly they would have little difficulty in tracing the boat to him, but he doubted that their attempts to identify the scorched remains would be likely to encompass the dental records of wanted Argentinian war criminals. Anyway, he now hoped, he had a cast-iron alibi in the form of Victoria's affirmation that they had spent the preceding three days at Fairview, waiting to pounce on CW when he returned. So far as he was concerned the story was that the boat had been stolen while he was away and the thief had been accidentally killed trying to destroy the evidence.

His intention in staging the explosion at the cottage had been to take Behan out of the game, permanently if possible. Luckily, no one had been killed and the injured had all been known London villains who, hopefully, would think the explosion to have been an unfortunate accident – an occupational hazard. All in all, while there were still some loose ends he reckoned that, once Campbell-West was banged-up, he would be able to claim some pretty healthy insurance money and then consider what to do with the rest of his life. With this much in mind he made his way back to where Chantelle waited patiently in the soft drizzle with the keys to the flat.

It was a small, comfortable place. A Thameside flat overlooking the fairy-lit spider's web of the Albert Bridge. As Chantelle went ahead she stooped to gather up the half-dozen letters that lay behind the door, putting them aside on the low table. Closing the door she went to the kitchen while he wandered idly about the flat. In the hall hung a photograph of a dozen or so young men in full combat dress and green berets, all smiling jauntily at the camera. In the centre David sported his newly won First Lieutenant's pips and the same old challenging grin. Latimer wondered how he would have felt about his relationship with Chantelle flourishing so strongly and so quickly after his death. He had liked and respected Collins and, while realistic enough not to agonise overlong on imponderables, still experienced the occasional qualm. One look at the picture told him everything. David would have been delighted. He grinned back at the picture and, absolved, he followed Chantelle into the kitchen.

'There's not much to eat, I'm afraid, but we've got coffee.'

'Coffee's fine,' he said, 'we can eat out later – there used to be a nice French place in the King's Road as I recall – we'll go there.' She handed him his cup and then drew up a high pine stool at the breakfast bar, looking around her.

'This was David's place really, I only came here if we were staying in town overnight. I don't suppose I've been here more than three times in the last eighteen months. He used it quite a bit, whenever he was flying in or out of the country.' She smiled sardonically, brushing a wisp of hair from her face. 'I think he used to bring his girl friends here sometimes.'

Latimer raised an eyebrow, grateful for her acknowledgement of the state of their relationship, yet not wanting to be drawn into their domestic arrangements nor, to his credit, to be untrue to his dead friend's memory. He was perfectly aware, however, that Collins had been no angel where the ladies were concerned. Indeed, he guessed it was this trait that made the acceptance of his bloody death and of the transfer of her affections to him that much easier. He remained silent and, sensing that she had made him a little ill at ease, she lightened the conversation.

'Right, Latimer, take me to dinner. I shall make every effort to get extremely drunk while you, on the other hand, will take great care not to; then, when we come back here, I want you to remind me exactly what making love in a proper bed is like. Performing the sexual act on board a bloody yacht is OK if nowhere else is available but, so far as I'm concerned, I'm better in conditions of comfort. I shall do my utmost to convince you of this when we return.'

As they made to leave, Chantelle cast an eye on the unopened letters. They were all addressed to Collins. One bore a bright, multi-coloured Brazilian stamp.

'I'll read those tomorrow,' she said, as he draped her coat about her shoulders.

Twenty Six

Guildhall, City of London

At ten o'clock on the Monday morning they duly arrived at Wood Street Police Station where Ellis, attired in his best blue suit in acknowledgement of the occasion, was waiting for them. Victoria, crowned by a magnificently broad-brimmed hat, was already in the inspector's office, her presence clearly making their host a little uneasy as he fussed about his official duties. To their relief the formalities of making official statements proved to be nothing more demanding than repeating the story they had delivered on the Saturday. This done, they walked the short distance to the Guildhall Magistrates Court where Campbell-West was expected to be charged later that morning.

It was the first time Latimer had trod the pavements of the City since the Algoan affair and it felt good. Despite a certain air of unease, it was almost like returning in triumph. They had achieved their avowed intention of nailing Campbell-West and, equally important, he was now guardedly optimistic about his own chances of avoiding any repercussions.

The scene outside the court was one of feverish activity as television crews tested equipment and radio men mumbled into microphones and fiddled with earpieces, preparing for the main event. As they settled themselves into a bench at the rear of the imposing court, Latimer saw that Sarah had already arrived and, sitting in the front of the court, apparently no longer wished to be associated with them or their cause. She was surrounded by the usual coterie of muck-rakers and legal hacks, whose numbers today were swelled and dignified by the presence of a sprinkling of more eminent gentlemen of the press, all keen to witness the arraigning of Campbell-West.

He wondered if the presence of these luminaries registered in the abacus of Sarah's mind. McColl might be dead but, were she to give the least indication that she was prepared to sell her story, every editor in Fleet Street would be reaching for his cheque book. What, he wondered, would her position be now that CW had finally been brought to justice? Would she still go ahead with her plan to expose him or, with David dead and her now safely home, would she be content with a negotiated maintenance settlement? In prison or out, CW could provide all the goodies essential to keep her and the child in a style to which she had long become accustomed. Assuming the deal with Chang had been successfully completed, there would be no shortage of funds available in the Campbell-West account even if the man himself was banged-up in a British jail. At eleven o'clock as the court rose and the three magistrates, two elderly men and a rather smartly dressed matron of slightly less antique appearance, took their seats on the bench, Latimer settled back and waited for the main attraction.

The first few cases to be dealt with were the usual hangover from the weekend, drunks who had become rowdy or unconscious within the sacred limits of the Square Mile or, in one instance, had decided to urinate in places not set aside for that purpose. These were quickly dealt with and there ensued a considerable murmuring and rustling of notepads at the front of the court as expectations rose among the vultures of Fleet Street. Chantelle gripped his hand as they leant forward, the better to witness CW's entrance.

There seemed to be a suggestion of confusion among the magistrates who stared in unison at the Clerk of the Court, eyebrows raised enquiringly. The Clerk was in deep conversation with a uniformed officer and for several minutes the attention of the entire court focussed on the pair. With a shrug the Clerk broke off the conversation and approached the bench, addressing the senior magistrate in whispers. From their position at the back of the court the dialogue was inaudible, yet clearly something was wrong for the Clerk's tidings were received with frowns, several hushed queries and, finally, an impatient snort. The magistrate, clearly at a loss, leant back in his seat, his eyes running over the increasingly fidgety assembly as the Clerk returned to his desk.

'What's up?' hissed Chantelle as the low murmuring of the assembled pressmen, a pack of curs sensing they were about to be deprived of a particularly juicy titbit, rose to a rebellious grumble. The mutiny was brought to sullen heel by a swift crack of the gavel and, as the rabble fell to a ragged silence, the Clerk of the Court stood up.

'Ladies and Gentlemen,' he said, generously giving many present the benefit of the doubt, 'I realise that the majority of you are here to report on the charging of Sir Peter Campbell-West.' He looked down at the slip of paper in his hand. 'We have just been informed that all charges against Sir Peter have been dropped. That's all we have been told, I'm afraid. I understand that a full statement will be issued by the Department of Public Prosecutions later today.'

An anguished howl rose from the assembled pressmen as they hurled questions at the Clerk and magistrates. They, unable to provide even half-acceptable answers, filed out with as much dignity as the situation allowed. Latimer looked at Chantelle, unable to believe his ears. Only Victoria remained impassive as though not the least surprised to find that their prey had apparently escaped justice yet again. Ellis appeared, red-faced and furious as he slid into the bench beside them.

'I don't believe it,' he raged, 'I just don't fucking believe it.'

'What the hell's going on?' Chantelle demanded. 'All charges dropped? They can't do that, can they? I mean, he's as guilty as sin.'

Ellis shook his head hopelessly. 'I'll tell you as we go. The car's waiting outside.'

'Where are we going?' Latimer began to fear the worst. Perhaps the whole story had come out and it was he who was to be charged. Ellis's answer was not enlightening.

'Heathrow. We're going to wave Campbell-West off – he's going back to Brazil.'

As they left the court Latimer caught a fleeting glimpse of Sarah, escorted by a powerfully built man dressed in peaked cap and dark blue chauffeur uniform, her face impassive as she slid into the rear of a silver Rolls that significantly sported CD plates. He had not been alone in observing her departure and all hell broke loose as pressmen screamed for taxis, almost coming to blows as they scrambled for seats and prepared to give pursuit. It occurred to Latimer that perhaps this unexpected upturn in Campbell-West's fortunes would make her less inclined to seek the public eye.

Ellis, at the wheel of the police car, had still not regained his composure as they drew away from the Guildhall in the wake of the Rolls and the harrying taxi fleet. Usually not given to profanities, his language made no allowance for the presence of the women and would have done credit to a sailor.

'Diplomatic fucking immunity,' he spluttered. 'Would you believe it? The slippery bastard has claimed diplomatic immunity.' The stunned silence in the car encouraged him to continue his tirade. 'The bastard claimed he was here on government business. Of course, hearing that, his brief's onto the Brazilian Embassy like shit off a shovel. They get

onto the Foreign Office and the next thing we know the
Foreign Office is on to the DPP. All charges are to be
dropped and the case of Sir Peter Campbell-West, who has
incidentally become a fucking Brazilian citizen overnight, is
officially closed.'

Chantelle shook her head in dumb disbelief, looking silently out of the window. All their efforts, the deaths of four
men, the fear and humiliation they had experienced at the
hands of Campbell-West's thugs, had all been for nothing.
The bastard was going to walk away scot free.

'Why are we going to Heathrow, anyway?' Victoria demanded hotly. 'I certainly have no intention of giving the
blaggard an opportunity to gloat over his triumph. You can
drop me at the next underground station, inspector. What I
need is a large gin and tonic and the next train back to
Oxford.'

Ellis's eyes searched her face in the driving mirror.

'He's not so insistent that you go along, Lady Cam …
Victoria. It's Mr Latimer and Mrs Kolowitz he's demanding
to see.' He fell silent, perhaps hoping they might offer some
explanation for this. None being presented he continued, 'I
don't suppose I'll ever know the full story of how you came
to take Campbell-West. I'm a police officer, so perhaps it's
better I don't. What he's saying is, if the pair of you go to
Heathrow he won't press kidnapping charges. In the normal
run of things I'd advise you to tell him to shove it but, well,
if he's got anything on you it might be better to let him have
his moment of glory.' He looked across at Latimer. 'You do
seem to have been a trifle unlucky of late, Mr Latimer – what
with your house and your boat getting done over like that.'
He looked directly into Latimer's eyes. 'I'd hate to see you
two end up in the shit after all this.'

The inspector, it would appear, was both a good deal more
human and a lot less gullible than they had, until then, given
him credit for. As Latimer considered the situation,

Chantelle made the decision for him. The powerhouse behind the whole crusade from the beginning she seemed uncharacteristically laid-back about these latest developments.

'You're right, inspector. Let's give the bastard his moment of glory and then maybe we can all get back to real life.'

As they sped down the M4, the sun slit through the thin cloud layer, its rays playing on their faces. Latimer looked over his shoulder at Chantelle. She lay back in her seat, eyes closed, a faintly bitter smile on her lips. He could imagine her thoughts. Everything had been for nothing.

At Heathrow they were escorted directly to the diplomatic suite, leaving Ellis and Victoria in the car.

Campbell-West sat in a high-backed seat, like a monarch on a throne, prepared to receive them. The large brandy balloon in his left hand might have passed for an orb of state, the long corona cigar in his left for a surrogate sceptre. At his side, Sarah viewed their approach across the hushed room with regal but restrained amusement, a supportive hand laid on his. The bottle of Perrier at her side indicated just how seriously she was taking her role of mother-to-be these days. No risks were to be taken with the heir apparent she carried within her. With a click of his fingers CW brought the steward scurrying to the table and a potent silence prevailed while the man served their drinks and departed.

'Well, well,' he crooned as the man left. 'Who would have thought the thing would end like this?' He drew on the corona and exhaled a curling cloud of blue smoke skyward. 'You know, I shall quite miss our battle of wits. It's been so stimulating to come up against opponents who have actually stretched me. I do hope you aren't going to be bad losers. I feel I am being exceptionally lenient in letting you off like this – my lawyers were all for throwing the book at you.' He brought his gaze to bear on Latimer, his mouth drawn down in sardonic amusement. 'You still don't know how I managed to get away with it, do you? Unfortunately, I suspect that neither of you fully comprehends the close and sometimes convoluted relationships that apply between governments and the international business community. I will do my best to explain.'

He swilled the brandy in its glass and, lifting it to his nose, savoured its fragrance. 'Since the Falklands campaign, the British Government has been notably short of friends in the South American continent. As I'm sure you both will recall from the old days in Algoa, there's a hell of a lot of money being spent on development down there and the Thatcher government, nothing if not businesslike, still wants a piece of the action. Well, since relations at government levels have been somewhat soured by our brave boys kicking the shit out of the Argies on the islands, they have of necessity been boosted at other, lower but no less effective, levels.

With my links in the City and at Westminster I have been instrumental in arranging British finance for hydro-electric schemes in Venezuela, a nuclear power station in Valparaiso and a chemical plant six hundred miles up the Amazon. I find it so gratifying to be of service to developing nations and to become immensely wealthy at the same time.

Currently the Brazilians are keen to sell their first home-grown military aircraft, the Tucara, to the Royal Air Force. It's an excellent basic trainer that meets all the Air Force's requirements. Moreover, the deal has an added attraction in that the Brazilians are prepared to accept fifty per cent of the payment in the form of North Sea oil.'

He sat back, giving his class time to assimilate the wisdom he was unfolding before them.

'You see. Unwittingly, your scheming has inconvenienced two governments. As the unofficial and unrecognised go-between, I should have finalised details of the deal on my return to Rio. When I realised I might be delayed and possibly detained, I took the precaution of appraising my contacts in

264

both countries. When two nations are about to settle a mutually advantageous deal of this magnitude, they are hardly likely to be prepared to see it fouled-up in the interests of petty personal revenge.'

Campbell-West raised his hand and in an instant the steward returned to clear the table and to bring fresh drinks. He looked slightly drunk, Latimer thought, his face flushed and his eyes pink-rimmed. It had been a traumatic couple of weeks and now, the crisis passed and the victory his, he was letting his hair down. Drained by the swift turn of events Latimer toyed briefly with the idea of slashing a glass across the man's throat, but all the fight had gone out of him, all the venom had seeped away. No, the thing was over and they had lost. If nothing else went wrong he would still have Chantelle and, with her, the prospect of some sort of future. Delighting in their silent acceptance of his total triumph, Campbell-West continued.

'Of course, I regret David's death. He was a most resourceful young man but his treatment of poor Groose and Sarah left me no alternative but to arrange his demise. As I'm sure you are both aware, I would have arranged a similar fate for the pair of you had you not proved so commendably devious in your actions. Anyway, thankfully all that is behind us so let us move on to happier considerations.'

He looked at his watch and threw back the fully-charged glass of brandy in one. 'Our flight should be called any moment now which, I suspect, means we will be saying goodbye for ever. What would please me greatly would be for us to split a bottle of bubbly before we go our different ways – just like the old days.'

Chantelle shrugged her shoulders indifferently.

'Why not? I guess you can afford it, CW, and we're not going anywhere special right now.'

The champagne, Dom Perignon, was delivered to the table and, jubilant, Campbell-West stood up, swaying slightly as he raised his glass, his mocking glance going from one to the other.

'To profit and pleasure.'

Without comment they sipped the champagne and, within seconds, the steward came over to advise Campbell-West that they should board their flight as soon as possible. Setting down his glass, he embraced them both with a final and hateful, valedictory smile, while Sarah stood up, hastily gathering together her hand-luggage, eager to be away. She had remained silent throughout the audience, perhaps fearful they might yet take such satisfaction as they could salvage by sowing seeds of doubt in CW's mind. Still blissfully unaware of his consort's treachery, Campbell-West crowed on.

'Well, I fear this is farewell, my friends. May I say you were a real challenge. Sadly you were out of your league from the start of the game. Nevermind, it's not who wins or loses – it's how you play the game, or so they say.' He turned to Sarah, relieving her of her insignificant hand-baggage in a display of husbandly concern. 'Well, my dear, I think it's time to be off.'

As they turned away, Chantelle caught his sleeve and he half-turned.

'Oh, I almost forgot, there's a letter here for you, CW. Don't bother to read it now, wait until you get on board. It's nothing important really.'

As he took the envelope from her, the faintest trace of a frown creased his brow.

'What is this?' he demanded stiffly.

'Nothing much,' she crooned sweetly, 'like I say, read it when you've got time.' For a second he hesitated, but Chantelle had by now turned her attention to the still half-full bottle of champagne. With an impatient snort he led Sarah towards the embarkation gate, thrusting the letter into his inside pocket as he went. An anxious Sarah looked back at them and Chantelle raised her glass.

'Be happy.'

'What was that?' asked Latimer softly, well aware that the woman who now sat sipping thoughtfully was not given to empty gestures. She fumbled in her handbag and handed him a folded piece of paper. He opened it and saw that it was a photocopy of the letter she had just handed to CW. It was from Sarah to David.

'My Dearest David,' it read. 'You cannot know how I am longing to be with you again. As I write this we are preparing for the trip to the Azores. This morning Peter gave me a fright by suggesting that perhaps I should not accompany him since it might put the baby at risk. Luckily, I was able to convince him there was no risk to the (our) child and he agreed to my coming along. He really is the most stupid of men yet blithely considers himself a superior being in every way. The meeting with Chang is still on and still expected to take place at the Almirante Hotel on the date previously agreed.

Take care, my love. I look forward to a time when we can be together all the time, a time when you are free of Chantelle and the three of us (I include the baby) can be a real family. I have lived a lie with Peter for so long now that I yearn only to be with you and away from this place. Since our time in Basle nothing has been the same for me and you fill my thoughts day and night. I long to be kidnapped.'

Latimer carefully refolded the sheet of paper and handed it back to Chantelle. Taking her hand he led her to the ceiling-height observation window that gave a view of the ungainly length of the 747. Having accepted the last of the stream of tourist class passengers into its capacious hull, the heavy pressurised doors slid solidly shut and the boarding ramp drew back.

Towards the nose of the aircraft, in the first-class section, a face that had once been handsome and impressive stared bleakly out at them from behind the clouded plastic of the oval window. Holding the letter up for them to see,

Campbell-West tore it in half and then in quarters before screwing it into a ball and, apparently, tossing it aside. Whether he had read it or not was impossible to tell, for no emotion was discernible in the grey eyes. It didn't matter; he had drunk from the poisoned chalice. Time and his own arrogance would do the rest.

As one they raised their glasses, their toast coming in unison as the engines of the giant aircraft rose to a banshee scream and, bouncing gently on its undercarriage, it eased its ponderous bulk away from the terminal building.

'Cheers CW!'

Twenty Seven

Rio de Janeiro

'In the name of the Father, the Son and the Holy Ghost, I baptise thee Peter Enrico ...' The Reverend Millichope's thin monotone rang among the rafters as the congregation moved closer to the font and the child in his arms whimpered under the baptismal water's cold kiss. It had been many a long year since the little Anglican church had housed such an exalted gathering. The convoy of chauffeured Rolls and Mercedes parked in the Ipanema sunshine outside, and the squads of security men who strolled amongst them with studied nonchalance, bore witness to the social consequence of the occasion.

Campbell-West ran an approving eye over his guests: with a Brazilian Secretary of State and the West German Ambassador for godparents his son already had his foot firmly on the first rung of the social ladder. Soon he would have to consider schools. As his gaze encompassed the great and the good a pair of eyes, warm and wide, met his and he smiled.

Marisa Falkenberg was a beautiful woman, young and full of life. Even the primly correct dress she wore in acknowledgement of the occasion could not disguise the sensuous lines of her ripe body. The daughter of a Swiss merchant banker she had, in the three months that had elapsed since Sarah Mendelsohn's tragic death, firmly established a relationship with Campbell-West that, while it yet remained intimate but platonic, held the undeniable promise of more.

In a week or so he would invite her up to Buena Vista, the vast estancia he had bought in Amazonia. At sixty he was once more confidently contemplating courtship and marriage, this time to a girl who, at twenty-four, was several years younger than his eldest daughter. Of course, with Sarah so recently dead, these things had to be handled with delicacy, but he felt he had played the grieving widower quite long enough. As the ceremony broke up the Reverend Millichope, blinking in the sunshine, shook his hand.

'You must take great comfort from your son, Sir Peter. His mother would have been so proud.'

Campbell-West nodded thoughtfully. 'Ah yes, my poor Sarah.'

'In life we are in the midst of death,' Millichope prattled tastelessly on and, seeing Marisa approaching, bearing his son and heir in her arms, Campbell-West was glad to excuse himself. He had to get back to the house, he explained, in readiness to receive his guests.

Sarah's death, three weeks after giving birth to a healthy eight-pound boy, had been a mystery. It had happened while Campbell-West had been away on business, salting away the profits of the deal with Chang. Servants had found her naked body lying in the flower beds beneath the third-floor verandah of the bedroom. She regularly sunbathed out there, loving the wide views of the Copacabana, though how she had come to fall no one could explain. It was whispered in the kitchens, however, that, despite her condition, she had grown noticeably over-fond of the gin bottle.

Death by misadventure was the coroner's verdict; an accident, possibly caused by a sudden attack of vertigo.

Campbell-West had been inconsolable, dropping out of the social scene entirely until the youthful Marisa Falkenberg, initially fascinated in the way young women often are by his unsavoury reputation, had coaxed him back into Rio society once again. Slowly, he had regained his zest for life and once more began to be seen in the casinos and restaurants he had frequented with Sarah, this time with Marisa on his arm. The jet-setters at the tables nudged each other with spiteful envy; the old goat had done it again.

As she sat at his side in the rear of the Merc, the sleeping child still cradled in her arms, she laid a comforting hand on his and he felt a warm glow of satisfaction. Everything was turning out so well.

The reception, held on the lawns behind the large colonial house that represented a further investment of his gains from the Chang deal, had been Marisa's idea. She had thrown all her considerable talents and energies into the project, determined to make it an event that would display her value to the English milord. She had other motives. By throwing the doors open and bringing the cream of Rio's social scene into the house she hoped to exorcise any lingering trace of Sarah's spirit that might still cling to its long, cool corridors. Three ambassadors, an English viscount, bankers and businessmen – her father amongst them – by the dozen, and a piquant sprinkling of the usual pretty, witty drones and parasites, without whom no Rio assembly would be complete, stood drinking champagne and laughing merrily at their own cleverness.

Campbell-West, deep in conversation with Marisa's father about the continuing weakness of the escudo, watched closely as she moved amongst the guests, presenting the child for their approval. Aware of his eyes upon her she dutifully played the little mother; it was a role, she knew, he had already cast her for and the very thought of being Lady Campbell-West brought a flush of excitement to her olive cheeks.

'Will you excuse me for one moment, Hugo?' he said, draining his glass with a flourish. 'I must make a telephone call – please, help yourself to the food, I shall be back directly.'

Going inside he walked through the lofty central hall and climbed the wide curved staircase to his office. Locking the door behind him he went to the windows, pulling them to and muffling the chatter that rose from the crowded garden below. Sitting behind the heavy desk he picked up the phone and dialled. Just one detail to be attended to and he would be free to return to the party and Marisa. Mr Chang, watching the sunrise over the Taipa bridge, was expecting his call.

'Good afternoon, Sir Peter.'

'Good morning, Mr Chang.' The stiff formality of their greeting and the ensuing silence underlined the tension. Chang spoke first.

'I have considered your offer, Sir Peter. It is not the sort of offer one man of honour makes to another. I am not accustomed to being threatened – you dishonour me.'

'Spare me the sob story, Chang. What I'm offering you is a very good deal. High-grade stuff – all you can handle. All you have to do is deliver twenty Crotale S19s. Or are you saying that you can't get hold of them?'

'It is not a matter of obtaining the missiles. The last deal was compromised. You exposed us all to great risk, I am not sure I wish to do business with you again, Sir Peter.'

'Mr Chang, as I have already pointed out on more than one occasion, if you will not supply the hardware there are others who will. I believe I already mentioned that Mr Ho in Hong Kong is only too keen to do business.'

'Mr Ho is my enemy.' There was no emotion in Chang's voice; it was a simple statement requiring no comment. Mr Ho, and others like him, had moved into Vancouver and San Francisco in a big way, the Hong Kong people were everywhere these days. They had the money and the connections to dominate the drugs trade on the west coast. If Campbell-West did business with Ho it would mean much

272

loss of face.

'Mr Ho will take all the stuff I can deliver.' Campbell-West continued. 'It's a good deal, Mr Chang. There are three thousand S19s lying around in armouries on Taiwan. The generals know there's not going to be any war – they're not going to miss twenty.'

'As I said, Sir Peter, the missiles are not a problem, it is security I am concerned with. The Azorean deal was very messy – you came close to compromising us all.'

'That was then. I'm a Brazilian citizen now and I have Brazilian Government credentials to protect me. The Azores, I agree, was tricky, but no one is going to come after me now. I am fireproof, Mr Chang – you, I suggest, are not.'

'If I agree to deliver the missiles, do I have your assurance that you will not at some future date supply Mr Ho?'

'You have my solemn word.' Ten thousand miles apart, both men smiled.

'Ring me tomorrow, Sir Peter. I'm sure we can reach a compromise.'

'I'm sure we can, Mr Chang.'

In the garden, the first of the guests was beginning to depart as the limousines snaked up the gravel drive to collect their wealthy owners. Security men unbuttoned their jackets and their eyes grew wary as they ushered their precious charges into the bulletproof security of the cars. There was no question about it, the reception had been a great success, everyone had had a most enjoyable afternoon. Last to leave, the Chilean consul was clearly drunk and effusive in his expressions of appreciation. As Campbell-West assisted the man into his car and waved him on his way, Marisa came to his side.

'Little Peter is asleep. I think it's been a very busy day for him,' she said and he laid a light, appreciative hand on her tanned shoulder.

'It's been a great success, my dear,' he took her hand, 'and it's all thanks to your hard work. I couldn't have done it without you.' He led her back towards the house and out into the gardens where the caterers were clearing away the debris. The late afternoon sun was warm and he slipped off his jacket, loosening his tie. He looked at her, so fresh and full of life; no point in putting things off. His tone was serious. What he was about to say was of great importance. 'I'm flying up to Buena Vista next week, Marisa. I was wondering if you'd care to come with me. Since Sarah died it's become rather a lonely life for an old man.'

She smiled up at him, caressing his cheek with a soft hand.

'You're not old, Peter. You've got more life in you than most men half your age.' She blushed, his proposition, if not unexpected, coming sooner than she had bargained for. She did not hesitate. 'I'd love to come with you.' Taking her gently by the shoulders he kissed her lightly, almost paternally, on the forehead.

That evening, after she had gone, Campbell-West sat and watched the sun die bloodily behind the circling hills. He had drunk the best part of a bottle of champagne and slipped easily into a pleasantly contemplative mood. In the space of one glorious afternoon he had resolved the two remaining question marks in his life: Chang had been brought to heel and Marisa as good as bedded. Life was good.

Sarah's death had been a sad affair, of course, but he had had no choice. He had, at first, been inclined to accept her protestations of innocence; to believe that the letter to Collins had been nothing more than a crude forgery, cobbled together by a vindictive Chantelle, intent on destroying their happiness.

As her pregnancy progressed, however, the nagging doubts festered and flourished and long before she had been delivered of the child he had made the decision and drawn up his plans. For a modest US$3,000 a Uruguayan killer had entered the house and tipped the half-drunk woman the three storeys from the verandah. The man, whom he had never met, had been a professional and no questions were raised; it had been quick and clean. Much as a dog owner might put down a sheep-worrying hound, he had, despite some sentimental regret, removed her from the equation that was his life.

His sombre musings were disturbed by a discreet cough at his shoulder and he turned to find the head of the catering staff, a wizened oriental, standing there.

'Everything is cleared away, Sir. We go now.' Campbell-West fumbled in his hip pocket, producing a roll of escudo notes. Peeling off ten bills he handed them to the man who nodded appreciatively.

'You've done a marvellous job. Thank all your staff for me, won't you?' Again the old man nodded, hesitating.

'One thing, Sir,' he produced a half-empty bottle of champagne; 'this was left over. Only just opened. Perhaps you would like me to leave it?' His eyes went to the glass in Campbell-West's hand. 'You have much to celebrate.'

'Thank you,' he smiled, holding it out to be filled. 'No point in wasting it, I suppose.' The man set the bottle by his chair and with a final nod of the head was gone, leaving him to his thoughts.

Emptying his glass and refilling it, he recalled his earlier conversation with Chang and frowned. The man had been right to be cautious, of course, the fiasco in the Azores had very nearly been the ruination of him. Latimer and Chantelle, a pair of blundering amateurs, had almost brought his whole world crashing down around his ears. His frown eased – almost, but not quite. In the end he had proved too clever for them, too well organised. A broad smile spread across his florid features and he staggered to his feet, surprised to find his legs buckling awkwardly under him: 'Whoops, must have drunk more than I thought.' He walked unsteadily out into the cool airs of the darkening garden, the stars shining like crystallised fireflies in the purple sky above.

'Yes,' he said, the words reverberating around the recesses of his skull, 'in the final analysis I was too clever for them.' He threw back his head and laughed aloud. 'Age and treachery will always triumph over youth and skill,' he roared, sinking to his knees in the damp grass, staring up at the lighted windows of the house which seemed, suddenly, to be separated from him by very thick, slightly flawed glass.

At the airport Mr Ling sat smoking in the departure lounge. He did not, he decided, like Brazil any more than he liked Canada. It did not matter. Once his business had been successfully attended to, Mr Chang had said he could return to Macau. No more serving food to arrogant dogfaces for him. Now he would have a pension for life and the freedom to come and go as he wished. The border was open now, perhaps he would return to Xiangtan and visit the graves of his parents.

Mr Ling checked his watch; there was one final detail to be attended to. Rising stiffly he walked to a phone booth.

'I have attended to your affairs here, Mr Chang.'

'You have done well, Ling.'

'There is a plane to Lisbon in an hour and one to London shortly after. I have tickets for both. What am I to do?'

There was no hesitation on Chang's part.

'I do not think that you need go to London. The account is closed. You may come home, Ling.'

Above him the flight-scheduling board shuffled itself with an almost imperceptible whirr. The Lisbon flight was announced. Taking up his overnight bag he filtered into the stream of departing humanity. Tomorrow he would be in Lisbon, and the day after that Macau.

Mr Ling smiled and thought of a tortoise that had shit on his hand.

Twenty Eight

River Snape, Suffolk

'Ole man ribber,' crooned Latimer, 'dat ole man ribber. He don't plant taters, he don't plant ...'

'I hardly think,' interrupted Chantelle from behind her paper, 'that cooking breakfast once in a while entitles you to identify with the slaves back on the old plantation.'

'An dem dat plants 'em,' continued Latimer, giving her a black power salute that went unnoticed, 'am soon forgotten.'

Outside, among the reeds that fringed the little Suffolk backwater, ducks quacked softly in the morning sunshine.

'Shit!' Chantelle's tone suggested surprise rather than actual excrement.

'No call to insult an ole darkie like dat, Miss Chantelle.'

'Campbell-West is dead.'

'What?'

She laid the paper flat on the chart table as Latimer, all thoughts of food forgotten, peered over her shoulder. She read aloud.

'Sir Peter Campbell-West, the British financier and businessman, died yesterday at his home in Rio de Janeiro, aged sixty one. Sir Peter, a former member of the CBI and a sheriff of the City of London, is believed to have suffered a heart attack. Obituary page 23.'

In silence she struggled with the unwieldy broadsheet.

When she had finally succeeded in folding it into submission, they stared down. From the page a half-plate image of Campbell-West stared smilingly out at them.

It was an oldish photograph, taken perhaps fifteen years previously, probably a PR mug shot from about the time he became chairman of Martin & Nicholson. He looked sleek and confident, his regimental tie neatly windsor knotted, a man whose word was definitely his bond, a man to whom 'utmost good faith' was a sacred credo. If the visual image flattered, however, it paled to insignificance beside the verbal blandishments that accompanied it.

'With the death of Sir Peter Campbell-West the world of international finance has lost one of its most influential and colourful characters, one who will be deeply mourned, especially by those of us privileged enough to have worked beside him. Peter Campbell-West was a man of great charm and charisma who worked unceasingly to improve Britain's trading relationships around the world ...'

'Not to mention lining his own fucking pockets and shitting on his friends,' said Latimer easily, strangely pleased to find that no real venom remained.

'Even though taking Brazilian citizenship in his later years,' Chantelle persisted, 'he continued to work tirelessly on behalf of British interests throughout the South American continent. Dynamic and bold, his flamboyant style of management sometimes led to disagreement with more conservative colleagues. Following the collapse of Algoan Financial Services in 1980 and the ensuing controversy, Sir Peter continued to work for better links between Britain's trading partners throughout the world.

While, inevitably, the British business community will remain largely unaware of his efforts on their behalf, those of us lucky enough to have known the man will always be grateful for the experience of working with him.

Sir Peter Campbell-West was an entrepreneur in the best

sense of that, today, often denigrated word. He was a man of integrity and vision who possessed that most valuable of assets – the ability to think on his feet.'

'Not to mention with his fingers in the till. Jesus Christ, who wrote this shit?' demanded Latimer, the smell of charred bacon taking him quickly back to the galley, 'Hans fucking Anderson? It's a total fairy story. He makes Campbell-West sound like a cross between Gandhi and Mother Theresa.'

'Well, the old bastard's dead now,' Chantelle said flatly.

Retrieving the blackened wafers of bacon he dropped two eggs, spitting and crackling, into the overheated fat.

'I suppose we should be pleased,' he said, although his words lacked conviction. 'The bastard did try to kill us both. Do you feel happy?'

'No, not really,' Chantelle lay the newspaper aside. 'I guess if we'd left well alone he'd have died anyway and Dave would be alive to enjoy the moment with us – Sarah too.'

He didn't reply. It was well over a year now since Collins had died and Campbell-West had breezed, scot-free, out of the country. Since then something like, but not exactly, normality had returned to their lives. He had made no real attempt to revive his career in finance but, thanks to the insurance on *Revenge* and his cottage, now boasted a modest portfolio of investments and this modern 30 foot cutter, *Nemesis*. The pair of them had settled into a relationship that was supportive and physically satisfying yet seemed, at times, strangely fragile. There were still ghosts.

'Apparently there's going to be a service of thanksgiving at St Mary Woolnoth the week after next,' Chantelle said airily. 'No flowers – donations to Oxfam.'

'By which time, we should be among the Greek islands, lying in the sun and drinking ouzo,' he said, perhaps a little too quickly. Once again he felt the unsettling presence of Collins and the past.

'We can go to Greece anytime.'

He stared at her, knowing it was crunch time. 'What are you saying?'

'We ... I can't leave it like this. It's not over, John, even now. I'm going to write that book after all. I'm going to write the definitive autobiography of Sir Peter Campbell-West. I'm going down to that service of thanksgiving – that'll be my starting point – and work my way back to the moment he came into the world. I'm going to put the whole rat-pack on warning.'

Latimer felt his precariously balanced world teetering.

'Why? What good will it do? He's dead, Chantelle. Nothing we do can touch him now.'

'It's not Campbell-West. It's the baby. It's David's child, John, and we owe it to him to make sure his son knows exactly who his real father was. There's Sarah too. You and I know CW too well to accept her death as an accident. That kid's going to grow up thinking the man who murdered both his real parents is his father.'

He stared at her. So that was it. She reached into the deep breast pocket of her fisherman's smock and handed him a small, silk-covered box. With it was a much-creased vellum citation. He prised the box open with a thumbnail. Inside, glistening on a bed of blue velvet, lay a small golden star.

'That arrived last month. Apparently some friend of David's from the marines, Mills or Miller, was killed in Ulster a couple of years back. That was among his effects. The Naval Benevolent Fund has been trying to return it to David ever since. I guess I was the nearest thing to next of kin.'

Latimer read the citation in silence, trying to comprehend the terror and carnage that lay behind the bland words. 'In all the time I knew him he never once mentioned any medals to me.'

'Nor to me.'

He looked at her closely, concerned that the old corrosive

poison might still be working behind the calm blue eyes. He took her in his arms, wrapping himself protectively about her, his face in the fragrance of her tousled hair.

'And you want to write the whole thing up?'

She nodded.

'Yes, and when he's old enough to understand I'm going to present the book and the medal to the child. I owe Dave that much.'

She was calm but determined and as he considered her words Latimer found himself hard put to fault her logic. They both owed Collins that much and more.

'I suppose it would mean a lot of research?'

She smiled up at him. 'Lots.'

'And travelling to all sorts of places?'

Her hands curled about his neck and she kissed him hotly on the mouth.

'Definitely. I want to go back to São Miguel for a start – there's a rather seedy bedroom there I'd like you to see.'